The Lost Fiancé Twist

SPENCER BROTHERS
BOOK ONE

ANA ASHLEY

To family.
The one we're born in.
The one we find.
The one that finds us.

About this book

Relationship status: it's complicated.

Being ghosted by the love of your life sucks. Zero out of ten, do not recommend.
One day, we're exchanging rings and picking honeymoon destinations, and the next, Emery is just...gone.

A year later, as I'm forcing myself to move on, I bump into him.
While my brothers would love to find creative ways to get the truth out of Emery, I just want answers.

When it becomes clear Emery isn't lying about losing his memory in a car accident, I have a choice to make.
Do I let him go or try to win him back?

The Lost Fiancé Twist is book one in Ana Ashley's new series featuring the charming and far-too-handsome-for-their-own-good Spencer Brothers.
Expect romance, heat, fun, and plenty of laughs from a loving but slightly too meddlesome family unit.

Prologue

LEX

A year ago

I f there were such a thing as the Boyfriend of the Year Award, I would be a finalist. Dead certain a contender for the big prize.

"And the winner is"—drumroll—*"Alexis Spencer: for his services to romance."*

The crowd would cheer, and I would proudly accept my award, but not before pulling the love of my life into my arms for a very public display of said romance.

Was I a little overconfident? Maybe. But I had everything planned with military precision.

"It's all yours, Mr. Spencer," Mr. Acker said, gesturing to the large open space inside the tree peony collection at the Botanical Gardens. "I hope he says yes."

"Thank you so much, Mr. Acker. I really appreciate you giving us exclusive access. This is my boyfriend's favorite place in the whole world, so it means a lot to me to do it here."

"You didn't give me much choice, son," he said, patting my shoulder before leaving me to my final preparations.

I may have been a little too persistent in my mission to get the groundskeeper's attention so I could secure the perfect location for the most important moment of my life. But I was going for Boyfriend of the Year, remember?

Maybe it was the box of cupcakes decorated with buttercream wildflowers or the coupon for a dinner for two at my parents' award-winning restaurant, Lusitana. It could have been the emails I'd sent weekly or the fact that I was getting so desperate that I'd sent Mr. Acker countless photos of Emery and me with the peonies in the background to show him exactly how important this place was to us.

I didn't care what had broken Mr. Acker's reluctance to close the area for these two hours. All I cared about was that it had worked.

In just half an hour, it would be me, Emery, and the country's most beautiful collection of tree peonies.

Not to mention the icing on the cake that was my Portuguese grandmother's pastéis de nata that I'd made myself using the recipe passed down for generations on my mother's side.

Thank you, Mom, for all the hours spent in the kitchen washing pots while you rattled on about our heritage and how there was no better food for the soul than Portuguese.

I checked the time again. My heart raced with nerves and anticipation.

"Só podemos avaliar a força do amor quando o sentimos," my grandmother used to say. The strength of love can only be measured when we feel it.

Of course, she only dished out such wise advice when there was a glass of Port and a slice of Madeira cake on offer. I'd made sure to have both when I confided in her that I was considering proposing to Emery.

Was it too early? We'd been dating for a year, but I couldn't imagine my life without him. My grandmother married when she was fourteen, and my parents were twenty-two when they got married.

At twenty-seven, I wasn't exactly old, but I wanted to officially start my life with the man I'd fallen head over heels for in this same place a year ago.

I felt the strength of that love. It was more than I'd ever felt for any other guy I'd dated. Hell, I didn't even feel that strongly about the advertising agency I started with my brothers, and that was saying something because my job was the second most important thing in my life.

The small table Mr. Acker provided me was dressed with a white table cloth. The bucket of ice on it contained an opened bottle of chilled white wine. Emery's favorite.

And on a plate I'd bought specifically for today, for the sole purpose of becoming our first heirloom, were six perfect pastéis de nata. I'd even brought a small pepper shaker filled with cinnamon. Avó, my grandmother, would disown me if I offered the delicious pastries without cinnamon.

The entire tree peony collection was stunning, so I could have picked any tree to get down on my knee for Emery, but our tree, the one that witnessed our meet cute? Today, it was blooming like it knew how important it was to show off its true wonder.

The sound of shuffling feet and hushed words got my attention.

When I'd asked Emery to meet me in the tree peony collection, I knew there was a chance he'd be late. His students had a test, and he always liked to give them extra time. Therefore, I didn't need to check my phone for messages or gather further clues about the identity of my uninvited guests.

"We're too early," Avó's voice said in a hushed but clipped tone. "Emery isn't here."

"I'm pretty sure we're not early. He said he had somewhere to be at six. It's six," my twin brother, Adam, added.

"Fuck, he's been dumped. Emery hasn't turned up."

"Shut up, Noah, he hasn't been dumped. I know these things."

I could almost hear our older brother roll his eyes. "Just because you shared a womb doesn't mean you're telepathic, Adam."

"Shush, you two. If my baby is hurting, I'm going to kill Emery. He seemed like such a nice boy," my mom said, disappointment lacing her voice.

"So he's your baby because he's been dumped, but when I lost my pet rabbit, you didn't even let me send out a search party," Noah said.

"That's because you left his cage door open on purpose, knowing he would run off next door to mate with their rabbit."

"I take mating rituals very seriously, and Pudding had...needs."

"And after he met his...needs," my mom said, "he returned home, so a search party was unnecessary. Just a very expensive vet bill and a prize-winning rabbit divested of her virtue. Not to mention a very angry neighbor."

"Those fluffy-tailed terrors destroyed all my lettuce. I should have put them all in a pot when I had the chance."

"Dad!" Adam cried out in indignation. He'd always been protective of the rabbits. More so than Noah, whose fault it was that they existed in the first place.

I pinched the bridge of my nose and sighed before turning toward the tree they were hiding behind.

"A herd of elephants would have been more discreet," I said.

"Told you he'd hear us. None of you can keep it down," Avó said as, one by one, they all came out from behind the bushy tree. Noah snorted. My mom hit him in the arm, so he hit Adam in turn.

"What are you all doing here?" I asked.

"We're celebrating, dear. We didn't want to miss your special moment. I won't pretend I'm not a little upset that you kept this from us, but we're here now. That's all that matters."

I groaned. "Mom, why did you think I didn't tell you?"

She shrugged.

"Because I knew you'd do this exact thing," I said, exasperation and slight panic building in my chest. They couldn't be here when Emery arrived. "How did you find out?"

My eyes landed on Adam. Avó came along with the rest of the crazy posse, but she was a vault. If there was anyone in my family who would've had the slightest hint about my plans, that would be my twin. We'd always been connected. Noah used to joke that he was lucky to not be a twin because at least he could have some privacy.

Adam immediately looked guilty. "Um...I could tell you've been a little off. Like, you're too nervous but also ridiculously happy, but I figured it was because things with Emery were going well, so maybe you wanted to take the next step but didn't know what to do."

"Things with Emery *are* going well...if you all don't ruin it for me," I said, running my hand through my hair, trying to figure out how to let them down gently. "Do you know how weird it is to have you all here?"

My mom's face filled with hurt, which made me feel like the bad guy—but come on. Can't a guy propose to his boyfriend on the anniversary of the day they met in private?

I wanted to open my heart to Emery Livingston. Let him know exactly how important he was to me. How I couldn't and didn't want to live without him. I wanted to marry him, have kids and grow old with him.

But dammit, I wanted to do it without an audience.

"We should all go," Adam said, and I gave him a smile that conveyed my thanks for his support.

"Aw, Lex is going to go all lovey-dovey, gooey marshmallowy for his guy," Noah joked.

"Just because you don't believe in anything more than a twenty-minute hookup doesn't mean other people don't want more from life."

"Whoa, little bro. Calm down, I was just saying—"

"It doesn't matter," I interrupted. "Please, guys, Emery is going to be here any minute now, and this really isn't how I planned to ask him to marry me."

"Marriage?" my mom asked while everyone looked at each other before they all started rapidly talking over each other, mixing English and Portuguese just like they did at every family dinner whenever something big was about to go down.

Why couldn't I come from a normal family?

"Yes!" I said, exasperated. "What did you think was going on here?" I gestured to the area around me. The table with the wine and pastries. My polished shoes, new slacks, and button-up shirt.

"We thought you were going to ask him to move in," Adam said. "Nellie from the bagel shop said she saw you get your keys cut last week, and River overheard you at the restaurant mumbling about closet space, which, if you ask me, is an impossible job in that matchbox you call an apartment. He said he suggested you could donate some clothes to Goodwill."

Ah, so River was my mole. He and Adam had been inseparable since we met in kindergarten when we were five. Noah even joked River was our triplet. It was ridiculous since River was a lot closer to Adam than me. Case in point, he'd mentioned the brief conversation we'd had at my parents' restaurant to my brother, who apparently had no twin loyalty.

"Okay, okay. Let's get outta here so my grandson can

propose to his man and start working on giving me some great-grandbabies."

"Avó!"

"What? I'm not getting any younger here."

"My god, you're all certifiable. If Emery ever figures out this is what he's in for if he marries me and then disappears into thin air, I'm never talking to you again. I'll disown you all," I said.

"Nonsense. That boy loves you, and I can guarantee he'd want to marry you any day, any time."

I couldn't help smiling at my mom's words. My reply didn't make it past my throat when I looked beyond the spot where my family stood.

"Lex?"

Emery stood a few feet behind my family. His eyes were wide open as he stared at me. For a moment, it was like no one else existed in the world but us.

"Did you mean it?" he asked, his voice shaky.

I narrowed the space between us in just a few steps. My family be damned. I wasn't going to miss this opportunity. I'd disown them later.

I took his hands in mine and brought them to my lips, kissing each of his warm palms in turn.

"It depends on what you heard, baby."

"You...you said"—he looked at my family behind us—"they said."

God, he was adorable when flustered. Emery was the kind of man who didn't like attention on him. He'd happily stand against the wall at a party, watching everyone have fun. And he'd one hundred percent prefer to skip the party over staying in with a movie and a tub of his favorite ice cream: peanut butter cup and chocolate brownie.

"Can we pretend they're not there?" I asked, but it was more of a plea.

He nodded, but it took a moment before his eyes returned to mine. His curly hair was wilder than usual. He'd probably run his fingers through it all afternoon while silently wishing all his students well on the test.

One of the many reasons I couldn't help loving this man.

"Emery, I came up with this elaborate scheme. The perfect location, the perfect chilled white wine, and the perfect food to win you over. The day we met, we almost got locked in here because we were so caught up talking. Then you offered to buy me ice cream. I'd never seen someone speak so passionately about ice cream or any other dairy product."

He smiled. I could swear my voice was too wobbly and my knees would buckle any time now, so I took a deep breath to continue.

"I knew that first day that you'd change my life. You were the person I'd been looking for since I saw Noah kiss a girl at school and decided I would only ever kiss the boy I was going to marry."

"We all know how that turned out," Noah mumbled.

I flipped him the bird and continued.

"You weren't the first boy I kissed, but I knew even before I kissed you for the first time that you would be the last one. So what do you say? Want to spend the rest of your life kissing just one boy?"

Emery let out a small gasp. I couldn't read his face as he looked at my family and then back at me.

"I mean me, in case you're wondering," I said, my heart competing for the Drummer of the Year Award.

Emery raised his hand to touch my cheek. His hand was warm, and when his thumb caressed my jaw, I shivered a little. He opened his mouth and closed it again before uttering the words that broke me.

"Lex...can we talk...somewhere else?"

Emery

Present time

"I need your help!" Ellie said, bursting into my empty classroom.

Only a moment ago, my eyes had rolled to the back of my head and I'd moaned as the smoky, spicy, savory chorizo tantalized my taste buds. The perfect filling for the fresh and crispy sourdough I'd bought this morning at the farmers' market on my way to work.

The farmers' market alone made my daily commute into Cliffborough worth it. Growing up outside the city, I remember being fascinated by what happened among the high-rise buildings, wondering why people were always so busy and running everywhere.

The reality was slightly different from what my imagination had made up while watching TV. Cliffborough retained a small-town vibe despite being a large city. At least that's how it felt to me because the buildings surrounding my school weren't that tall and people seemed a lot more chill than on TV.

Sure, the business district was full of high-rise buildings, but it wasn't an area I visited often. Besides, the river surrounding most of the city was more appealing to me.

And the farmers' market bread? It was as close as I could get to being somewhere on the Mediterranean coast while on my lunch break.

I knew my imaginary escape wouldn't last long. It never did. Not when in the classroom across the hall from mine, my best friend, Ellie, had spent the morning making weird hand gestures through the door's glass panel that I had yet to decipher.

"You're beyond help, Ellie."

She rolled her eyes and sat on the front-row desk closest to mine. "I'm serious. This is a DEFCON 4 situation, possibly in need of an upgrade. If I don't get this right, it could become DEFCON 1. The end of days. Armageddon."

"You were the answer to my prayers. The ticket to a new world. I'm sorry I'll never enjoy your freshness in its full capacity." I gazed longingly at my sandwich before placing it down to give full attention to my now soon-to-be-ex-best friend due to the fact she was interrupting my lunch. "There are very few situations in which I'd call out the end of days, so what is this one?"

"I told you about my sister, right?"

"You told me many things. Most I won't repeat out loud."

"Victoria just got engaged." Ellie threw her hands up in the air like I was supposed to get the true seriousness of the situation.

I gestured for her to go on.

"Ugh, you know how she's like the princess that gets everything she wants, right?"

"You have told me, yes."

"Her boyfriend, well, I guess it's fiancé now, proposed, and of course, she said yes."

"I'm still failing to see the need for any kind of DEFCON. Is that even how DEFCON works?" I asked.

She reached over and grabbed my sandwich right from my warm hands. Well, from the desk, but it was *my* sandwich. The scent of fresh bread had teased me all morning. I loved my students, but I'd been literally counting the minutes until lunchtime.

"Don't you dare take a bite, or I will never speak to you again, Eleanor Elizabeth Stanton," I said, full-naming her for effect, knowing how much she hated it.

She put the sandwich back like it was a bomb about to detonate. It was good to know she understood the precarious state of our six-month-old friendship at this very moment.

I took a bite and gestured for her to continue her story. Maybe I could pretend to listen while I traveled back to the sunny shores of the Mediterranean coast. Portugal, Spain, or maybe Sicily. Hmm...

"Okay, here's the thing," she started. "Victoria's boyfriend is great. I don't know what he sees in her, but I guess that's his funeral, right? But his family is also really nice. I've only met them a couple of times. They own that restaurant I've been telling you about for months."

I moaned a reply. I *really* was listening to her, but damn, the sandwich was nirvana. She must have accepted it as an agreement because she continued. Hand gestures and all.

"There's an engagement party this weekend. I don't have anything suitable to wear."

"I'm sure that's not true. Have I even seen you wear the same outfit twice?"

Ellie was super creative, and she had this theory that she could teach her students many important lessons through fashion. To be precise, the clothes she made herself and wore to school every day.

Her shoulders slumped a little, revealing a vulnerability I hadn't often seen in the feisty girl who befriended me six months ago on my first day at this school.

After the car accident that changed my whole life one year ago, saying I'd been a nervous wreck on my first day in this school was an understatement. I hadn't even needed to tell Ellie the reason for my anxiety before she took me under her wing.

"What's really wrong, Ellie?"

She sighed. "I don't want to look like the black sheep in the family, okay? Usually, I'd wear it like a badge of honor, but Adam's family is actually nice, so I find myself in the uncommon conundrum of caring about what people think about what I wear."

My brain felt fuzzy for a moment when she said the name Adam. It happened sometimes. It was like it was searching for a memory but not knowing where it was, so it left me feeling off balance.

I focused on my friend because this wasn't about me.

"Do you have time to make something yourself, or do we need to go shopping?" I asked.

"Ugh. I think I need to go shopping. If you tell anyone, I swear I'll kill you."

"Who would I tell?"

She was my only friend. Or at least the only one I'd made since the accident. Maybe there were other friends out there. Maybe someone called Adam. But there was no way for me to be sure. The accident took everything away from me, and I was still hoping to find the start of the breadcrumb trail that led to my lost life.

A few hours later, I dragged a reluctant Ellie into a shopping mall with the promise of ice cream therapy to make up for the horror of buying a ready-to-wear outfit for the party.

"You'd think you don't actually need to get something to wear for an event," I teased, bumping her arm after she scoffed at the tenth dress I'd suggested.

"None of these are perfect."

"Then pick one and make it perfect."

Her eyes bulged. "Oh my god, Em. You're right!" She put the dress down on the rack and pulled me by my hand out of the store and back into the first store we went into.

She picked the second dress I showed her and took it to the checkout.

"I can't believe I could have been eating ice cream for the last eight dresses."

"You should have had your brilliant idea earlier." She handed her card to the guy at the register. "I know exactly how to make this the best dress ever."

By the time we walked into The Ice Cream Parlor, I knew more than I ever thought I needed to know about fabric.

"Hi, Emery. I wondered if I'd see you this week," Patrick said as we approached the counter.

"Um, yeah, we're on an unplanned mission, but you know how I feel about ice cream."

He smiled and crooked his head a little. "I sure do. What can I get you today? The usual?"

"Yes, please."

Ellie coughed. "Can I have my usual too?"

Patrick looked at her as if he'd only just seen her. "Of course, darling. Remind me what it is again?"

"Strawberry shortcake with melted chocolate on top," she answered, not even trying to disguise her annoyance.

We took our ice cream to the seating area in the middle of the mall since the parlor didn't have seating space.

"Patrick couldn't be more obvious if he tried," Ellie said. "And you couldn't be more oblivious."

"What do you mean?"

"Don't play coy, Livingston. You know Patrick would drop to his knees and give you a blowjob if you half-crooked your little finger in his direction."

I laughed. Ellie thought every other guy out there was gay and into me.

"I'm pretty sure that's not true. He was only being friendly. Maybe he appreciates someone who appreciates ice cream."

She snorted. "He *appreciates* you. I bet he has wet dreams about you licking his ice cream. And no, that's not a euphemism. He's probably kinky like that. He'd kneel at your feet, holding a scoop of salted caramel and toffee—your favorite, of course. He'd say, 'Lick it, Master,' and hopelessly wait for you to finish so he could lick you in return."

"What kind of books have you been reading?" I asked, half laughing, half trying not to choke as I saw the toffee pieces in my ice cream in a different light.

"The best kind. The current one is about this guy who's really poor, and he falls in love with this super-rich guy with a kink for satin panties. It's like a gay Cinderella story with hot sex and a naughty twist. You should read it."

I pretended to be uninterested, but I was definitely curious. Reading had become one of the few ways I could escape when I was home.

Living with my parents was becoming stifling. The constant checks. The lack of privacy.

Maybe I should start looking for my own place in Cliffborough. The daily commute to school was made bearable by listening to my favorite audiobooks, but it also made my working days really long. Besides, what twenty-seven-year-old man still lived with his parents?

"You're doing that thing again," Ellie said.

"What thing?"

"When you're thinking about something so hard that the space between your brows creases. It's like you're trying to talk yourself into something and then talk yourself out of it. Maybe you should ask Patrick out."

I almost coughed up my ice cream. "What? No. You know I'm not ready to date. And I wasn't thinking about him."

"First," she said, pointing her spoon at me, "no one's talking about dating. You can let Patrick show you how much practice he's had licking"—the woman with two kids at the table next to ours looked at us with disapproval—"ice cream."

"No way. And second?"

"Second, you can come with me to the engagement party as my date."

"I'm sorry." I coughed again. "What?"

"Yes! That's it, you're coming with me. That way, you can filter anything I might be about to say or do. Help me fly under the radar so my sister leaves me alone. Not that I'm likely to even be asked to be a bridesmaid. I'm sure she won't even miss me if I don't make it to the wedding."

"Don't say that."

She gave me a look that told me she would very much be welcome to not attend the wedding if it was up to her sister.

"You're not really selling it to me, El."

"How about if I tell you Adam has a twin brother who's not only very single, he's also gay?"

I laughed. "I think we've established I'm not ready for that."

It was something I'd brought up at my therapy sessions. The last relationship I remember being in couldn't exactly be called a relationship when it had been merely two gay college roommates taking advantage of close quarters.

"No," she said, pointing at me with that damned spoon

again. "*You* established that. I'm establishing that you need to go out there and experience life."

"Ellie, it was because I was *experiencing life* that I ended up in a major accident and lost three years of my life."

Suddenly, the rest of my ice cream lost its appeal. I didn't even know if that was true, but how could a young twenty-six-year-old responsible adult wrap their car around a tree unless they were, as Ellie put it, *experiencing life*. Being irresponsible.

Ellie pushed her chair closer and linked her arm with mine.

"I'm sorry, Em. I didn't mean to push you. I can't imagine how hard it must be for you."

"I know."

"But...you can't be in this limbo forever. You need to live your life and open yourself up to new things. Good things."

She was right. It had taken me months after leaving the hospital to consider applying for a job. My parents hadn't wanted me to do it, but I couldn't continue staying home all day doing nothing.

I hadn't regretted that decision a single time. Even when we'd had a snowstorm last winter that made it almost impossible to get from my parents' estate into the city. I never missed a class. I just missed...what I didn't know was missing.

"Fine. I'll be your date. But can we just enjoy ourselves without any ulterior motives?"

"We can, Em. We definitely can." She placed a kiss on my cheek, and everything was better again.

"One thing, Ellie."

"Okay?"

"You should pair your dress with that red scarf with the skulls in bow ties. Don't let go of yourself to please other people."

She leaned her head on my shoulder and sighed. "You

should listen to your own words, honey. Sometimes, they make a lot of sense."

"I'll try. What's the worst that can happen, hey?"

Lex

"I can have the first concept with you on Monday, Mr. Knox. Just need a few tweaks before I'm ready to press send," I said into the phone, looking at the clock above my office door. Ten minutes to five. Which meant my brothers would barge in any moment now.

"Please call me Reed," he said with a soft laugh. "Mr. Knox makes me sound like I'm my grandfather."

"From what you said, he seemed like a great man."

"He was. Thank you, Lex. I loved your ideas, so I'm looking forward to seeing what you come up with."

"We're honored that you're trusting us with your brand. My mother sends her thanks for the honey samples you gave us. She's making a honey cake and can't wait to see how the lavender flavor will taste."

Working out the concept for a new brand was one of my favorite things to do. The blank page, the limitless ideas, the chance to put my stamp on someone's business. It was pure fun.

But working with an established business like Knox Farm gave me a different challenge because I wanted to capture the true essence of Reed's business. A business that had been started by his grandfather and was expanding into newer avenues under Reed's care.

I could tell how important the farm was to Reed and how he wanted to make his late grandfather proud. And if there was one thing I truly understood, it was family.

From how my parents' restaurant was woven from the core of our family to the business I'd started with my brothers when Adam and I finished college, family had always been the most important thing in my life.

Even when said brothers marched into my office looking like they were up to anything but something good.

"Bro, time to pack up," Noah said.

I leaned back in my chair and pointed at the clock. "Great example you're setting, big boss."

"Dude, it's Friday. Everyone knows the rules. Do what you must, but if you must not, then go home when you want to." He pointed at me and Adam, and then himself. "We created that rule specifically for days like today."

He was right. We all worked hard but never forgot that everyone needed to unwind, including the dozen people we employed at the agency and us.

The only problem was that I wasn't feeling that social. If I were honest, I hadn't been feeling social for a whole year. Being ghosted by the man who promised to love and marry you would do that to a person.

"Fine. Give me five so I can grab my stuff. I'll meet you downstairs," I said. Adam's smile alone was worth pretending that everything was fine. That I was fine.

It wasn't every day that your twin brother got engaged, right? What self-respecting brother wouldn't help him get drunk off his ass before he faced his fiancée's family in less than twenty-four hours?

Five minutes later, I was wrapping my arm around Adam's

shoulder and messing his hair. "Come on, let's get you wasted."

"No way, man. If I go home drunk, Victoria will cut off my balls, flatten them like a pancake, wrap them in a box, and hand them back to me."

"That's oddly specific," Noah said, "but whatever you guys are into, it's not our business."

There was absolutely no way Noah would let Adam get home in a state less than deplorable. I could see it in his eyes.

I loved our big brother, but he didn't do anything by half-measure. He worked hard and played even harder. I didn't want to think too much about how many people he'd hooked up with in the past and how many had come back for seconds. Adam and I, on the other hand, had always been the romantics. We wanted to find the love of our lives, get married, and live happily ever after.

Adam had a shot with Victoria, but me? After Emery, there would be no one. I couldn't risk my heart again.

Tanner's was, as usual, full of loud and happy people ready to start their weekend. We'd tried other bars in the business district, but Tanner's was conveniently located a block from work and served the best buffalo wings in the city.

We walked through the crowd until we reached the bar. Tanner, the owner, was pulling a draft beer. His short blond hair and baby face looked so out of place in the bar, like he was better suited for an Abercrombie photoshoot than pulling beers. His tattooed arms, however, were a total contradiction to the rest of his look. I'd always wondered if he had other tattoos on his body.

He winked at Noah when he saw us.

"Dude, is there anyone in this town you haven't slept with?" Adam asked.

"Who says I slept with Tanner?"

I snorted. "The way he's looking at you like he wants to spill that beer all over your chest and then lick it clean."

Noah kept his eyes on Tanner as he said, "You got that right, little bro. He sure wants. Maybe tonight will be his lucky night."

We found a table after a small group left and ordered a couple dozen wings and beer while Noah continued to communicate with Tanner using the power of his eyebrows alone.

"Do you ever keep it in your pants?" I asked.

"Why would I when it's so much fun to whip it out and watch the reaction as they fall at my feet."

"Not that you're cocky about it," Adam said.

"Besides," Noah said, "with Adam off the market and you living as a monk, someone has to meet the sexual needs of the people in this town."

"I hear Mrs. Poach is ready to get back on the dating scene after she kicked her husband out for cheating on her with the postman," Adam said, talking about our parents' neighbor.

"I'm not living like a monk. And isn't Mrs. Poach like seventy?"

Noah raised his glass. "Hey, even older ladies have needs. I won't be the one to meet them, but leave poor Josephine out of this."

I raised my glass to my lips, savoring the cold beer. There was nothing like it after a day inside the four walls of my office. "This is just what I needed."

"I think what you need is to get laid," Noah said.

"Give it a rest," Adam said. When I met his eyes, I saw twelve months of concern in a single look.

"Sorry, bud." Noah put his hand on my shoulder. "I don't mean to push you, but I want to see you happy, and this version of you isn't happy."

Out of both my brothers, I always thought Adam would

be the first to break. The first to tell me I needed to make an effort and get out there. Date. Be happy.

As if it was that easy.

"Do you think I haven't tried? That I haven't given myself a hundred pep talks?" I glanced at all the people around us. The easy smiles, the flirty looks over the top of a beer bottle. "I thought my life would turn out a lot different from what it has. I don't want to bring the mood down, but I'm not ready to put myself out there, okay?"

My eyes tracked the front door of the bar. For a moment, I let myself believe Emery would be the next person through it. Walking in with his wild curly hair, eyes searching for me. He'd be late because he got distracted grading his students' homework, but as soon as he saw me, his smile would light up the room, telling everyone that he belonged with me.

Instead, it was a different familiar face that I saw.

"Hey, guys. Thank fuck you've got beer and food. I swear I get more trouble from your dad than you all do, and I'm not even his son. I'm starving."

River's sudden arrival put an end to the conversation. Adam visibly relaxed and Noah returned to his brow mime conversation with Tanner.

"What's he done now?" I asked.

"Who?" River sucked a wing into his mouth and took a large swig of the beer Adam had ordered for him. "Oh, your dad. He needs to stop micromanaging the restaurant. I can't get the staff to do what I need them to do when he goes behind my back and gives them everything they want. I spent all afternoon trying to fill a Saturday shift in two weeks because he gave three people the day off."

I shook my head. "I don't miss the weekends we had to help out before we opened the agency. Working at the restaurant is no life. I don't know how you do it full-time. No amount of money would get me to go back."

"Thanks." He raised a brow and looked at Adam, who shrugged and smiled back. "I love how you're all super interested in the business you will inherit one day."

Adam put his arm around River. "Nah, the old man is going to leave the restaurant to you. You're practically one of us, and he knows we have the agency. If there's anyone capable of carrying on the Lusitana legacy, it's you."

"One of you...right." He removed Adam's arm from his shoulder.

"Yeah, you're like our brother from another mother."

Adam seemed oblivious to River stiffening next to him. I wondered what that was about. They'd been best friends since we were kids, and as far as I was aware, they never fought about anything. Ever.

"I'll be right back. Gotta take a leak," River said, heading toward the restroom.

Adam took his phone out, and I saw Victoria's name pop up. He declined the call.

"Is River okay?" I asked.

"What? Sure, why wouldn't he be?" Adam asked. "You mean the stuff about Dad? You know he complains, but he loves Dad, and he loves the restaurant. A lot more than we do."

"Hell yeah. The years of servitude ended when I went to college," Noah said. "Thank fuck for River. And thank you for forcing him to hang out with you in kindergarten." He raised his glass in a mock toast.

It was probably nothing, but River had seemed a little off to me. Maybe I was hypersensitive to people's moods because I'd been faking my own for a year, but I was certain something was up.

When he returned from the restroom, the conversation changed to the engagement party. Noah declared we needed a double round of drinks if we were going to talk about anything wedding-related.

"I'm sorry to say this, Adam, but to have the party at the Botanical Gardens is incredibly insensitive," Noah said after finishing his second beer.

Adam's shoulders sank. "I know, man. I tried to get Victoria to change her mind. Even offered Lusitana as an alternative, but she wouldn't budge."

River gave me a sympathetic look.

I hadn't been to the Botanical Gardens since the day I proposed to Emery, and the thought of returning for not just a party but my twin brother's engagement party made my stomach roll with nausea.

But I couldn't tell Adam that. He already felt bad enough.

"It's fine. It's just a location. Nothing more. Besides, I agree with Victoria that it's the perfect setting for an engagement party."

Noah opened his mouth to speak, but I stopped him. "Look, I don't want everyone to walk on eggshells around me. I'm not the first man to be dumped after a proposal, and I certainly won't be the last. Who knows, once I break the seal by going back to the gardens, I might be tempted to try other things."

Three pairs of caring eyes stared back at me. None of them believed the bullshit I'd just spat out, but they seemed too afraid to call it out.

Thank fuck for small mercies.

"Let's toast to Adam's balls being chained forever," I said, raising my glass.

Despite Noah's plans, no one got anywhere close to being drunk. I stopped after my third beer, and with the number of wings consumed, I probably walked out of the bar more sober than when I'd walked in.

River only had two beers before he took Adam back to the

apartment he shared with Victoria, and Noah and his flirty eyebrows were last seen on their way to the bar where Tanner was serving drinks shirtless.

I guessed that answered the question about the tattoos. Tanner did have a bunch of them all over his chest. It was interesting that if he wore a long-sleeved shirt, no one would ever guess what was underneath, and with his preppy all-American good looks, he could pass for a choir boy.

That was how I felt most days. Wearing a long-sleeved shirt to cover up what was really hiding underneath. A broken-hearted man.

As usual, the only thing welcoming me home was the goldfish Emery had won for me at a fair last year. We'd spent the afternoon walking around, eating cotton candy, and talking about why people wasted money on all the games no one ever won.

That was until he saw the tiny goldfish at the shooting booth and spent a hundred dollars trying to win the poor thing so he could rescue him from living out his days as a shooting booth prize.

Goldie had lived longer than expected and was a daily reminder of what I'd lost, but I couldn't help loving the little guy. Sometimes, I wished I was a goldfish like him, swimming in the tank, being fed at regular intervals, with no expectations to achieve anything more in life other than live it.

After grabbing a shower and feeding Goldie, I was too tired to work and not in the mood to watch TV.

The picture frames on the wall outside my bedroom caught my attention. Most days, I actively ignored them, but I was too unsettled by the conversation with my brothers and the thought of going back to the Botanical Gardens tomorrow.

Emery and me at the beach on Mountview Lake.

Emery and me at the fair with Goldie inside his plastic bag.

Emery and me talking as we danced at my parents' wedding anniversary.

That one hurt the most because that was the moment I'd decided I wanted to spend the rest of my life with him.

"Na vida tens que lutar pelo que queres, meu filho, porque ninguém to vai dar." *In life, you have to fight for what you want because no one's gonna give it to you.* Those were my avó's words when I'd told her my plans. That was just before she'd opened the fridge and cut a perfect square right from the middle of the yet-uncut chocolate brownie my mom had made.

Then she gave me half the slice, and only after I'd finished it did she blackmail me into confessing to my mom that I'd taken the whole thing.

Why would I confess to a whole crime when I'd only been an accessory to half of it? Because I loved my grandmother more than life itself, and she knew it.

She was right. If I wanted to live more than the half-life I was living now, I needed to fight for it.

I took the photos off the wall and put them in the nearest drawer, away from sight. Maybe one day, I could look at them again without feeling hurt.

Today was not that day.

But today marked the start of a lot of changes for Alexis Spencer.

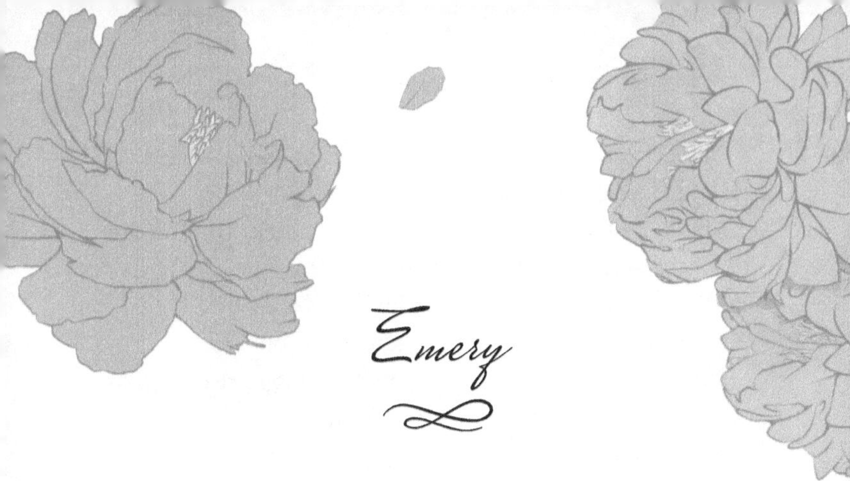

Emery

Any hope of getting out of the house undetected was quashed when I heard my name being called as I was almost to the front door.

"Emery, sweetheart, join me for a cup of tea," my mom said in that voice that meant it wasn't a question. Or at least not a request I wanted to challenge.

"Hi, Mom," I said, dragging myself into the kitchen, where she was pouring tea into two porcelain cups. I didn't even like tea, but I knew it would break her heart if I refused the drink, so as usual, I joined her.

"Were you going somewhere, darling? It's getting late."

It took everything in me not to remind her that leaving the house at five o'clock on a Saturday was neither late nor unusual for a man my age.

But I got it. She worried. She had reason to. After all, she'd almost lost me a year ago.

I just found it hard to walk the line between being thankful to my parents for everything they'd done for me and wishing for the courage to tell them I needed my independence.

"Ellie has a family event and asked if I could go with her," I said. "I won't be back late."

"Ellie…? Oh, that girl with the weird clothes you brought here once? I didn't realize you were that close."

"We work together, Mom, and we're friends."

"And you're going all the way to Cliffborough?"

"Yes." Cliffborough was only an hour-long drive from us, but to my mother, it may well be on Mars.

She stared at me over the rim of her teacup with those piercing green eyes I inherited. Her strawberry-red curls, something else I inherited from her, had been styled into submission. I had never understood why she despised them on such a deep level. I rarely saw her hair in anything less than a straight line, down only as far as the top of her shoulders.

"Hmm. Well, if you're not in a rush, there's something I want to talk to you about."

I *was* in a hurry, but from experience, there was no way to get out of a conversation with my mom.

My dad, on the other hand, was either hiding in his office working or had left this morning to play golf with his friends and hadn't yet returned. It was hard to tell when the house was quieter than a mausoleum most of the time.

"I don't want to be late, Mom."

"This won't take long."

Her gaze pinned me to my chair. I swirled the spoon around the pinkish water in the cup and took a sip. A sugar cube would make the tea much more bearable, but then I'd have to contend with a comment about how it ruined the flavor.

"I'm all ears then."

"As you may have noticed, your dad isn't getting any younger."

Oh god, not this conversation again.

"Mom—"

"Your dad built the company for you, Emery. It's time you take on some of the work and start learning how to manage the business and then take over managing the family's assets when the time comes."

"I can't just leave my job, Mom."

"I understand, and I agree that taking the teaching job was a good stepping stone back into the workplace. A way to help your recovery. It was your idea to return to teaching to get back on your feet. You said no one ever achieved anything by sitting at home doing nothing. You said you wanted to work with your father. This was your decision, Emery. He put all the steps in place for you and agreed to let you finish the year so you're not letting the school down, but as soon as the year ends, you're working with your father."

I stared at the cooling tea in front of me, unable to reply. She was right.

Did I remember making that decision? No. But past Emery had wanted it, so who was I to question it?

Three months. They were giving me three months until the weight of my surname came crashing down on me.

"Don't look so dejected, my dear. Any young man in your position would be delighted to have such an opportunity. You've never wanted for anything in your life. Your father and I have been there for you every single moment. It's time for you to do your part now."

I nodded. She smiled and stood, taking her empty tea cup to the sink. I followed with mine, grateful for the small mercy that she hadn't commented on my single sip of the tasteless drink.

"Oh, by the way," she said, pushing her hair behind her ear even though there wasn't a single lock out of place, "Jeanelle Rhys-Myr's son has just come back from Europe. He's the one who's been studying international law and business. You should take him out and show him around. He could use a friend after being away for so long."

A friend. What a loaded concept when coming from my mom.

"I'm not sure, Mom. The guy probably has his own friends and doesn't want a babysitter. He grew up around here, didn't he?"

"He spent most of his time at a boarding school before going to Europe for his degree, so he doesn't know anyone local. Be a good friend, Emery."

It wasn't even a wild shot to guess that my mother's intentions had nothing to do with me being a good friend and everything to do with her wanting to set me up with her best friend's son.

"I'll think about it," I said, kissing her cheek. Before she had a chance to say anything, I walked out of the house and practically ran to my car.

Sometimes it felt like my life was so heavy that one single conversation with my mom had the chance to finally turn me into a pancake. And not the fluffy kind. More the kind that was thick, heavy, and flat.

That was me. A walking, talking pancake. Squashed by the pressure of my obligation to my parents and their legacy.

"Snap out of it, Emery," I said to myself as I turned on the car. In an hour, I'd be in Cliffborough, where I could finally breathe. I tried to question my brain about that, but it still wasn't cooperating.

My therapist had told me to follow my instincts whenever a place, person, or object felt familiar, even if I didn't know why.

"It will come back to you, Emery. Sometimes the brain just needs a jumpstart. Like a car with a dead battery," he'd said.

A year after the accident, I was still waiting for the jumpstart, and my battery felt like it would never jolt back to life.

The only option was to accept my life as it was now. A clean slate, my mom had called it.

My therapist had agreed.

Then why did I have this pain in my chest that felt a lot like grief? Like I'd lost something so important in my life that the lack of it was becoming physically painful, even when I had no idea what it was.

I was almost at the end of the private drive from my parents' place onto the main road when I saw a familiar face. I slowed the car to a stop.

"Hey, Mr. Kowalski, isn't it about time you finished for the day?"

"Oh hello, Emery. I'm almost done here. You know how your mother loves the hedges to stay neat." He put the hedge trimmer down, rotating his wrists. Gardening was hard work for a man his age, but as far as I knew, he was reluctant to take retirement. "And where are you headed to? Anywhere fun?"

"Just going into the city to see a friend."

He nodded. "You always did like the city. Counting the days until you could leave. That was you since you were a little boy."

"I remember that."

"I suppose you'll be moving back soon now that you have your job and all," he said.

What?

"What do you mean?" I asked.

Mr. Kowalski's brows narrowed for a moment. "I suppose you don't remember that. I'm sorry, son. I forget what happened."

"That's okay, but what did you mean when you said about me moving back?"

"Well," he said, scratching his short beard, "you moved out to the city about two years ago. It was very sudden. I don't get up in the family business, as you know, but you were here one day and gone the next. Then the accident happened, and you were back."

"Mr. Kowalski, can I ask you a favor? Can you keep this conversation between us?"

"Of course, son."

I waved him goodbye and got back on the road. His words replayed in my head all the way into the city. Had I moved out? Why hadn't my mom said anything? Surely, I would have noticed if I'd only recently moved back.

"Welcome home, Emery," Mom said, opening the door to my room.

"Thanks, Mom."

I looked around. Everything was familiar. Same bed. Blanket over the chair in the corner. A stack of books on the desk. But I couldn't shake off the feeling that I wasn't coming home.

"Everything is as you left it. Your clothes are in the closet. I'm going downstairs to check on dinner. Settle in, and I'll call you when it's ready."

"Okay. Thank you."

She gave me one last look before leaving the room. How weird that she pointed out where my clothes were, like it wasn't obvious.

I took a deep breath and looked out into the garden outside my window.

After three months in the hospital, I was finally out. Physically, I felt fine. But the rest? The doctor had advised me to get a therapist to talk through everything that happened.

I laughed to myself. If only I could remember what happened.

All I knew was that I couldn't shake the feeling that something wasn't right.

I forced myself to be present and focus on Ellie and the dinner.

The Botanical Gardens were easy to find. The parking lot

was busy, but I was able to find a spot. Ellie hadn't messaged yet, so I was probably early, despite my mother's brief distraction.

Apparently, the dinner was in a room adjacent to the rose garden, but I didn't want to go in without Ellie. I got out of the car, took my phone out, and sent her a message as I walked toward the big building.

The metal frame with glass panels that made up the building entrance looked somewhat familiar. I knew I hadn't been to the Botanical Gardens since my accident, so I wondered if maybe this was a place I used to visit before the accident.

I paid for my entry ticket while waiting for Ellie's reply. It wasn't until after that I realized I probably didn't need it since we were attending a private function, but at least I could check out the inside of the building.

I picked up a leaflet with the map and walked around the lobby area. It was a semi-open-plan place with a glass roof above an area with a tree and some plants, giving it an outdoor feel.

My phone dinged with a message.

ELLIE

Five minutes. Helping the hot server with his drinks tray.

EMERY

You think he can last five minutes when you're wearing the dress I know you're wearing?

ELLIE

I'm actually helping him, but now you're giving me ideas. See you in ten.

. . .

I chuckled to myself, putting the phone away.

Ten minutes later, there was no sign of Ellie, so I went to the restroom. I was coming out when someone bumped into me on their way in.

"Sorry," the guy said quickly. A shiver went up my spine, and I turned to make sure he was okay, but all I saw was the back of his head. Dirty-blond hair, slightly tousled, and then he was inside.

I shrugged it off and walked toward the middle of the lobby. Maybe I could find the Rose Room and make my way there to meet Ellie instead of waiting.

The Botanical Gardens' areas were well labeled, so it shouldn't be difficult to find my way.

Those moments when my brain tried to kickstart still caught me unaware every time. It put me off balance, and I hated it as much as I welcomed the opportunity for a memory to return.

So when my eyes fell on the sign for the tree peony collection and a weird flash, followed by a series of images passed in front of my eyes, I felt like my world had been flipped upside down.

A group of people with their backs to me.

A guy without a face facing me but standing on the other side of the group.

Peonies. Hundreds of peonies in bloom. Those I saw clearly.

I didn't realize I'd collapsed until I opened my eyes and saw I was on the ground.

"Are you okay?" a man asked, kneeling beside me. "I noticed you looking at the sign, and suddenly, it was as if your legs failed you. Do you want me to call an ambulance?"

Take a deep breath, Emery.

"Um...no..." I looked around, thankful when I didn't see

anyone else. "I'm okay." I stood, and the man helped me to a bench nearby. "I just need a moment. I'm okay, I promise."

"I don't want to leave you alone, but I need to go," he said apologetically. I nodded.

"My friend will be here any moment. I'll wait for her here."

"If you're sure."

I raised my hand to shake his and noticed my trembling fingers. I closed my hand and took a deep breath, and when the man was out of sight, I called Ellie.

"Hey, Emmy-Boo. Please tell me you're not giving up on me and going. The wicked bride from the Southside is driving me nuts, and I'm about ready to leave this party. Sorry to take so long. I'll be with you in a minute."

"Ellie," I said, my voice shaky.

"Emery, what's up? Where are you?"

"Outside, the large hallway off the lobby. I...something weird happened. I think I remembered something."

She gasped. "You're shitting me? This is huge. Let me find Adam to apologize for leaving the dinner."

"No! No, you can't do that. Your family will be upset."

"They'll live."

Even though I felt really bad for Ellie, I was also relieved. I needed to tell Ellie what I'd remembered because I didn't trust my brain to not forget it again.

I also needed help deciphering it.

Who was the guy without a face?

I forced myself to continue into the restroom. It was bad enough that my anxiety was through the roof and I was hanging on by a thread. Imagining Emery was the stranger with the curly hair I'd just bumped into was a new low level.

I ran cold water over my face and went back out, but instead of returning to the Rose Room, I walked past the ticket area in the lobby and out of the building.

Men and women in white shirts and black slacks walked in and out of a door on the side of the building.

Bingo.

I followed them. No one challenged me when I walked in through the catering area. With my white shirt and dark gray slacks, I could pass as one of them. I grabbed a bottle of champagne and a tray of truffles and went back out.

"Hey, where are you going? The function is that way," someone said, stopping me.

"Um, yeah, there are a couple of guests outside. I figured they didn't want to be left out. They look kinda important."

The guy stared at me for a moment.

"Okay, fine, but come right back. The bride's throwing a

hissy fit, and we need all hands on deck in the actual function room."

"All right, boss."

I didn't have a plan, so I followed my feet until I was back inside the building in the same place I'd stood a year ago.

My heart thundered as I followed Emery from the tree peony collection toward the parking lot.

His hand was warm on mine and his grip was firm. He hadn't let go. That was a good sign, right?

The pond on the other side of the parking lot was always full of people having picnics on the grass in the summer, but today, it was mostly empty.

The sun was slowly coming down, giving the sky an orange-red hue. I could already see the blue poking out from behind the mountains in the distance. Or maybe it was my imagination.

Emery walked us toward one of the gazebos. Most were covered in rose bushes, ivy, and other climbing plants that provided some shade or, in our case, privacy.

Privacy for what?

Was he going to let me down gently?

Maybe I'd misread our whole relationship. Maybe Emery didn't love me the way I loved him. Maybe he wasn't ready to get married yet, or at all.

Fuck. Had I messed it all up with the proposal?

"Can I take it back? Can we pretend today didn't happen? Please, Emery." My voice broke as I rambled. "I blame my grandmother for turning me into a hopeless romantic. She's told me all these stories about her and my granddad and my parents and true love and happy ever afters. My parents are so happy. I wanted the same, I...I made you pastéis de nata." I blurted that last one so loud that Emery stopped and turned around.

He pulled me closer until we were nose to nose, staring into each other's eyes.

"Did you really mean what you said?" he asked. The closest gazebo was only a few feet away.

"Yes, I made you pastéis de nata. They're really good. Maybe my best batch yet."

He chuckled, pulling away and dragging me into the gazebo. "Do you want to marry me?" His hand cradled my cheek. "Do you want to take it back?"

I swallowed. "I would be the happiest man on earth if I had the chance to spend the rest of my life with you. Married or not."

"I want to marry you too."

"Is it because of the pastéis de nata?" I exhaled for what felt like the first time since we'd left my family behind in the tree peony collection.

"You got me. I always said if a man ever baked pastéis de nata for me, I'd marry him. You're basically giving me no other option." He leaned forward and pressed his lips against mine.

It could have been nerves from planning the proposal, the near miss when I thought he would say no, or maybe it was just the effect Emery had on me, but I suddenly needed him like I needed my next breath.

A fire unfurled in my gut, extending to every single nerve ending. I deepened the kiss, pushing Emery against the corner of the gazebo that offered privacy from prying eyes.

I wasn't naive enough to trust that my family wouldn't follow us. They'd give us enough distance that they couldn't necessarily hear our whispered conversation, but they'd be watching.

"Jesus, Lex, we need to get out of here," Emery rasped into my mouth.

"You won't hear me complain."

"No," he said, pulling his mouth away and placing my

hand on his crotch, groaning when I pressed my palm against his erection. "We need to get out of here, and I can't like this."

"I can take care of it, baby."

"Lex!"

"Fine. But I'm taking you to my place right now. I need you naked as a matter of priority." I pulled away from him reluctantly.

He looked adorably mussed, like he'd been devoured by the big bad wolf. I was no wolf, and at five foot eleven, I wasn't exactly big, but the plans I had for when we got to my place would definitely fall under the bad umbrella.

"There's only one thing," he said, his expression suddenly changing. "I didn't want to do this in front of your family because—"

"They're too much. Trust me, I know. We can avoid them. I'll message Adam, and he'll make sure we have a clear route to the parking lot," I said, taking his hand before I looked toward the building to ensure we wouldn't be ambushed.

I couldn't believe he'd actually said yes. Emery wanted to be my husband. Okay, so the proposal hadn't exactly gone as I'd planned, thanks to my meddling family, but I'd gotten a yes, and that was all that mattered.

"Wait. It's not that." Emery pulled on my hand, stopping me before I dragged us out.

"What is it?"

"I need to go away to deal with a family...thing. Do you think...maybe...we could keep the engagement between us until I'm back?"

I looked at Emery but wasn't sure what I was looking for in his expression.

As if he could tell what I was thinking before I thought it, he said, "I love you so much, Lex. I would never do anything to hurt you. It's just a couple of days. I promise when I'm back, we can celebrate the engagement properly. Hell, we can even move in *together. My lease is up for renewal next month."* He shrugged. *"If you want to spend the rest of your life with me, you better get used to seeing me every day, right?"*

I smiled, tugging him closer. "Every single day, baby. For the rest of our lives."

Those words replayed in my mind over and over again as I stared at the peony blooms in front of me.

"We can move in together. I love you so much, Lex." And the worst of all. *"I would never hurt you."*

The bubbles in my large gulp of champagne went up my nose, making me cough. I hated champagne, but it had seemed like a good idea to take the bottle when I walked past the server opening it to fill a tray of glasses. As had taking the full tray of chocolate truffles.

I'd heard Avó complain between her teeth that these fancy truffles didn't shine a candle on the many Portuguese traditional pastries. Naturally, she was incensed about the crime committed against good food, and naturally, I'd taken it upon myself to help her cause by making a large chunk of said truffles disappear into my belly.

There was a very good chance I'd barf into the nearest peony any moment now.

I groaned when I heard the echo of footsteps behind me.

"Leave me alone."

"Can't do that, little brother. It's my engagement party, and if you're broody, I'm broody. Blame Mom and Dad. Or genetics, or some shit," Adam said, sitting on the floor beside me.

"I'm not broody."

"Then why are you in the tree peony collection surrounded by a half-eaten truffle tray and an admittedly too-full-for-broody champagne bottle?" Adam picked up the bottle and took a long swig. "Damn, this is the good stuff. I don't even want to think how much it's costing me."

In his light-gray suit, dress shoes, and over-styled hair, I almost didn't recognize my twin.

"I'm...healing," I said, taking two truffles and stuffing them into my mouth.

"Oh really? Because that looks a lot like you're eating your emotions, and *that*"—he pointed to the tray beside me—"isn't even the good stuff. Don't let Avó catch you eating those."

"I'm helping her, actually. These need to disappear into the black hole that is my body. I'm providing a service to our heritage."

Adam helped himself to a few truffles, and for a while, it was just the two of us, the bottle of champagne, and the tray of truffles.

The longer we sat in silence, the harder it was for me to not feel like I was ruining my brother's day. The decision I'd made last night had crumbled as soon as I stepped into the Botanical Gardens, but enough was enough. If I wanted my life to change, I needed to allow change to happen.

Fuck Emery. I deserved more.

"Come on," I said, standing all of a sudden.

"Huh?"

"You were right, and I'm really sorry for keeping you away from your important day. Today isn't about me. I've moped, and I've had enough."

Adam stared at me in disbelief, but he must have seen the resolution on my face because he hugged me tight. We were making our way back to the party when Ellie, Victoria's sister, approached us.

"Hey, um..."

"Adam?" I asked, pointing at my brother.

She smiled and shrugged. "It's still hard to tell you two apart. Sorry."

"Are you looking for Victoria?" Adam asked.

"Actually, I was looking for you. I want to apologize for leaving early, but my friend needs me."

I'd always gotten the impression that Victoria and her sister weren't exactly close. Ellie had always struck me as a nice, down-to-earth woman, if a little eccentric.

"Is everything okay? Can we help in any way?" I asked.

Her forehead creased, but she shook her head. "No. He had a really bad accident last year and lost his memory. He was actually coming today as my plus one, but he had some kind of episode or flashback or something. I just need to be with him and make sure he's okay."

Adam, by far the most tactile of us, hugged Ellie straight away.

"Go help your friend. We hope he's okay," he said.

"Knowing him, he probably remembered that his favorite ice cream isn't salted caramel with toffee chunks after all." She chuckled, but it was easy to see she was worried.

"Is there anyone you want us to inform that you're gone?" I asked.

"I'll message my parents later." She turned to go back toward the exit before she turned to us again. "Hey, Lex, do you know the farmers' market by the old cinema on Sloane Square?"

"Yeah, I usually go there on Sunday mornings. Why?"

She seemed to think about something for a moment. "No reason. I've been looking for a new artisan baker and wondered if it's worth checking that market."

I smiled. "It's definitely the place to be for all your carb needs."

"Now you're talking. Might bump into you there."

She turned around and left, speeding up her pace as she went.

"Huh."

I looked at Adam. "What do you mean?"

"If I didn't know that she knows you're gay, I'd have thought she was flirting with you."

I laughed. "The truffles have gone to your head. Come on, let's go find the love of your life."

"Victoria?"

It was my turn to laugh. "No. River. He'll keep me company while you schmooze your in-laws. God knows Noah is probably already defiling some dark corner and showing the tropical plants a good time."

He elbowed me, and for the first time in a long time, I laughed because I wanted to, not because I felt I had to.

"I hope you're ready for the epicurean gangbang of your life so far." Ellie clapped her hands in front of her chest as I approached our meeting spot by the farmers' market.

"I'm not sure if I should be scared that you're terming it a gangbang or that you're assuming this will happen more than once. And who says epicurean and gangbang in the same sentence?"

"Don't be a mood pooper, Em. I thought you'd be a little happier at the prospect of carbs and coffee."

I wasn't in a mood as such…I'd just had a tough week. Between what Mr. Kowalski had said last weekend, the weird flashback memory, and failing to get my mom off my back about taking her friend's son out, I felt like an old wet cloth. Wrung out and slightly frayed at the edges.

"And I thought we were here to buy vegetables," I said.

She wrapped her arm around mine, pulling me across the street. "Coffee comes from beans. That's a vegetable, right? The Coffee Cart's brownies are made with avocado. That's a vegetable."

"Coffee beans are the pit of the fruit that grows on coffee trees and avocados are fruits."

I didn't have to look at her to know she was rolling her eyes.

"Don't go all teacher on me. It's the weekend, and we're off, so let's have a good time. Come on, this is just what you need."

I raised a brow and snorted.

"*Fine*," she said, overly dramatic. "*I* need the brownie and the coffee. What can I say? Last night's dessert kept me up all night."

"How many times do I have to tell you Tinder and Uber Eats aren't the same thing?"

She pulled me closer. "Tell that to the guy who spent all night with his mouth on my—"

I covered her mouth with my hand. "No! No, I don't need to know the details of your...gastronomic experiences." I shuddered. I loved Ellie, but she had no filter and no shame.

Despite her apparent need for coffee, our first stop was at a stall that sold honey-based products.

"Hey, Callan," she said to the big guy behind the display table low enough that it was almost a whisper. "You have the stuff?"

"Hi, Ellie. Like I would ever forget my best customer." He grabbed a bag from under the table and handed it to her. "I trust that's all in order."

She tapped her nose like they were doing some secret exchange and then handed him some folded bills.

"Same time next month?" he asked.

"Until you finally give in and let me take you out."

"You know I have a pretty demanding man in my life who takes up all my attention. A pretty girl like you deserves more." He winked, and a small dimple appeared on his cheek.

I watched their exchange and Ellie's uncharacteristic blush

but waited until we were out of earshot before I poked her on her ribs.

"Anything you want to share?"

"No. This honey is all mine. I go through two jars a month, and the lavender soap isn't your scent."

"You know that's not what I meant."

Around us, people moved between stalls like a practiced dance. I just held on to Ellie so we wouldn't get separated in the crowd. Especially since I was now super curious about her and Mr. Honey Man.

She shrugged. "Nothing to tell. I may have an itsy-bitsy crush on Callan, but I know it'll never go anywhere."

"Why not?"

"Because he's a widowed father of a toddler who lives for his job. We're just friends, and you know me. I can't resist a good man or woman with dark eyes and a plaid flannel shirt."

"Not to mention the dimple."

She rolled her eyes and bit her lip. "That dimple, right?"

"So tell me about last night's meal. The PG stuff, please," I begged as we walked the length of the marker toward the Coffee Cart.

"His name is Ten, which is short for Tennessee."

"Is that a real name?"

She snorted. "Apparently, it is. And so is his huge"—she looked around for sensitive ears—"dick."

"Ellie," I warned.

"Just stating the facts. It's just biology, so don't go all blushing virgin on me. Anyway, Ten has the killer combination of LBD."

"Little black dress?"

"Looks. Brain. Dick."

"You mean he's hot but can hold a conversation, especially when naked."

She laughed. "Exactly. So naturally, I didn't want to have

anything to do with him. Can you imagine meeting up and finding out he's actually a thirty-five-year-old manchild who still lives with his mother and refuses to eat anything but ramen?"

"You've given this some thought."

"If you bothered to look at your Tinder profile, you'd understand."

It was my turn to laugh. "I don't have a Tinder profile."

Her evil smile only reassured me that I couldn't trust her.

"Eleanor Elizabeth Stanton, what have you done? No. Don't tell me. I prefer to be oblivious. If I don't see it, it doesn't exist."

"I'll say nothing."

"So, how did you get past your manchild issue?"

A couple of stalls away from where we were headed, my eyes fell on a guy. He was turned away, but something about him drew me in. He looked up from the vegetables to the guy running the stall and smiled. My lungs forgot what air was and my brain mushed into a pulp.

Hot damn.

"...so the guy said if I was up for it, he knew a girl I'd like. I never told him about, you know, my preferences, so I don't know if this is a sex thing or a preference thing. It's fine either way, you know. Fun is fun, but sometimes a girl just wants to find her people and fuck her way around town. Fuck every-one. Fuck the mailman, fuck the plumber, fuck the lady that helps the kids cross the road, fuck the grandma–"

"What?" I asked, suddenly paying attention to the number of fucks she'd just said. "Fuck whose grandma?"

"Don't worry, I don't have a grandma kink. I was just trying to grab your attention. Who are you looking at?"

I pointed in the direction of the mystery man.

"Oh, holy coincidence. I couldn't have timed it better if I'd tried," she said, sounding weirdly excited.

"What do you mean?"

"That's Lex. He's Adam's twin. I was going to introduce you two last weekend, but..."

She didn't need to finish what she was going to say. I'd been feeling super bad all week for taking her away from her family, even though she'd assured me that listening to each detail of my flashback over and over again had been a much better use of her time. Not to mention the gallon of ice cream we ate together when we got back to her place.

Ellie walked up to the guy with me right behind her, hoping for only a DEFCON 5 level of embarrassment.

"Hey, Lex, how great to see you here again. Let me introduce you to my friend Emery. You'd have met him last—" She didn't finish her sentence because Lex turned at the same time I held my hand out to shake his, accidentally knocking the coffee he was holding.

The cup fell to the ground with a plop. The lid came off, spilling most of the coffee onto Lex's leg.

"Oh crap, I'm so sorry. Did you get burned?" I asked, looking around for tissues or a cloth. Maybe the Coffee Cart had something we could use. They'd have a wet cloth somewhere. Trust my fucking clumsiness to burn the first guy I'd felt an instant attraction to in forever. Or at least since I could remember.

"I...uh...I..." he stammered.

"Oh god, please don't apologize. It'll be mortifying if you do. It was totally my fault. I should have paid more attention."

He kept staring at me like he'd seen a ghost, which was when reality dawned.

It was the first time something like this had happened since the accident, but statistically, it was bound to happen.

"Shit. We've met before, haven't we?" I groaned, rubbing my eyes before looking at his stunning baby blues. God, the guy was... Everything about him screamed composure and quiet confidence, from the way his hair was styled—slightly longer on top but combed in place—to the clothes he wore: tan chinos and a denim shirt.

He didn't say anything, so in my need to fill up the conversation void, I told him what happened to me. "I was in an accident a year ago. It was pretty bad, so the doctors put me in a coma until the swelling in my brain came down. When I woke up, I couldn't remember anything about the accident or before. I basically lost the last three years of my life."

"You...lost...?"

"Yeah. I can't remember anything." I sighed. "I hope if we met before, I wasn't a dick to you or anything."

His brows furrowed. He didn't seem bothered about the coffee splashes on his jeans. "You...um...no, we haven't..."

"Well, you've met now," Ellie said, her eyes moving from me to Lex. "I was going to introduce you last weekend, but we left before you got to meet."

She seemed oblivious to the intense stare Lex was giving me. I felt my insides heat, although I wasn't sure if it was because I was feeling all kinds of attraction to him or if he had superpowers and was physically heating me up from the inside out with the invisible lasers in his eyes.

"Nice to meet you," Lex said, holding out his hand.

I held out mine, pretending the little spark I felt when we touched was all in my head because it had been so long since I'd been attracted to another guy that I'd regressed to feeling like a teenager.

"Nice to meet you too, Lex."

"Lex, can I borrow your phone?" Ellie asked, and Lex handed it to her without breaking eye contact with me. It was intense, but I...didn't hate it.

Lex's gaze moved away from mine and he scratched the back of his neck. Maybe he wasn't as confident as he looked. I kinda liked that.

Not that anything was going to happen. I mean, he was...
so way out of my league.

"Okay, so, Lex, you now have Emery's phone number so
you can reconnect again. You can both thank me in your
wedding speech," Ellie said.

"What?" Lex practically squeaked, his eyes finally
connecting with mine before moving away again.

I took a breath before I gave myself a brain injury.

"Anyway, we must get going. Right, Em? We have that...
thing before lunch." Ellie took my arm and practically pushed
me in the direction we'd just walked from.

I looked behind us and saw Lex staring at me again. He
looked...lost.

"Why did you do that? I didn't even have the chance to
offer to buy him a new coffee," I said.

She patted my arm. "Trust me. He's going to be thinking
about the guy who should have bought him an apology coffee
until he can't stop himself from calling you."

"Why do I want him to be thinking about me? Especially
as the guy who spilled hot coffee all over him."

Ellie tutted. "Because Lex is single and gorgeous, and
you're single and gorgeous. You're both super nice people, so
I'm not letting either of you get wasted on a douchebag when
you can be with each other."

"What is it with the women in my life wanting to set me
up with men I don't know?" I groaned. "Now *I* need a coffee
and probably two muffins to make up for this trauma."

We went inside the first coffee shop with a free table,
which, according to Ellie, was a minor miracle on market days.

This farmers' market was different from the one by the
school. Everything seemed a lot more upmarket, while my
usual hangout by the school felt a lot more personal. I knew
the farmers grew their own stuff and there was no one advertising websites and online stores.

Ellie came back with two coffees and a box of pastries.

"Pick what you want. I'm taking the rest home. I need to carb up for tomorrow. Ten's spending Sunday with me. Now tell me what's up with your mom."

I leaned back on my chair and took a long sip of my cinnamon latte. "She wants me to take her friend's son out. He's been in Europe for years, but he's back now, and apparently, he doesn't know anyone."

"Why don't you want to do it? You've met the guy and don't like him, is that it?"

"No. I haven't met him."

"Then take him out and get your mom off your back."

I laughed. "I thought you wanted to set me up with Lex. You know, the guy who I actually have proof of hotness."

"You're the one who said you're not ready for a relationship. I don't see the harm in going out with your mom's guy just for fun. You don't need to do anything. And then, if Lex calls, you go out with him."

I traced the handle on my coffee cup with my thumb. "I don't know."

"You don't have to have all the answers, Em. You're allowed to figure it out as you go." She took a huge bite out of a filled doughnut, marking the end of the conversation.

I picked out a chocolate muffin and peeled the paper off before using my hands to split it in half.

Could I do it? Could I try?

If the memory flash was a one-off, I needed to accept that I had to move forward with my life and look at the future instead of constantly trying to rebuild my past from scraps.

I looked at my phone where a message from my mother showed unread.

Unlocking the phone, I replied.

EMERY

Can I have Frederick's number?

Thirty minutes after I was left staring at Emery's back in the farmers' market, I was back in my apartment, carving a path into the wooden floor by pacing back and forth between my open-plan kitchen and living room.

The groceries I'd bought were carelessly thrown in the fridge and a kale leaf was trapped in the door, but caring about food was the last thing on my mind.

The doorbell rang once before my brothers and River spilled inside using the key I'd given them for emergencies.

"Why did I have to steal four steaks from the restaurant?" River asked, going straight for the fridge. "If I get fired over this, I'm taking you all down with me."

"It was a Code Red," Adam said.

"Code Red," River repeated in awe.

"Yup, that beautiful moment when one of us is in need, and the rest will drop everything and come rushing with food and booze," Noah said.

"Oh man, remember the first time we called it?" Adam asked. "Lex thought we'd killed Mom's goldfish. We spent a whole day going around the neighborhood asking for money in exchange for jobs so we could get enough to buy a new goldfish like Mom wouldn't notice that old Paprica had been replaced with a much younger fish."

"That was epic," Noah said. "Dad said we were cursed, and Mom argued our entrepreneurial efforts meant we were destined for great things."

"How old were you?" River asked.

"Guys," Adam shouted, staring at me, and they all turned around like they'd only just noticed where they were. "Code Red, remember?"

Kudos for twin telepathy.

"Sorry, bro. Okay, you all take a seat, and I'll grab the beer," Noah said, heading to the door.

"Where are you going?" I asked.

"The car. I left them in the cooler."

"Why didn't you bring them in?"

"In case we needed to go to the hospital." He stared at me like it was obvious.

"We had this discussion on the way," River said. "If we ended up in the hospital, we wouldn't bring the beer in because we'd need them all to keep the steaks cool."

"Why would we end up in the hospital?"

River gave me a you-called-Code-Red look.

My brothers were deranged. River wasn't any better. I was starting to think I should have called my grandmother to talk me through this situation.

Once Noah came back with the beer, they all settled. Adam and River on the big couch, Noah on the chair, and me on the floor.

Whenever we all hung out at my place, there was enough seating for the four of us, but I was too unsettled and would probably get up to walk around some more, so I didn't bother claiming my usual spot next to Adam.

"Okay, little bro, what's up?" Adam asked.

"I went to the farmers' market this morning and bumped into Ellie."

"Victoria's sister?"

"Yeah. She wanted to introduce me to a friend…" I paused to take a breath because the image of Emery's face when I turned around was still burning in my head.

He looked so much the same but different. Same wild curly hair, same green eyes, but he wasn't the same Emery.

"And he's cute, but you don't know how to ask him out," Noah said, cutting through my thoughts.

"You want some tips on what to cook for the guy on your first date," River added.

"Nah," Adam said. "Those aren't Code Red reasons."

Noah raised his beer to his lips. "You need sex tips. It's been a while, and you're nervous. I get you, bro. I mean, I don't think I've ever been there, but I sympathize."

"You're such a manwhore," Adam said.

"Why? Just because I enjoy sex?"

"Don't you ever get tired?" Adam asked.

"Of what? Enjoying myself? Life's too short." He put his empty beer on the coffee table and sat back on the chair.

"It was Emery," I blurted out.

What followed was complete silence.

They all looked at each other before River said, "Are you sure?"

"Of course I'm sure. Do you think I'd forget the man I'm in love with in just a year?"

Noah sighed, and Adam looked at me with pity. I was going to fucking punch them.

"Lex…"

I stood up. "Fuck you all. I don't need your pity."

"What do you need?" Adam asked.

"Help figuring out what to do next."

"What do you mean?" Noah asked. "Do you want the

let's-find-out-where-he-lives-so-we-can-kick-his-ass option or... wait, don't tell me you're thinking of..."

"Ignore him, he's always ready to fuck or fight someone," Adam said. "Tell us exactly what happened at the market."

"He made me spill my coffee, and then he apologized. I froze. Didn't know what to do or say." I ran my hands through my hair, pacing the space between the living room and the kitchen again. "Apparently, he had an accident a year ago and was in a coma. When he woke up, he didn't have any memory of what happened. It seems he's lost the last three years."

"That's...wow," River said. "How is that possible?"

What could I say? That I hadn't realized how little I'd known about Emery until I couldn't get hold of him? That a few days after he said he had to go see his family, his phone was disconnected and his apartment emptied? That I'd been prepared to marry a man who had never really opened up about his past or family, when family is so important to me? And more to the point, I was happy with that because I was so blindingly in love?

"I don't know, but the way he reacted to seeing me? That wasn't fake. He really didn't know who I was," I said.

"Do you think he's lying to get out of the situation? Imagine going to the weekend farmers' market and bumping into your ex. The ex you ghosted for no reason," Noah said. "Hell, I'd pretend I didn't know you either, just to get away. I could be wrong, but I may have pulled that stunt before."

I rolled my eyes. "I doubt that was the case with Emery. I knew him, remember? I knew his face better than I know mine, and I've spent my life staring at it through Adam."

I just didn't know everything else.

"There's only one way to find out if he is telling the truth. Ask Ellie," Adam said.

"I have his new number. Ellie put it in my phone."

"Then call him and meet him to talk," River said.

Noah raised his hand. "I think you should call him and ask him out. Take him to one of the places you went together and see how he acts. You'll be able to tell if he's lying."

"What, and pretend they weren't in a relationship?" River asked. "What happened to good old-fashioned conversation?"

"You said it, dude. Old-fashioned," Noah said.

"I'm not sure about that. It feels wrong, like I'd be tricking him or something."

"Look at it from the guy's point of view. He wakes up with no memory of the last few years, so he doesn't know if he was in love with someone, if he was single, if he was a douche to people. Everything is a reset. You can't blame him for something he doesn't know he did."

Noah nodded. "You have a point, River, but how could he not know? Didn't he check his phone? There would have been messages, photos, contacts. How about his place? Didn't he have someone's spare toothbrush in the bathroom? Clothes that weren't his size?"

"I agree," Adam said, and River looked at him. "Can't argue with that reasoning."

"So what do I do?"

Three pairs of eyes stared at me before Adam spoke. "I think you already know."

Did I? Was I trying to talk myself out of contacting Emery because I was afraid of what I would find out? Or was it because part of me still hoped our story would get a different ending?

"Fuck it. I'll fire up the grill. River, get the steaks. Let's get shitfaced."

It wasn't until I woke up the next morning that I regretted not stopping Noah when he went back to his car to get a bottle of scotch he apparently kept for emergencies.

When I'd questioned it, he'd just said, "*We're opening the bottle now, aren't we?"* And that was that. The existence of the twelve-year-old scotch in his car was justified.

Today wasn't the day to drive to work. Or arrive on time, for that matter.

When I finally got in, there was a note on my screen saying we had a meeting in the conference room at twelve. I looked at my watch, and it was ten minutes past.

Since I was already late, I stopped by the small kitchen we shared and filled a cup with fresh coffee.

I had no recollection of a meeting today. We didn't usually book meetings on Mondays. This was the day we'd picked to either visit clients or catch up with emails and work.

The faces of my whole family turned to me when I walked into the conference room. Well, apart from Adam, Noah, and River, who were wearing sunglasses indoors and using their hands to prop up their heads.

"What happened?" I asked, reaching for the nearest chair.

"Nothing happened yet," my dad said. "Your mom, grandmother, and I came to the city's best advertising and PR agency to find it's being run by an immature group of young men who think it's okay to turn up to work in this deplorable state."

"Technically, it's my day off," River said, raising one hand.

"It hurts to roll my eyes," Noah groaned.

"You think this is funny?" Dad asked in his I'm-the-boss-of-this-household voice. "You're lucky we're not some other clients."

"Dad, we're quite capable of managing our own schedule. We always put our best image forward with our clients," I said.

"Exactly. Our clients don't just turn up. And you're not even a client," Adam said.

I glanced in his direction only to catch Victoria's murderous gaze. What was she doing here?

"Good weekend, Victoria?" I asked.

"It was until Adam came home smelling like a distillery threw up on him. You all better get this out of your system before the wedding," she said.

I noticed Avó's lips twitch, not in a good way. No one told off her boys unless it was preapproved, something Victoria didn't know yet.

"You called this meeting, so let's get on with it so we can all get to work," I said, and Noah snorted. Yeah, little work was going to get done today all because yesterday...

A sharp pain hit my brain when I remembered the reason we were all hungover.

"Next month is the thirtieth anniversary of Lusitana," Mom said, putting to rest the family chatter to focus on business. "We want to hire you to manage the celebrations. We want advertising, our celebrity customers to talk about our food on their social networks, and we want to host a family dinner and invite all our best and most loyal customers."

Noah, Adam, and I all looked at each other. We'd always done stuff for the business in the past, but we were too busy right now to take on something this big.

"When did you decide this?" River asked.

"Last Tuesday at the weekly meeting," Dad said.

"I was at the weekly meeting, and this wasn't discussed."

Dad looked at River and patted his shoulder. "We talked about it after, on our way home. We were going to mention it to you, but we thought we might as well wait to tell all our kids at the same time."

River tried to disguise his frustration, but he wasn't sober enough. Victoria threw him a sideways glance before intervening.

"This is such an important date for Lusitana. I'm sure you, more than anyone, want to see the celebration be a success. Why would you put this in anyone else's hands, right?"

"She's right," Adam said.

Two hours and a round of coffee and pastries later, we were finally waving our parents goodbye.

River followed out because he wanted to stop by the restaurant, and Victoria said she had only dropped by to see how Adam was doing before meeting a friend for lunch.

"Talk about being driven to the edge of the cliff and given a push," Noah said.

"Whose idea was it for us to work as waiters to show our customers we're still very much a family business?" I asked, staring at Adam.

"Sorry."

"For someone who's not family yet, Victoria sure has a lot to say about ours," Noah said.

I couldn't entirely disagree with Noah. This should have been a family meeting. Or maybe I needed to get used to the idea that Victoria would soon be family and had a right to give her opinion, especially when she seemed to be taking this celebration much more seriously than the three of us.

Adam stood up.

"Thanks, guys," I said before they both disappeared into their offices

"For what?"

"Not telling the parents about Emery. I'm still trying to process it."

"We've got your back," Adam said. "I have work to do. Let's put a meeting on the calendar to discuss the Lusitana anniversary. They haven't given us a lot of time, so we're going to have to pull all the strings to make it happen." And then he was gone.

"What's wrong with you?" I asked Noah. My feelings toward Victoria fluctuated as much as her apparent moods, but Adam's happiness was more important.

"What does he see in her? He's not even himself when she's around."

"That's Adam's business, not ours." I stood to go to my office.

"Have you decided what you're going to do about Emery?" he asked.

I sighed. "I'm not sure. I think I have."

"What are you going to do?"

"The only thing I can."

Emery

I took hesitant steps across the road toward the Italian restaurant I'd suggested after calling my mother's best friend's son.

Picking a restaurant in Cliffborough put us on neutral ground, and if this date went south, then at least I'd be going down with a belly full of pasta and didn't have to drive that far to crash at Ellie's if I didn't feel like driving back home.

Frederick Rhys-Myr had been pleasant enough on the phone. I'd cringed when it became clear he wasn't expecting my call, but as soon as I'd introduced myself, there'd been a complete change.

His British accent was a turn-on, I'll admit. I didn't know how much time Frederick had spent in the UK, but clearly, he'd picked up the accent, even if it slipped a little on the odd word.

Ellie wanted me to put myself out there, right? Going out with a well-traveled guy, who could probably hold a conversation, wasn't a bad place to start.

It didn't mean I wasn't nervous as hell. I couldn't

remember the last time I went on a date. Literally. And those I remembered...I'd happily forget them, given the choice.

I'd parked my car on a side street nearby, thanking my lucky stars for the available spot. This area by the river bordered the financial district, so it was always a guess as to whether it would be busy with everyone going out after work or empty because they deserted the city for a weekend in the country.

As I approached the restaurant, the door opened. I stepped aside until I noticed the person coming out smiling at me.

"You must be Emery. Oh my, aren't you just adorable? *Mwah. Mwah.*"

The air kisses and super high-pitched voice took me by surprise, making me jump.

Who even does air kisses? Do Europeans air kiss?

"Mother never said her friend had such a darling son. I'd have returned from Europe sooner," he continued, placing his hand on my arm and running it down until he caught my hand, bringing it to his lips.

"Um...right...nice to meet you, Frederick," I said, trying to process the man in front of me.

He was not at all what I was expecting. In fact, he was downright confusing. Tall, with broad shoulders, a tapered waist, light-blue eyes, and almost black hair. If he wasn't wearing the strangest ensemble of gray chinos and patterned shirt combined with a neck scarf, I'd say he would be any gay man's dream. Not to mention the loafers and no socks situation.

But that shirt? God, it made my eyes hurt.

"Shall I take you inside? We have the best table in the restaurant, and I was assured plenty of privacy to dine in peace. Don't you hate it when you're trying to hold a conversation and keep getting interrupted by other people being noisy? It's a positively ghastly experience."

I didn't know what to say, so I followed him inside until we arrived at a table for two set in an alcove that looked like a separate room from the rest of the diners.

A server came to see us as soon as we sat down.

"Good eve— Wow, darling, what are you wearing? That shirt screams baby gay trying too hard," the server said, his mouth gaping at Frederick.

He was a tiny thing of a man with bigger balls than me because there was no way I'd ever have the guts to say what he just had to someone easily twice his size.

"I beg your pardon?" Frederick asked.

I rested my elbows on the table so I could cover my mouth with my hands and keep from laughing.

"I mean, it's none of my business, but everyone knows you need a mix of annuals and perennials to make a garden really work for you." He pointed at the various flowers on the shirt.

"Huh?"

"Anyway, what can I get you?"

The server finally turned to me, giving me a what-the-hell-are-you-doing-with-this-dude smile.

I looked at Frederick, who was still frowning at the oblivious server, and then turned back to the server. "Can we have a menu, please?"

"Oh yes, of course. Silly me. I'll be right back."

"He's a tad rude, isn't he?" Frederick asked when the server left.

I laughed. "I think he's just a little eccentric."

Frederick looked down at his shirt. "Is it that hideous?"

I scrunched my nose. "I can't say it would be my first choice, but you do you. If you like it, own it."

"I thought you'd like it." His shoulders sagged a little, and I felt like a dick.

"Why did you think I'd like it?" It was not the question to ask, but I was curious why he'd made that assumption.

"Um, because you're...um—"

"Here you are," the server said, interrupting us. "You can start with the antipasto or go straight for the main dish. I'm a main dish kinda guy. Why beat around the bush with a limp salad when what you really want is the eggplant special, right?"

I snorted. "Good point. What are your specials?"

"The eight-and-a-quarter-inch pizza comes in all flavors. The spaghetti meatballs are to die for, and if I ask the chef, he'll put in an extra ball for you." He winked in Frederick's direction, and I stifled a laugh. "The whole-wheat fettuccine is also good if you hate yourself, and let me see"—he tapped his chin—"oh yeah, my name is Ren with an *R*. I probably should have said it earlier."

"How come the pizza is eight and a quarter inches? The menu says it's nine," Frederick asked, looking over the fancy menu.

Ren looked around and, when he seemed satisfied, cleared his throat and said, "Honey, I know what nine inches feels like, and those pizzas? They're far from nine inches. Besides, eight and a quarter inches will not fill you up. Not a man like you."

Frederick coughed, his face going redder than a tomato ripened under the Italian sun. "I think it's time for us to leave."

"Will you give us a moment?" I asked Ren, who smiled and left us, singing something under his breath. "The menu is good here. Can't we stay?"

"Fine," Frederick said, his voice suddenly two octaves lower. He seemed to correct himself immediately. "Of course, darling. Anything for you. I am really looking forward to getting to know you better."

He raised his hand to call Ren, who came running like we were the most important diners. There was a weird silence once Ren, who was oddly quiet this time, took our orders of ziti and caesar salad and left us alone again.

"Um...so, how's living in Europe?" I asked.

Frederick preened at my question. "It was wonderful. Europe is so liberal, so open, so educated. And the fashion?" He put a hand to his heart, letting out a long sigh.

For a while, I let him ramble about his life in London and how much he traveled around Europe. I tried to be interested in what he was saying, but my mind kept going back to the farmers' market, wishing Lex had used the number Ellie gave him to ask me out.

Shit. Stop being rude, Emery. Think of a question. Be friendly. After all, he's here and he's not a douche.

"And you did a business degree?" I asked.

"Yes, but enough about me. Tell me about yourself."

"Um, I'm an elementary teacher. I love teaching." I played with my fork, wondering what else to tell him. I didn't want to bring up the amnesia because that would lead to more questions I didn't know how to answer.

I suddenly felt very unprepared to navigate this part of my life. Sometimes it felt like coming out all over again.

Hey, I'm Emery and I'm gay, and by the way, I also don't remember a chunk of my life, but tell me about you.

"Do you mind...um, will you excuse me? I just need to use the restroom."

"Sure."

I didn't miss his shoulders sagging once again as I walked away.

Was I messing this up? Was he interested? I didn't get the feeling that he was that into me. No matter how often he called me darling or dear in his part-British accent.

"Emery?"

Even though we'd only met once and he'd barely spoken, I recognized the voice immediately.

"Lex, hi."

He stood by the front desk, hands in his jean pockets. Once again, I couldn't quite decipher his piercing gaze. Maybe I had a thing for blue eyes. I thought Frederick's eyes were really nice too. But Lex's eyes were...something else.

"Are you here on a date?" I asked, cringing at my question.

He shook his head. "No, just picking up dinner. I don't live far from here. Their ziti is the best, and I wasn't in the mood to cook for myself."

"Oh."

"You're here on your own?" he asked.

I looked toward my table, thankful I couldn't see my date from here. "No, I'm um...with a friend."

He nodded. "A date?"

"No, he's just. Kinda. I don't know."

He raised his brows and smiled. "You don't know if you're on a date?"

"I am. He's a family friend."

We were interrupted by a woman. "Mr. Spencer? Here's your box. Enjoy."

Lex took the box and stared at it for a moment before looking at me again. "I guess I should let you get back to your date."

"Yeah."

This was ridiculous. We'd met for a total of ten minutes with no meaningful conversation or exchange of basic information. I knew nothing about the guy other than his name and that he was the twin brother of Ellie's future brother-in-law.

Why did my stomach get all twisted when I was around him?

"I should get..."

"Yeah. Enjoy the rest of your date," he said before heading

for the door, looking behind once before disappearing onto the street.

When I got to the restroom, I checked my phone. As expected, there were a dozen messages from Ellie.

ELLIE

So...what does he look like? Asking for a friend.

That friend is me.

Come on, Em. The suspense is killing me!

Wait...are you dead?

No, don't answer that. Do I need to send out a search and rescue party?

oh...OH! You're hooking up with him!

You go, girl! I expect all the sordid details on my desk on Monday.

I rolled my eyes and put the phone away. I'd let her think whatever she wanted.

Before I went back out, I looked at myself in the mirror. My hair was its usual untamed mess and my freckles still made a good impression of a connect-the-dots picture, but my eyes were somewhat brighter than usual.

Apparently, despite the awkwardness of being on a date for the first time since I remembered, having my stomach flip for another man was enough to bring a little spark to my life. Now, if only the person from the date and the one giving me butterflies were the same.

Sigh.

When I returned to the table, the food was there, and Ren and Frederick seemed to be in some kind of standoff.

"Oh, um, I don't know your name," Ren said to me.

"I'm Emery."

"So, Emery, as I was saying to this person over here"—he pointed at Frederick—"I can help him. I don't go around offering my services to just anyone I meet, but honey, he needs serious help...and those eyes." He bit his lip and rolled his eyes. "Those eyes deserve better than being washed out in that... that...what fabric is that shirt made of? Does he know natural fibers are a thing?"

"I am here, you know?"

Ren huffed. "But you're not listening. The flowers are all wrong."

"If they bother you so much, then here." Frederick took off his shirt and handed it to Ren, whose eyes practically bulged at the sight of Frederick's sculpted torso now visible through his undershirt.

I laughed. "Should I give you some space?" I pointed at the two. This was turning out to be the most fun date I ever remembered having.

"No!" they both said.

"Oh, for fuck's sake, I'm not even gay," Frederick said, dropping his high-pitched voice and, more importantly, his British accent.

"I knew it was a fake accent," Ren said, pointing a finger at my date. "No self-respecting British person would ever wear those horrendous flowers on a date."

"You're not gay?" I asked, dumbfounded. Had this whole dating thing been a joke to him? "Why did you come?"

"Because...um—"

"I'll give you some privacy," Ren said.

"Now you're leaving. Thanks for pulling the pin out of the grenade," Frederick barked.

I was still processing everything when Ren turned around to Frederick. "Honey, if you ever need to figure things out, call me. Like I said, I can help you, and I know what to do with nine inches." He threw Frederick's shirt back to him.

I stood and dropped enough money on the table to cover the bill. "I think we should call it a night."

The cool evening breeze did nothing to make me feel less stupid, gullible, or naive. No wonder I hadn't felt a connection with Frederick. He was faking everything, from his accent to his sexuality. Was he even Mrs. Rhys-Myr's son? Or had I called the wrong number, and he'd decided to play along for shits and giggles?

"Emery, wait."

I stopped because I didn't want him to make a scene in front of the people eating on the restaurant's outside deck.

"Please let me explain," he begged.

"It doesn't matter. You're not gay, and I wasn't interested anyway. You just...you made me feel like a fool."

He sighed. "I'm so sorry. That wasn't my intention."

"What was your intention?"

He ran his hands over the hideous shirt he'd put back on but didn't bother to button up before shoving them in the pockets of his chinos.

"Years ago, I accidentally came out as gay to my mom to get her off my back. It's a long story, but after I did it, she left me alone. She didn't even care when I applied for colleges in London."

That was not okay, and I felt bad for him, but he hadn't needed to deceive me too, had he? I crossed my arms and gestured for him to continue.

"None of her friends had sons, so it was a safe bet. I'd never need to pretend, and I figured one day I'd come out and say I'd met a girl I liked. Except that as soon as I came back, all she talked about was you. How I needed to meet you because you were such a good man, and I needed to settle down and all that. I never thought you'd call me, so when you did, I panicked. Then I figured if I was over-the-top obnoxious, you wouldn't want to see me again."

"What if I'd liked you?"

He came forward and touched my arm. "I would have told the truth. You have to believe me. I wouldn't have deceived you like that, Emery."

I nodded. "Okay. I guess I am sorry you felt you needed to do that. I know how moms can be...challenging."

"Can we still be friends?" he asked, and it was the first time all night that I felt like I saw the real Frederick.

"Of course."

"Do you want a ride home? Or I can walk you to your car."

I shook my head. "No, thank you. I'm going to walk for a while before I go home."

The door of the restaurant opened and Ren came running out. He gave Frederick a murderous look and then turned to me.

"Here," he said, holding a box.

"What's this?"

"Your dinner."

I smiled and took the box. "Thank you."

"Yours is in the trash. Maybe you can go out back and find it. Don't forget to accidentally drop that shirt in it," Ren said before walking back inside the restaurant.

"You know. I think he doesn't like me very much."

I laughed. "What do you think gave it away?"

He smiled back, and I liked it. So he was straight. That was okay because even when I'd thought he was gay, my belly hadn't reacted to him like it had to Lex.

"Friends?" I asked.

"Friends." Frederick gave me a kiss on the cheek and left.

Maybe the night wouldn't turn out so bad anymore. I could sit by the river and eat my pasta, then drive home late enough to avoid being grilled about the date by my mom.

With that decision made, I crossed the road and found myself once again face to face with the man in charge of the butterflies in my belly.

"Lex?"

Lex

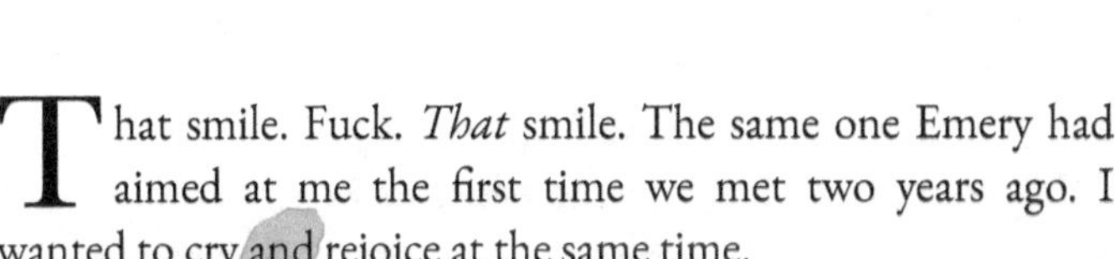

That smile. Fuck. *That* smile. The same one Emery had aimed at me the first time we met two years ago. I wanted to cry and rejoice at the same time.

"You're...here," he said.

"I am. Um, I decided to have my ziti out here since it's such a beautiful evening."

I couldn't exactly confess that I'd started walking home but hadn't made it half a block before turning back. I hadn't been able to see Emery and his date from the restaurant window, which only fueled my curiosity. Who was the guy? Was Emery having a good time? Was this a new thing, or was it serious?

The compulsion to stay had been bigger than my willpower, and in the end, with my cooling dinner in my hands, I'd sat on the bench on the other side of the street after returning to the restaurant to ask for a plastic fork.

His smile widened. "Ziti is my favorite."

I know.

"Are you okay? I don't want to pry, but things didn't look too happy over there," I asked.

"Yeah, I'm okay. I'm a little hungry, though, so I was going to sit by the river and have my dinner." He raised a box like the one that had held my dinner.

"Can I join you?"

"Sure."

We crossed the bridge to the north side, where there was a nice riverwalk with plenty of benches and lights.

"I take it your date didn't go that well," I said, desperate to know exactly what had happened and why Emery had been in the restaurant for such a long time but hadn't had dinner. Not to mention the tense conversation I'd witnessed from afar.

"You could say that. He wasn't exactly my type."

"Too many flowers?"

He snorted. "Not gay."

"I'm sorry, what? You said he's not gay?"

Emery pointed to a picnic table, so we sat opposite each other. He removed the fork stuck to the box with tape and then opened it. I could smell the fresh pasta.

"God, this smells divine," he said, digging in straight away. "So yeah, he's not gay. And don't let his poor choice of shirt cloud your judgment. That was all an act."

"Why did he ask you out then?"

Emery looked up from the food. "What makes you think he asked me out?"

"Anyone would be a fool not to."

The soft glow from the lights hanging along the river revealed the blush creeping across his face. I didn't need more light to know exactly what it looked like. I'd mapped all the colors of Emery before and knew them all by heart.

"I asked him out, actually."

"And you didn't know he wasn't gay?"

He shook his head. "No. I've never met him before. I just wanted to...get my mom off my back and try out dating."

"Try out...dating?"

"I haven't dated since the accident. I'm seeing a therapist to help me deal with everything that happened, and—I'm sure you don't want to hear my sad story."

I want to know everything. I want to know where you've been, why I never found out about the accident, why you left your apartment. I want to know if there's still a chance... That's what I wanted to say, but instead, I said, "You can tell me anything you feel comfortable with."

He sighed before putting his fork down. "I guess we were just two guys trying to find a way to escape the expectations put upon us. So I can't be upset that he lied. And he came clean in the end."

"Expectations can be hard to live up to."

He nodded. "Ellie mentioned your twin brother, Adam, and there's another brother?"

"Yeah, Noah. He's the oldest. And then there's my mom, dad, and grandma. Not to mention all the uncles, aunts, and cousins we have in Portugal. It's a big family with a lot of history and traditions, so I know all about expectations."

Emery rested his crossed hands under his chin. "You're Portuguese?"

"Yeah. Well, I'm half-Portuguese. My dad is American."

"Wow. I've always wanted to visit the Mediterranean countries."

I know.

Going down the road of talking about things I already knew added a layer of deception I wasn't comfortable with. As it was, the longer I spent with Emery, the more I wanted to blurt out the truth. Or at least my truth.

I wanted to know what he hadn't told me when we'd been together.

"Tell me about your family," I asked instead.

Emery pushed all the sundried tomatoes aside, which made me smile.

"They're not meant to be all shriveled like that. It's just wrong. Tomatoes are meant to be juicy. This is—"

"The devil's work," I continued for him before I could stop myself.

"How did you know I was going to say that?" he asked.

Because you said it every time you had ziti, but you still only picked ziti from any Italian menu.

"Lucky guess. My grandmother doesn't like mushrooms. She calls them the devil's work. She says nothing natural is meant to be both slimy and edible."

Emery smiled. "I like mushrooms. Anyway, you asked about my family. It's just me and my parents. I don't have any siblings."

"Ah, the only-child curse," I joked. "So, tell me, what do you do?"

"Do you want to walk? This food was great but filling, and I couldn't resist eating it all."

"Minus the tomatoes."

He smiled. "Minus the tomatoes."

He dropped his almost-empty food box into a nearby trashcan, and we walked to the path by the river. "I'm an elementary teacher. I work at the same school as Ellie. That's how we met, actually."

Emery's face lit up the same way it had every time he'd talked about his students when we'd been together. As weird as it may seem, I liked that he was still teaching.

"So you remember things like your education?"

"Kinda. I don't remember my master's studies, so I'm taking online classes to catch up and reading through the materials."

"How about all the work you must have done to complete it?"

He shrugged. "I don't know what happened to it."

Another puzzle. Another question without an answer, although this time for both of us. I knew he'd had all his materials meticulously ordered and kept in a box in his apartment.

I rested my hand on his shoulder and squeezed. "I'm really sorry that happened to you." I knew I shouldn't touch him, but I was desperate for some kind of connection, and a friendly shoulder squeeze was okay, right?

He didn't say anything, but the sagging of his shoulders told me everything I needed to know. He continued walking beside me, pointing out the various new businesses that had sprung up on the riverfront. At least that he remembered.

"How about ice cream?" I asked.

"It's like you know me inside and out." He beamed.

If only he knew. Although, apparently, there was a big side of him I hadn't known. Such as everything about his family. He'd always avoided the topic, and since we'd spent so much time with my family, they'd become his family too.

It wasn't until I couldn't get in touch with him that I realized how little I knew about his family and his past.

"What's your favorite ice cream flavor?" I asked.

"Definitely caramel with toffee chunks. That place in the shopping mall in the Greenfield area. The Ice Cream Parlor? They have the best ice cream."

I grabbed his hand and pulled him away from the riverfront.

"Where are we going?"

"To the real best ice cream place in the world."

He laughed. "I'll be the judge of that."

The place I was taking him to had only opened a few months ago. I liked that I could give Emery this first experience of Margot's amazing ice cream. I wouldn't be so confident if I hadn't tasted multiple samples while working on her grand opening campaign.

"Did you know it takes twelve pints of milk to make just a gallon of ice cream?" Emery asked.

"Nope."

"Did you know chocolate ice cream was invented before vanilla?"

I laughed. "How many facts do you know about ice cream?"

He scrunched his nose. "A lot."

Margot was, as usual, busy catering to a big line of ice cream lovers. It wasn't difficult to become addicted to her stuff.

"Do you want to guess how many licks it takes to finish a scoop of ice cream?" Emery whispered while we waited in line.

"Two-hundred," I guessed.

He shook his head. "Fifty."

"No way." I tried doing the math in my head. "That's not enough."

"Maybe you just have a smaller tongue than the average person," he said, snorting.

I pulled him closer and whispered in his ear. "How about I let you test it out?"

He shivered and leaned into me. His eyes met mine, and a tiny crease appeared between his brows like he couldn't under-stand how we'd got to where we were.

One tiny move and my lips would be on his. What would it be to kiss this Emery? An Emery that looked so much the same but also not.

"Lex! I didn't realize it was that windy out there. What blew you this way?" Margot asked.

"My friend here doesn't believe me when I say your ice cream is the best in the world."

She pursed her lips. "Ah, a nonbeliever."

Emery blushed, making his freckles stand out even more. "I was only saying that my favorite ice cream is—"

"Nope," Margot interrupted. "Let me show you what your favorite ice cream is."

She grabbed a waffle cone and picked two flavors from the selection, mixing them with her spatula in a bowl before creating two perfect scoops and placing them on top of the cone.

"I guess that's a hundred licks, huh?" I said.

Emery blushed even harder, taking the ice cream cone from Margot.

When he licked it the first time, it was like watching a child enter the circus. His expression was full of wonder. Like life as he knew it had been flipped upside down.

"You weren't wrong," he said. "What kind of magic is this?"

Margot handed me a cone and waved me off when I tried to pay.

"It's all organic ingredients and a passion for good ice cream. Although I think I've met my match. I should be careful that you'll open an ice cream store next to mine."

"I prefer eating it, thank you," Emery said. "What's this flavor?"

"Peanut butter cup and chocolate brownie. I make the cups and the brownies myself," Margot said proudly.

"You're incredibly talented and a superstar," I told her on our way out.

"What he said," Emery said, his mouth full of ice cream.

We stayed on the path in front of the stores but started walking back to the bridge.

For a while, it was just silence while we enjoyed our ice cream. Every time I glanced at Emery, he looked like he was trying to figure out how the ice cream was so good.

I knew I didn't have much time until we went our separate ways again. My anxiety spiked. Just like when we met at the market, I didn't know if I would see him again.

"Thank you so much for the walk and the ice cream, Lex. I think I have a new favorite flavor."

I bit my lip. He used to get peanut butter ice cream and add peanut butter cups and any leftover brownies I had at my place. There was no doubt Margot's ice cream was better than the store-bought home-created variety.

"I really enjoyed my evening too, Emery."

We arrived at the end of the bridge.

"I'm walking that way," I said, pointing toward my apartment.

"I'm parked the other way," he said.

Every second we stared at each other was a second I used to memorize his face, searching for any new freckles. I hoped this wouldn't be the end.

"So..." he started. "Are you going to use that number Ellie saved to your phone?"

I smiled. "Let me think. You don't look as upset now as you did when you walked out of the restaurant, and I approve of your choice of favorite ice cream. I think I might just use it."

He leaned over and kissed my cheek. "You do that."

And then he walked away, turning back when he was a few feet away, smiling.

"See you soon, Lex."

"See you soon, Emery."

Had we been destined to meet again, regardless? It would only be a matter of time until Ellie mentioned her friend by name or brought him to one of my family's Sunday lunches.

The whole time I'd thought it was over, it seemed we'd only been on standby, waiting for the right cog to move.

Nothing has started. Not until you come clean.

I just had to figure out a way to do it without hurting Emery with my lies because there was one thing I was absolutely sure of.

Emery wasn't lying. He really didn't remember me.

I just needed to figure out what had happened after the accident. Who or what had made him disappear from everything he'd known in a way he didn't seem to question.

91

Emery

"Hey, Em. Listen, I was hoping you could help me organize—wait," Ellie said as I walked into the teacher's lounge.

Most days, I ate lunch in my classroom while catching up on work and then joined the teachers for the rest of the break.

Today, I'd felt like a change. I was on top of my grading and it was a sunny day. I wanted to grab a coffee from the teacher's lounge and maybe sit outside.

"What do you need help with?" I asked.

"Never mind that. I need to know what's put that smile on your face."

I didn't have a smile. Did I? Okay, so I was in a good mood. Sue me.

"You're imagining things. What was it you needed help with? I'll ask only this time, and then you're on your own."

She groaned. "Fine. I'm in charge of the activities on the last day of the year before the summer break. I was wondering if you wanted to help me out with it."

"Yeah, that sounds fun."

"Great! Now tell me what's making you happy." She

gasped. "I can't believe I forgot. Did the date with your mom's guy go well? I still haven't forgiven you for not answering my messages or calls, but if you were getting lucky, I might give you a pass."

"He's not my mom's guy, and that just sounds all kinds of wrong."

She waved me off. "Don't deflect, Livingston. Spill the beans."

"There are no beans to be spilled." I headed to the coffee maker, where another teacher patiently waited for the coffee to brew. "Hey, Nadine, how's things?"

"Hi, Emery. Same as always. Kids be kids and coffee be the fuel."

Nadine was approaching retirement, but you'd think she was actually dreading the day it happened. The woman lived for her students. Teachers like her had inspired me to become one even when I'd hated the private school I'd attended closer to home.

"What have you got there?" She was holding a leaflet.

"Oh, my favorite restaurant, Lusitana, is hosting an anniversary party next month. You can enter to win a five-course meal and the proceeds all go to an LGBTQ+ charity."

"That's such a great idea," I said.

"Yeah, shame I probably won't make it. My husband has a work trip that weekend, and I don't want to go alone. You see, this is where he proposed so many years ago. Lusitana had just opened, and the word about their amazing food hadn't gotten out yet. We were one of the few people there, and the owners, Jack and Carla, made it such a special night."

My heart skipped a little beat, as it always did whenever Nadine mentioned her husband and their life together. As she'd said, they hadn't been blessed with children but had a life full of love and adventure.

"Nadine, if you're happy with a second-best replacement, I'd love to take you to that dinner," I said.

"Oh my goodness, really?"

The coffee maker finished spluttering, so I grabbed two mugs and poured us a cup each.

"Yes. It sounds like a great cause, and it's not entirely selfless. I want to grill you about your teaching career."

She laughed. "You have yourself a deal." She gave me a kiss on the cheek and patted my arm. "You better dress up for the occasion."

"For my first date with a girl? You bet I will."

Watching her leave the room with a smile was the highlight of my day because as soon as I sat on the old couch next to Ellie, I was met with her don't-bullshit-me-Livingston face.

"Have you ever considered Botox, Eleanor? One day, those wrinkles will start creasing your forehead," I joked.

"You come in smiling, ask Nadine out, and now you're making jokes? Unless you've suddenly found yourself a new best friend, I think it's time you spilled it."

"Botox is no joke," I said, snorting into the coffee cup. Ellie hit my arm, making me almost spill the coffee.

"By the way, did you know that Lusitana is Lex's parents' restaurant?"

"Oh really?" I asked, taking a sip of my coffee and trying to look like this was information I wasn't at all interested in.

"Yes, *really*. But it's your other date I want to know about."

Today, she wore a dress patterned with images of garden tools. Spades, rakes, hoes, pitchforks, you name it. If I were to take a guess, her class was currently learning about agriculture, plants, and how to grow things.

Maybe I could distract her by asking about her class until it was time to pick up our students from lunch. Her gaze told me *no fucking chance.*

"Okay, fine. My date with Frederick was somewhat of a disaster." I gave her a breakdown of the weekend's events until the conversation outside the restaurant.

"So he's straight," she said.

"It seems so."

"But he has gorgeous blue eyes, jet-black hair, and abs."

"That go on for days."

She burst into laughter. "I think I need to meet this guy."

"I thought you were into your Mr. Southern State."

"I am. I saw Ten again, and we had a great time. But a girl needs to keep her options open, right? In case Tennessee's weather becomes suddenly chilly."

I laughed. "You're certifiable."

"Thanks. So your date flopped. How are you so happy?"

There was no point hiding anything from Ellie. I just hoped she didn't make a big deal out of it.

"I saw Lex."

Ellie waited patiently as I told her about having my dinner on the riverside bench with Lex, our walk, and ice cream. When she could no longer contain herself, she punched the air, looking super smug.

"I knew it! I should have set you two up earlier."

I rolled my eyes. "You didn't set us up. We met randomly at the market and then at the restaurant."

She smirked. "Yeah, because I didn't know there was a super high chance he'd be at the market."

"You know, no one likes a smarty-pants."

"Although..." she started.

"Although, what?"

Ellie turned on the couch to face me. "I should probably not tell you this because it's personal, but I like Lex and love you. Victoria said that last year, Lex had a really bad breakup. The guy just left him or something."

"That's...I'm so sorry that happened to him. What does it have to do with me?"

"Nothing. Just...be careful. With his feelings and yours."

I nodded. The last thing I wanted was to hurt anyone, least of all Lex.

Ellie was getting way ahead of herself if she thought we were anywhere near the region of feelings. Maybe her next lesson should be geography.

"Gotta go pick up the kids before we're late," I said, standing.

Ellie's words stayed with me until my class distracted me with their antics. I really should write down some of the lines my kids said because they would make a great stand-up comedy routine.

On the drive home out of the city, I wondered if Lex would make good on his promise to use my phone number. It had been two days since we met and my phone was annoyingly silent.

Selfishly, I wanted to know more about Lex. He had this intensity about him when his focus was on me, but it was different when he talked about his work or his brothers. I wanted to understand him, but for that, I needed to spend more time with him. Since Ellie hadn't used the opportunity when she was saving my number to his phone to actually message or call me, I didn't have his number.

"Emery." My mother sang as soon as I was through the door.

I sighed and followed her voice to the kitchen, where I found her chopping vegetables with a chef who often came over to cook with her.

"Hi, Mom."

"Hello, dear. Good day at work?"

"Yeah, it was. The kids are working on a project to build a windmill—"

"That's nice. I want to hear all about your date with Frederick. You didn't come home until very late, so I'm assuming it went well."

I sighed. I shouldn't be surprised that she'd be more interested in knowing about the date than something I was doing at work.

"Yes, Mom. He's a really nice guy."

She stopped her practiced moves on the chopping board and looked at me.

"Just nice?"

I gazed at the chef, who was professional enough to continue working like he wasn't listening to the conversation. I always wondered about that. People who work in other's homes and are expected to fade into the background.

It made me uneasy because some conversations were private, and I was pretty sure the guy would rather not be present for it than have to pretend he wasn't there.

"You don't want me to go into every single detail, do you?" I asked, trying to inject meaning into my voice so she wouldn't pry further. If I could trust my mother to be one thing, that was prude.

She laughed. "Oh no, goodness. Not that. I just want to know if you got along. Are you going to go out again?"

"We got along, and I don't know." I walked back to the door.

"I do. Jeanelle and her husband are coming over for dinner. I told them to bring Frederick. After all, it's only right that we meet him."

I ran my fingers through my hair, feeling the pull in my scalp when they got tangled in my curls. "It's a weekday, Mom. I have work to do."

"Everyone eats dinner, Emery. Make sure you're down here by eight-thirty."

"Yes, Mom."

I went up to my room, angry and frustrated. My great day was turning out to be not so great. I really did want to do some research tonight to help the kids with their project. They were building a windmill and wanted to figure out a way to make it work using solar energy.

Two hours later, after a calming shower and some reading, I came down to greet our guests for the evening.

Frederick was dressed more appropriately this time. Even though I believed anyone should wear whatever they felt comfortable with, that really had been a hideous shirt.

"Good fashion choice," I said into his ear when he greeted me with a kiss on the cheek.

His chuckle tickled my ear. "Don't worry. The criminal shirt is in the trash."

"Aw, don't they look so great together?" Mrs. Rhys-Myr said, clutching her hands to her chest.

"Mother, we had this conversation already. Let things progress naturally," Frederick said. "Now, if you could excuse us. I'd like to have a quick word with Emery privately."

"Of course, dear," my mom said all too chirpily. "Emery, take Frederick to the library."

His pleading eyes made me sad, so I did as I was told.

As soon as I closed the library door behind us, Frederick plopped down on the couch.

"I'm so sorry, Emery. She wouldn't leave it alone. I said we were just friends, but she wouldn't have any of it."

I sighed. "I don't know why they're so hell-bent on us getting together."

"Knowing my mother, it's some kind of competition with the other women in her country club. I bet someone has a wedding coming up."

"How do you know?" I asked, and he looked at me like it was obvious. Both our mothers were socialites with carefully drafted public lives.

"What if we faked it?" he asked.

"What? Are you crazy?" That had bad idea written all over it.

"Yeah, you're right. They'd probably have our wedding planned in two weeks, and then we'd have to go through with it." He looked so defeated I was one puppy-dog look away from agreeing to it.

My phone dinged in my pocket, so I took it out. The message was from an unknown number, but as soon as I opened it, I knew who it was.

LEX

Hey, Mr. Peanut Butter Brownie. How do you feel about cemeteries?

I laughed.

"What's funny?" Frederick asked.

"Nothing. Sorry, let me just answer this."

EMERY

It's Mr. Peanut Butter Brownie Ice Cream to you. And it depends on the POV.

LEX

That's too long. Maybe I'll call you PBBIC. Although that doesn't roll off the tongue. Peanut it is. And don't worry, I'm not planning on a killing and burying spree.

EMERY

Of course. That's double the job. You
should hire someone for the burying part.
Digging soil must be a messy job.

LEX

I don't mind messy jobs, but you didn't
answer my question.

EMERY

Why do I get the feeling that the answer is
more dangerous than possibly being
murdered?

LEX

Meet me at St. George's Cemetery on
Saturday at 8?

EMERY

Okay.

His reply was a smiley face and a peanut emoji.

"You're seeing someone," Frederick said without any bite
or resentment in his voice.

"No. Not really. We just met."

"But you like him."

"Yeah, he's nice." I couldn't stop my growing smile, even
more when Frederick returned it. I thought about what he'd
said for a moment. "This will probably backfire, but...what if
we did it?"

"Did what?"

"Pretended to date. Like the slowest dating in the whole
world of dating history. Snail pace. No mention of engage-
ments or weddings. We'll be virgins until further notice."

He snorted. "That ship sailed a long time ago."

I shrugged. "What do you say?"

"Dude, I'd kiss you if I was into guys."

"The lady doth protest too much for a straight gal...guy."

He laughed. "Nah. But I'll fake date you. There's nothing more time-consuming than your mother trying to marry you off to the nearest eligible bachelor when you're busy looking for a job. Just the diversion tactics alone are SWAT-team-worthy. Not that I've ever been inclined to join law enforcement."

"Well," I said, standing and holding out my hand. "I hope you took some acting classes in Europe."

He stood and took my hand, kissing the back of it gently. "Lead the way, my dear."

Stepping into my parents' kitchen was like stepping into another world. Unlike the modern decor of the rest of my childhood home, which my parents had redone after Adam and I went to college, the kitchen had remained much the same.

They'd painted the walls and restained the kitchen cupboards, changed the vinyl tablecloth and cleaned the terracotta floor tiles, but once it was all done, the kitchen was just a cleaner version of its former self.

As my dad always said, there was no point changing what wasn't broken, and the kitchen certainly wasn't broken. It was the most used room in the house, and often, when we all came over for a meal, none of us even stepped into the living room.

The kitchen was the living heart of the house and usually in it was the soul that kept it alive.

"Hi, Mom," I approached from behind, kissing her on the cheek.

"Olá meu filho, tudo bem?"

"Yes, Mom, everything's okay. Can I help?"

She pointed at the bowl filled with peas from the garden.

"Avó picked them this morning and I'm adding them to the stew. If you can shell them for me, that would be great."

I sat at the large dining table and got to work. My school friends had found the vinyl tablecloth tacked to the table weird. I hadn't questioned it because it was all I knew, but after visiting my friends' houses, I realized how different ours was.

Yes, it wasn't as pretty as seeing the wooden table underneath, but we'd had all our meals, birthday parties, and done arts and crafts around this big table, and at no point had my parents stressed over anything being damaged. A wet cloth and cleaning spray did the job.

"Where's Dad?"

"In the garage, hiding."

I laughed. "From you?"

"He'll stay there if he knows what's good for him."

"Oh no, what did he do this time?"

"He was in charge of the laundry, and now all my underwear is pink. It's not like he hasn't done laundry a million times before or like I didn't tell him to check that his new red shirt wasn't with the rest because I was going to wash it by hand tomorrow. But no, he insisted it wouldn't bleed." She raised her hands like she was talking to God herself.

"How many times do you have to tell him, right?" I asked, knowing by heart the words she'd uttered a million times before.

"Precisely. Where are your brothers?" she asked.

I gasped. "Mother, you lost your children? Everyone knows not to leave them to the care of the youngest one." She threw a wet dishcloth at me, hitting my face with a wet plop. "This is child abuse."

"I'll show you child abuse when I send you home before you try my lavender honey cake."

I stood and wrapped my hands around her waist. "I love you, Mamã. Tu és tão linda. Perfeita."

"Your compliments will get you nowhere unless I get those peas."

"Yes, ma'am."

"I knew he'd be sucking up to her."

Mom and I turned to the kitchen door where Noah and Adam stood.

"Oh, come here, you two," she said, and in a heartbeat, we all surrounded her in a big group hug. "Meu deus, it's so good to have you all home with me."

"So where's that cake then?" Noah asked.

"Noah Spencer, you will not have cake before lunch. Now go check on your dad and make sure he's not doing something else he's not supposed to."

He rolled his eyes and left through the kitchen door to the garage.

"Where's Avó Jacinta?" Adam asked.

"She's in her room watching the Sunday mass on TV. Once she's done her prayers, she'll come down."

Adam joined me at the table, helping with the peas.

My family was Catholic, and my brothers and I had all been baptized, but the only practicing one was my grandmother. I loved that despite everything she'd been through, from losing my grandfather so young and raising a family on her own in a foreign country to supporting her grandchildren as we came out as queer, her faith never left her.

She knew the difference between good and bad. The bad was everywhere and the good was inside her. That's how I saw it. She was our own saint. An imperfect one with a naughty streak and a passion for chocolate brownies.

When Mom left the kitchen in the same direction as Noah, probably not trusting that Noah wouldn't take Dad's side, Adam turned to me in a hushed tone. "Have you thought about what you're going to do about Emery?"

The question was so unexpected I almost dropped a bunch of peas on the floor.

"Shhh, I don't want them to know. Not until I've figured it out."

"When will that be?"

I huffed. "I don't know. I saw him last weekend."

"You did? Where?"

"He was on a date at the Italian restaurant by the river."

"He was what?"

I raised my hand to stop him from reaching the wrong conclusions. "That doesn't matter. The date didn't end well, but I was there after. We ended up going for a walk and then had ice cream."

Adam gestured for me to continue. I paused when I thought I heard a noise upstairs.

"He really doesn't remember me."

"How was it being with him? Was it weird?"

I let out a breath. "It was good. Like I was getting to know him again. Imagine getting a second chance at falling for the love of your life. What would you do?"

He shook his head. "I don't know. I mean, in theory, it's a beautiful thing. But what happens when the truth comes out?"

"I know. I know."

"Are you going to see him again?" he asked.

"Yes, tonight."

"Are you going to tell him?"

I paused. "I don't know. How would you feel if you forgot that you knew Victoria and thought you'd just met her, but then she tells you about your relationship?"

"It would definitely be a biggie to take in."

"What if this Emery could never fall in love with me? What if the first time around was a fluke?"

He sat back in his chair. "Are you really worried about that?"

"Of course I am. Wouldn't you be? Do you believe without a shadow of a doubt that Victoria would fall in love with you in every single version of her life?"

He narrowed his eyes, his gaze fixed on the tablecloth's pattern. "I really don't know. What if the problem isn't him, it's you? Are you still in love with him or the idea of how he was before? If the accident changed him because he's missing vital information from the last three years, would you still fall for him?"

"Where are those two? By all that is saint, I swear most days I'm running a daycare center instead of a household."

We both turned to our grandmother, who had suddenly appeared in the kitchen.

"Ah, os meus netinhos estão em casa," she said.

I stood up to pull her into a hug. "Yes, Avó, we're here. Are you all done with your date with God?"

She gave me a well-deserved smack on the butt. "Don't you mock my faith, neto. If I don't pray for you all, no one will."

"Hey, Avó, guess what I bought for you," Adam said, pointing to a box I hadn't noticed he'd carried in.

Avó practically ran to the counter, squealing when she opened the box I saw contained four bolas de berlin, her favorite Portuguese filled doughnuts.

"Kiss ass," I muttered.

Adam stuck his tongue out. "You should have thought of it yourself."

"Anyway, where's that fiancée of yours, Adam?" Avó asked.

"She was busy with work so she couldn't come. She'll come next time."

The look Avó gave him said an entire novel of words. Considering Victoria was marrying Adam, she didn't seem like a family person, which was odd because her sister, Ellie, seemed like the kind of person who'd live for a good family dinner. Dysfunction and all.

So far, Victoria had only come to my parents' place for a meal the day Adam introduced her to the family. They'd been dating for a couple of months, and he thought things would get serious.

It wasn't my place to say anything, but I had a feeling Adam knew how the family felt. We wanted to welcome Victoria into the family, but it wasn't easy when she kept away from us and, occasionally, Adam.

"Come on, boys, let's set the table for lunch, and then you can help me pick the book for this month's book club," Avó said. "It's my turn to pick, and I want something scandalous."

"Will I need to bleach my eyes afterward?" Adam asked.

"On second thought, maybe this is a better job for Lex."

"Why?" we both asked.

She went to the cupboard to get drinking glasses out while I went for the plates and Adam the cutlery.

"Because I want a spicy gay romance. At the engagement party, I was speaking to Ellie. She's a dear, isn't she? Fiery. Full of spirit. Anyway, she was talking about a series of books where the boys are in Portugal. They're best friends in child-hood and then separate for years. One comes to America and then returns home after his parents die."

We both stared at Avó.

"What?" she asked.

"Avó, River reads those books. They're kinda spicy," Adam said.

"The spicier, the better. I want those old women in the club to get their heart rates up. It'll be like cardio."

I snorted. She wasn't wrong there. The gay romance novels I'd read so far could be pretty explicit. Although the thought of my grandmother reading them was super weird. Judging by Adam's expression, he thought the same.

"You should read some of them too, Adam. You might learn a few things," she said, and I burst out laughing.

"Avó!"

"What? I don't believe for a second he's a virgin."

"I can't find Dad," Noah said, returning from the garage with two bottles of red wine. No doubt, one for lunch and one as an apology to Mom. "Who's a virgin?"

"No one's a virgin," Adam groaned. "Christ."

"Don't take the Lord's name in vain, Adam Spencer."

"Sorry, Avó. Anyway, it's not like I haven't read those books."

I nearly dropped a plate. "I'm sorry, what?"

"What books?" Mom asked, coming into the kitchen followed by Dad, who looked a little red in the cheeks. Well, she'd found him all right, and from the look of him, she'd either told him off again, or they'd made up. I suspected it was the latter, which wasn't a thought I wanted to entertain.

"Adam reads gay porn books," Noah said.

"That's not what I said."

"Has anyone put the peas in the stew?"

"No."

"Do I—"

"Have to do everything around here?" everyone said after Mom.

God, it was good to be home.

"Go wash your hands before lunch while I sort the peas out," she commanded, and we all spilled out of the kitchen toward the bathroom.

"Does it sometimes feel like we haven't moved out?" Adam said.

"Back in the day, you didn't read porn, so no, it doesn't feel like we haven't moved out," Noah said.

"Did you do it while I was in the room?" I gasped, adding kindle to the fire.

"Oh, for the love of—" He stopped himself before Avó overheard him curse. "River was going on about this one book, so I read it. It was a little weird reading about two guys, but the story was fine. That's all."

Noah met my gaze as we washed our hands.

After Adam walked out, threatening to complain to Mom, Noah turned to me.

"You okay?"

"Yeah, why?"

"Just checking, you know. About the whole Emery thing."

"Don't worry, Adam has already done the brotherly due diligence."

He nodded. "Just...you know I'm here for you, right?"

"Okay, so can you tell me, what would a guy wear to a date with his former boyfriend who doesn't remember him? Is dressy casual trying too hard? Casual *casual* not hard enough?"

"Baby bro, you'll have to impress the guy all over again."

I laughed. "That's what I thought."

We joined the family for lunch before I gave an excuse and left early, with Adam and Noah covering for me.

As soon as I got home, I grabbed a shower and picked the clothes I was going to wear that evening. Now, if only it was as easy to stop my brain from thinking that Emery wouldn't turn up.

Emery

"Y ou're here."

I had to take a moment to catch my breath. "Yes. Sorry, traffic getting into the city was insane, and I had to park a little far, but I'm here."

"I'm glad you made it." Lex smiled, shifting on his feet.

"Did you think I wouldn't?"

"No. No! Of course not."

I wasn't sure about that, but I didn't press it. After all, I was here.

"Why are we in a cemetery instead of Margot's ice cream place? And should I be worried I may not make it back home tonight?"

He laughed, and the tension in his shoulders dissipated a little. Had he really been worried I wouldn't show? And then I remembered Ellie's words about Lex's boyfriend leaving him.

"No Margot for you today, but there's a diner nearby that makes the best waffles, so if you're hungry after the tour, we can go there."

"Tour?"

Lex held his hands up, shaking them and making eerie

115

sounds. "Welcome to St. George's Ghost Tour. Muahahaha."

"Ghost tour?" I looked at the other people around us, and apart from one group of girls all wearing *Bachelorette Party* T-shirts, everyone else seemed to be in pairs.

"Are these all couples on dates?"

"I guess so."

I felt a little rush of butterflies in my stomach. "Are *we*...on a date?"

Lex put his arm over my shoulder and pulled me closer. I came perilously close to showing people things they had no business seeing. Dick stirring things because Lex was easily the most beautiful man I'd ever met, and he had a dose of nice to go with it. Basically, any gay man's kryptonite.

When he whispered in my ear, I stopped breathing.

"I don't know, what do you think? We have mood lighting and plenty of places to hide and make out. If it looks and feels like a date..."

"It must be a date," I finished, and he smiled. Those butterflies were having a field day in my belly.

A spotlight shone on a pedestal by the entry gate to the cemetery, followed by the amplified sound of what seemed like hearts beating.

Everyone turned to the light. The sound dimmed a little, and then a black cat jumped onto the pedestal.

"Good evening, everyone. I'm Damien Blackdye, and I'll be your guide tonight. Before we go inside, you can pick up a flashlight to help you see where to put your feet in."

In? Does he mean on?

A glance at Lex told me he picked up on the same thing.

"It's a talking cat," I said.

"I'm pretty sure it's fake." He shrugged. "It's fake, right?"

"There's a full moon tonight," Damien continued, "so you probably won't need the flashlight, but it's always useful." Someone went around with a bag distributing flashlights, so we took one. "The rules are simple: listen out for any sounds or lights. The ghosts love to show off to an audience. But don't touch anything. Remember that people's family and friends are buried here. Show them the respect they deserve. Try not to wander off because the tour won't stop to go find you, and you'll have to catch up on your own. Oh, and have fun."

"Our tour guide is a creepy talking cat?" I asked, hoping to see a human appear from behind the shadows.

"Maybe it's a possessed cat."

"Or a cat apparition."

"What kind of life do you think he led to get stuck in the in-between with a job herding humans around a cemetery?" I shook with laughter, which earned me a look from an elderly couple.

"Do you think they're here to scope out the real estate?" Lex asked, nodding in their direction.

"Oh my god, you didn't just say that."

We held back a little, waiting for everyone to follow the cat into the cemetery through the small side gate.

The same guy who had distributed the flashlights stood at the front of the group. The cat was perched on his shoulder.

"This is Lucifer, my business partner."

The man didn't move, and in the dark, it was hard to see who was talking.

"Which one's which?" I asked under my breath.

"I say the guy is Lucifer. I think the cat owns him. If you see him blink a lot, that's probably a call for help."

I elbowed Lex to make him stop. I didn't want to get kicked out before the tour even started.

Everyone followed Damien, or Lucifer, as he went between a row of graves. He shared a few stories about the people buried there, but no ghosts joined the tour.

The bachelorette-party girls kept scaring each other

because every time one of them touched another one, they'd all jump.

"I guess I should keep you close," Lex said in a low voice.

"Because of the ghosts?"

"Because you're holding our only flashlight."

"Ah, of course."

Damien-slash-Lucifer stopped in a circle-like space. All the graves faced the middle, and there was just enough space for everyone to stand.

"This grave here doesn't look like the grave of someone who achieved much in life, but did you know the man buried here claimed to have invented the lightbulb?" he asked.

"I thought Thomas Edison invented the lightbulb," the man in the older couple said.

"Everyone knows that while Thomas Edison invented the first practical light bulb, a few other inventors paved the way. In fact, Alessandro Volta, who's credited as inventing the electric battery, Humphrey Davy, James Bowman Lindsay, Warren de la Rue, William Staite, and Joseph Swan all paved the way," I muttered under my breath.

I felt my cheeks warm when I saw the way Lex was staring at me. "Sorry. It's a habit from teaching."

"It's cute. I like it."

And I liked the way his gaze made my belly tighten. How long could I legitimately leave it until I stole a kiss? I could overlook the fact we were surrounded by dead people and it was dark.

"What are you thinking about?" he asked.

"Nothing."

"Then why are you blushing?" He ran a hand over my cheek. "Your face is warm."

I swallowed. *Kiss me, dammit.*

"It's a warm evening, and you're hot."

He laughed. "You really think so?"

"I mean, your temperature. Because you're so close and… I'll shut up now." God, could I be more embarrassing?

"Nah, I think you think I'm hot."

Someone near us made a shushing as Lucifer-slash-Damien explained, "John Masterson III sold all his belongings to travel to New Jersey where Thomas Edison had his lab. He wanted to work with the great inventors and leave his mark on history. The few records available don't say much about young John. His family were merchants and made a lot of money trading carpets and upholstery. According to a diary found in his home after he died, he claimed that Thomas stole his idea for the lightbulb. After leaving New Jersey, he spent the rest of his money trying to prove it. He died destitute."

"But is he a ghost?" one of the bachelorette-party girls asked. "I haven't seen any ghosts yet."

"Shut up, Tracy. We signed up for the *concept* of the ghosts, not for the real thing," another one said.

I tried to remain unaffected as Lex ran his hand down my arm until his fingers brushed mine. God, he smelled so nice. If I didn't know any better, I'd say he smelled familiar, which was a ridiculous thought. Either way, I hoped we'd spend a lot more of the evening this close together.

The flashlight almost fell to the ground as I trembled under the contact, but he caught it and pressed the little button to turn it off.

"What—"

"Shh," he whispered in my ear. "Follow me."

No one seemed to notice as we slowly took a few steps back until we were on an intersecting path. Lex took my hand and led me away until we were out of sight of the group.

He turned the flashlight on, pointing it to the graves.

"What are you looking for?" I asked.

"Who. I'm looking for someone."

The longer he searched, the farther away from the group

we became until we could no longer hear the guide or people talking.

"This is eerie," I said.

He chuckled. "It's meant to be. It's a cemetery. Ah, here," he said.

I followed the light until I saw two graves side by side, and all around them were the most beautiful peonies. They were all closed because it was night, but I could make out the different colors.

"This is beautiful," I said, my heart unexplainably stuck in my throat. "Who are they?"

Lex pulled me closer, wrapping his arm around me so we were practically nose to nose. "This is Vincent and Clara. Clara's favorite flower was the peony. Her brother, Vincent, worked at the Botanical Gardens when it first opened in 1865. He was in charge of what is now the tree peony collection. Clara died quite young, never having seen her brother's peonies bloom, so with permission from the gardens, Vincent took cuts from his trees and planted them here, knowing that eventually Clara would be surrounded by her favorite flowers. He never married, so when he died, he was buried next to his sister."

I hugged Lex. The warmth of his body seeped through to mine. "That's such a beautiful story. Thank you for bringing me here. Did you know peonies are my favorite flowers?"

He nodded. Or at least I think I felt him nod against me. It was hard to tell because he was holding me back so tight.

When he pulled back, I looked into his eyes. The moon made them look dark, but I could see an emotion in them I couldn't read.

"If this was a date, how would you rate it from one to five?" he asked. "One being that you won't see me ever again and five being that we'll most definitely see each other again and maybe..."

I bit my lip so I didn't moan when his arm caressed my back, moving from my shoulder blades down to the small of my back. That maybe was promising, and I was definitely in the market to find out what a five meant.

"Um, so far, I'd say a three," I said.

"Three? Man, I need to up my game."

"I haven't seen any ghosts," I said. "You get a point deducted for that."

"But I showed you the peonies," he said, bringing his hand up to trace my lips with his thumb.

"Fair enough. A four then."

"I'd really like to go for a five. What does a guy have to do to get a five?"

The energy around us crackled. This could be the point of no return. The moment I'd been waiting for since I met Lex. Because yes, no man in his right mind wouldn't immediately zero in on his lips and wonder what they tasted like.

They'd been the focus of many of my dreams over the past couple of weeks. I'd even jerked off to the thought of them in the shower.

"I think...you know," I said, my voice a bare whisper in the night.

"Emery..." His voice cracked. "Please promise me you won't leave."

I had no idea what he was talking about, other than maybe what Ellie had mentioned about his ex, but it was an easy promise to make. I had no intention of being anywhere far from Lex. In fact, the closer, the better, which is why I wrapped my arms around him tighter.

His lips crashed onto mine, taking my breath away. I sank into him, the hard planes of his body turning my brain into a soft mush. I wanted to imagine what Lex would look like without his clothes, but I was far too gone for any conscious thought.

The unmistakable outline of his erection pressed against mine.

I brought my hand up to his cheek, deepening the kiss, opening for him, allowing him to explore the recesses of my mouth. Lex tasted like lust and heat and all the forbidden things I couldn't help feeling drawn to.

The kiss could have lasted hours. I couldn't tell. Maybe we'd even get locked inside the cemetery. I didn't care. I'd kiss him until the sun was up.

"Lex," I moaned into his lips, needing more and knowing it wasn't possible here.

When he pulled away, he was breathing heavily.

The flashlight flickered on the ground, making us both jump. I didn't even know when that had happened.

"That's probably the ghost of John Masterson the Third proving a point," I said. "You've definitely earned your five."

"Oh, Emery." He kissed me again, a chaste kiss that felt much more intimate and personal than the first one. His fingers laced through my curls, making my scalp tingle.

"I can see your freckles even in the moonlight," he said when he finally stopped the kiss.

I didn't know what to say other than, *Can we kiss some more? Elsewhere, where we can get naked?*

A realization hit me. I hadn't panicked when he kissed me. Unlike all the other times when I'd avoided any kind of intimacy or even getting close to another man because I was afraid I wasn't whole enough, this time, it had been different.

I didn't need to feel whole to feel wanted by Lex.

My romantic heart warned me this had all the signs for the love story of a lifetime or a broken heart, but worrying about which it would be was something for tomorrow's Emery.

Today's Emery was going to keep kissing Lex until it was time for waffles.

Lex

Working with my brothers meant that at any given time, one or both would barge into my office like a small herd of elephants.

As Mom always described it, I did the pictures, Adam did the words, and Noah did the schmoozing.

Apparently, as one of the graphic designers and the art director for our agency, I had no need for space or privacy, and my time somehow stretched further than theirs.

Adam was one of our copywriters and also the creative director. He was often seen through the glass windows of his office pacing and talking to himself. He said he found the words better if he walked them, whatever that meant. The only person allowed to interrupt when he was like that was River, who was always happy to get drafted into helping him.

Noah was the accounts director. The money and networking guy. Thanks to him, we'd landed some of the most sought-after accounts in the city and had worked on some really interesting projects. If there was a man who could make a living from low-key flirting, that was my brother.

My job was to create all the artwork for our clients, so I

didn't need silence to come up with words. In fact, I usually had the radio playing in the background. I also didn't need to always be on the go and talking to people like Noah. Which somehow meant I was fair game.

But there were days when the perks of being the go-to boy paid off, like today.

I parked by Emery's school just as the bell signaling the end of the day rang. I was early, but I didn't care. I got out of the car and leaned against the door, taking in my surroundings.

Emery's old school had a similar layout, making the post-class activity easy to see from the parking lot. The rush of kids running to their parents. The best friends holding hands and always hugging before they went their separate ways. The body language of the parents that told many stories of school-gate drama.

So many lifelong memories were made at school. I'd certainly been privileged to have my brother and River beside me all the way through. There were a lot of memories I'd cherish forever and a few I'd rather forget.

I heard a ding from the car, so I put my arm through the window and grabbed my phone from the holder.

EMERY

You do know I don't finish for an hour.

I smiled at the image in my head of Emery looking out his classroom window and seeing me outside by my car.

LEX

I heard the ice cream truck go past earlier.
The kids will clear before you can spell
push pop.

EMERY

Get me one, and I'll be less thorough with
my cleaning duties.

LEX

No can do. I have a small tub of a certain
flavor of ice cream from a certain ice cream
place that is a certain someone's new
favorite.

EMERY

Damn you. On my way out!!!

I laughed, and for a moment, I felt like the old Lex. The one who stood by the gates of a school waiting for his boyfriend to come out so they could go for a walk by the river, out on a date, or just a date with a shopping cart followed by a cozy night in, eating ice cream and watching movies.

A few minutes later, Emery marched down the steps toward the school gate. A few parents stopped him to chat, and every time, he'd glance at me and smile apologetically, even as he gave them his full attention.

"You know," I said, "I thought I was going to have to go out there and take you by force."

He laughed. "Lucky that Ellie was happy to cover for me. Although I confess, I'd be partial to a kidnapper armed with my new favorite ice cream."

"Good to know." I extended my hand, and he took it. I pulled him until he was close enough to smell his cologne but at the appropriate distance for outside an elementary school.

"Come on, let's go somewhere I can kiss you. It's been seventy-two hours, and I'm having withdrawal symptoms."

A gorgeous blush crept up his face, highlighting his freckles. God, how I loved his freckles.

"Where are we going? Your message earlier was a little cryptic."

He toyed with his hair, and I wanted nothing more than to break the remaining distance between us, replace his hands with mine, and kiss him senseless.

"Have you ever been to the Van Stern Stained Glass Museum?"

"No, but that sounds super interesting. Is that where we're going?"

I nodded and then opened the passenger door of my car, where on the seat was a cool bag packed with ice to keep Emery's ice cream from melting.

He bounced on his toes. "Oh my god, you weren't lying!"

"I never lie when it comes to ice cream," I said, pushing aside the ugly voice in my head that was shouting, *But you lie about everything else.*

I walked around to the driver's seat. Emery was practically bouncing as he locked his seatbelt in place.

"How far away is this museum? I don't know if I can wait to eat the ice cream," he said, toying with the zipper pull on the bag.

I laughed. "It's thirty minutes outside of the city. You can have the ice cream in the car. Otherwise, it might melt."

It was not possible for someone to look happier than Emery at the prospect of being able to eat his ice cream straight away. As I pulled away from the school, he pulled the carton of ice cream from the bag and removed the lid.

"I want to say that I'll share this with you, but I'm not sure I like you enough yet to make that kind of sacrifice," he said, cutting through the scoop with the spoon.

"Yet, huh? So there's still hope you might like me more than ice cream."

He moaned. "Oh my god, this is even better than I remember. Yeah, you have a lot to live up to."

"I'm up for the challenge."

"Good to know," he said, repeating my words.

The busy city roads gave way to the quieter countryside. While the city wasn't a huge metropolis, I always loved going out into the country, which didn't happen as often as I liked.

Another reason why taking my brother's place for this meeting when he'd said he'd accidentally double-booked himself had been a good idea.

"Oh, this is the way to my place." Emery pointed at an intersection we passed. "It's another thirty minutes in that direction."

It took everything in me not to react, but I had to know more.

"Tell me about it. You live alone?" I asked.

"No, I live with my parents."

"Since the accident?"

"No...I don't know."

He put the lid on the empty carton, placed it in the bag, and put that in the footwell between his feet.

I took my eyes off the road for a quick glance at him. He was staring straight ahead at the road.

"You don't remember?"

He let out a long breath. "I remember coming back home after college. My parents are...quite protective of me, so after I finished college, I came back, hoping to get a job teaching locally. After the accident, I was still at my parents' place."

"What do you mean *still*?"

I saw him shrug from the corner of my eye.

"I always thought that once they got used to me being an adult with a job, they'd accept that I would eventually move out and get my own place. Something in my gut tells me I did, but I lost those memories. Also…"

I placed my hand on his leg. He was radiating tension and stress. As much as I wanted to know everything about the parts I was missing, I could tell he was also missing them. We were like two people working on the same puzzle, except one of us didn't know the other was working on it too.

"I don't know how it feels to walk in your shoes, Emery. I hope one day you'll remember it all."

"I'm starting to think those memories are lost, but also that maybe I don't need to find all the answers in my head," he said, sounding resigned.

"What do you mean? About the answers."

"Our gardener, Mr. Kowalski, said something to me the day I was supposed to join Ellie at your brother's engage-ment party. He said I always wanted to live in the city when I was younger, which is true. My parents loathe the city. They say it's dirty and lower class. Then he said I would probably want to go back now that I had my job there." He rubbed his hands on his thighs, so I held on to one and squeezed it tight.

He continued. "If I would want to go back, it means I was there to start with, right? The problem is that I can't find any evidence in my stuff that I've ever lived anywhere other than my parents' home. All my college books are there, my clothes. It doesn't make sense."

We were only a couple of miles from the museum, so I knew our conversation would end there.

"Have you asked your parents about it?"

He didn't answer, but I saw him shake his head.

I didn't press the subject further since we were pulling up to the museum's parking lot.

There weren't a lot of cars around, likely because it was getting close to the end of the day. I picked a spot where the car wasn't facing the building, and as soon as I put the car in Park, I turned to Emery.

"I'm going to kiss you now because I can't wait a second longer," Emery said.

He snaked his arm around my shoulders, and with his hand on the back of my neck, he guided my mouth onto his. I sank into him, letting him take charge of the kiss.

I met his tongue, giving it teasing lashes with my own, but I let him lead the kiss and take everything he needed.

How was it possible that kissing Emery felt both familiar and new?

When we parted, Emery's lips were swollen and his eyelids were heavy with lust. God, I *knew* that face. In the past, I would have known what to do with that face.

Now? I had to hope I didn't say or do anything to scare him off. I couldn't afford to lose him again, even though he was barely mine.

"Wow," he said. "Kissing you is...fuck. We should get out of the car before I do something really inappropriate."

I chuckled. "Hold that thought." Then I kissed him gently before opening the car door.

The museum looked like it had been a large family home once upon a time. The kind you'd see in the South. Stairs led to a wraparound porch with a set of double doors with windows on either side. Not surprisingly, they were fully made of stained glass.

"This is beautiful, Lex," Emery said as we walked up the steps.

I realized then I hadn't told him exactly why we were there.

"I have a confession to make," I said.

"There's more ice cream in the trunk of the car?"

I laughed at the way he wiggled his eyebrows.

"Afraid not. This is both a work and pleasure visit. My

brother, Noah, had a meeting with the owner of the museum for a project they're considering us for. He couldn't come, so he asked Adam, except Victoria also arranged for them to visit a few wedding venues, so as the odd man out, I got the assignment."

"It must be great to have siblings," Emery said with a hint of playful sarcasm.

"Today it is. If it's okay with you, I'll leave you to explore the museum while I have the meeting, but after, we've been invited to join their stained glass decoration demonstration. I don't believe they offer ice cream, but snacks are included."

Emery winked. "You had me at snacks. Lead the way."

I lost Emery to the stained glass panels in the room adjacent to the lobby as soon as we walked in, so I headed to the reception desk.

"Hi, I'm Alexis Spencer from Spencer Brothers Agency. I have an appointment with Mr. Van Stern."

"Of course, if you want to follow me, please," the man behind the desk said.

"Is it okay for my friend to wander around? We're scheduled for the demonstration after the meeting," I said. I'd checked before we came, but I wanted to make sure Emery wouldn't get in trouble for walking around since the museum would likely close within the next thirty minutes.

"Of course, sir. We'll make sure he doesn't get lost. There are a lot of windows in this place. After a while, they all start to look alike."

The man had to be in his seventies, and I liked his sense of humor. He took me down a hallway with closed doors on either side all the way along until we reached the one at the end.

He opened the door. "Mr. Van Stern, Mr. Spencer is here."

"Thank you, Charlie," the man standing by the window

behind the desk said, and Charlie nodded, leaving me with the museum owner.

"Good afternoon, Mr. Van Stern." I walked into the spacious office, holding out my hand.

Someone old, stiff, maybe wearing a tweed jacket. That was how I'd pictured the owner of a stained glass museum in my head.

Tall, dark eyes, a heavy-on-the-salt-lighter-on-the-pepper beard, and carefully styled hair. A man who filled a suit like he could command authority in any place. Lior Van Stern was definitely not what I'd expected.

If I had to guess, I'd put him in his late forties.

"Please, call me Lior," he said, shaking my hand and pointing to the chair in front of his desk while he took the chair with his suit jacket draped over the back. "I trust that everyone has been accommodating for your visit."

"Yes, everyone's been great with the arrangements. They've scheduled me and a friend for your stained glass decoration demonstration. My apologies for my brother's absence. Unfortunately, he was double-booked today."

And I was going to kill him because Lior was friendly but a little intimidating. This is why we left this part of the job to Noah. He knew how to handle himself with just about anyone.

"It happens. I'm glad you're able to experience the demonstration. I've fought hard to bring that project to life, which is why it's so important to me that we take it into the spotlight. Hopefully, we can get the workshops and courses off the ground soon."

Lior exuded confidence and old money. I would never place him in the kind of environment visited by families and art students, but the way his eyes brightened as he spoke about his passion project, even as he seemed to try to portray a professional emotional distance, was telling. This was important to him on a personal level.

"Tell me something about the history of the museum that I can't find via a Google search or your public website."

His lips were set in a straight line, and for the second time since I'd arrived, he glanced at his computer screen. Then he reached under it and pressed a button.

"Let me give you a personal tour."

"I'm all yours," I said, following as he stood.

I heard a barely-there chuckle.

Lior Van Stern was most definitely an enigmatic man, but as much as I was keen on learning everything about the museum from him—after all, I was here on a job—it was the other man walking around the building on his own I couldn't keep my thoughts away from.

E verywhere I turned, there was light and color. It was magical.

With the sun lower in the sky, the colors somehow seemed more intense. Every window, panel, or door told a story. Some rooms had themes, while others seemed like an eclectic mix of anything else that made the artist's creative juices flow.

I'd read the information boards and learned that all the stained glass creations belonged to Mr. Georg Van Stern. It had to have taken him years to make everything. Was he the guy Lex was meeting?

Lex had told me a little about his work with his brothers at the agency. It seemed strange that he was the one to come instead of Noah, but I wasn't going to complain about a free visit to this place and the demonstration afterward.

This was another one of the many places within a short driving distance from where I grew up that I hadn't known existed. How had I never noticed that my parents had kept me so isolated from the world around us when I was growing up?

My life's memories seemed to be formed from a curated

list of experiences that were appropriate for someone carrying the Livingston legacy.

I carried it around like a weighted blanket in hundred-degree weather. Heavy, too hot, and leaving me short of breath.

After taking hundreds of photos and inquiring about the possibility of doing a school field trip to the museum, I stepped outside the museum into the garden.

Even there, the stained glass creations didn't stop. Statues made out of iron and glass adorned every corner.

I spotted an arch with a bench underneath. The color show reflecting off the graveled path was stunning, although I wondered about the fire hazard of all the glass reflecting the sun onto the grass nearby at certain times of the day.

I had just sat down when my phone started ringing. It was the number for my therapist's office.

"Hello?"

"Hi, Emery, this is Dr. Solani. I had a patient cancel a session, so I was reviewing a few cases, yours being one of them. I thought I'd give you a call to check in on you."

"Oh, thank you, I appreciate that. I've actually been meaning to call to move up my next session."

"Has there been a change in your situation?" She sounded hopeful. My parents had insisted on hiring Dr. Solani to help me after the accident. They'd hoped she would steer me in the direction they wanted, but thankfully, she was a true professional, and I enjoyed our sessions. They were exhausting, but I always had something to work or focus on, and I felt like I was making progress.

"Um, yes, you can say that." I paused for a moment to think about how to explain everything that had happened recently. "In a nutshell, I had a flashback but can't decipher what it means or if it's even real. Then I met someone, a guy I am ridiculously attracted to and has the magic power to make me feel more at home with him than anyone else. But also, it's too early in any relationship to have these feelings, so I'm mostly just confused and trying to go with it. Oh, and I think my parents lied to me about where I lived before the accident."

There was silence on the other side. I could only imagine Dr. Solani was making her usual notes or probably gawking at the amount of information I'd thrown at her in just a few phrases.

"I'm glad I called. It seems like there's a lot to unpack here. Do you want to book a session? I could fit you in this week."

"Yes, please. That would be great."

"Okay, I'll get my assistant to send you my availability after this call. Is there anything you want to discuss now or ask me?"

"Yes. It's about the guy I'm seeing." I told Dr. Solani how I met Lex at the farmers' market and the two subsequent times. "I am inexplicably attracted to him. Not just the kind where I find him hot. I mean, I do, but—" I raised my hand to touch my face. My cheeks were burning. Was it weird to talk to your therapist about this? "I feel like there's more. The kind of feelings that are so strong and deep they could change you. You know how you suggested that I lean on the things that make me feel good and try not to question them? I'm trying to do that with Lex, but I'm scared."

"I understand. Do you think if you'd met Lex before the accident, you'd still be attracted to him in the same way?"

"Yes," I replied with certainty. "I may not remember what happened in the last three years, but I know I would've always been attracted to him."

"Maybe he's the link between past Emery and present Emery."

I thought about it for a moment. "If I know I would have been attracted to him before, then whatever happened between doesn't matter because I'm still the same person..."

"Sounds like a realization. How do you feel about that?"

I smiled to myself, my eyes following the colored patterns of the glass reflection on the gravel. "I...I think I like that."

"Good. I'd like you to focus on that feeling until we meet again, and not just where it comes to Lex. See if you can use it in other areas of your life. We can talk about it at the next session."

"Thank you, Dr. Solani."

"My pleasure. Speak soon, Emery."

Shortly after the call ended, I received an email from Dr. Solani's assistant with her available dates. Unfortunately, I couldn't do any of the session times because I was working, so I asked for the following week.

While I waited, I thought about her words. Being around Lex made me feel settled like it was where I belonged. I craved seeing him. We'd been together for as many hours as you could count with the fingers of both hands, but there hadn't been awkward moments.

Lex tried to get to know me, and he truly listened. He didn't make any judgments or offer solutions to my amnesia. He accepted that I was who I was.

But it was too early, right? God, we hadn't even done anything more than kissing.

But they'd been the best kisses of my entire life.

Hot, needy, soul-consuming. What would it be like to take things further with Lex? Since my accident, I'd felt I wasn't ready to have sex with anyone. I couldn't even explain why. I just didn't feel like myself.

What if when we got to it, I realized I didn't want to bottom or top or I gave bad blowjobs? It sounded stupid even as I thought it. There was no such thing as bad sex if it ended in an orgasm, but there were different levels of intimacy.

Whatever this connection with Lex was, I wasn't going to stop myself from enjoying it. I just needed a plan.

I turned on the bench when I heard footsteps on the gravel.

"Hey, you all done?" I asked Lex as he approached.

"I am."

"How did it go?"

He sat next to me, leaning back on the bench and pulling me close. "It was really interesting. We've got a big project on our hands, but the meeting was far too long. I wanted the chance to explore the museum with you."

"I took about a million photos, so I can show them to you later."

"I'd like that," he said, smiling. "How about we join the demonstration? It starts in five minutes."

We walked back into the museum and discovered a group gathered by the reception desk. Someone had brought over a cart with fresh coffee and pastries, so we helped ourselves.

"Ice cream and pastries? Nothing like a balanced diet," I joked.

"I'll take you to a salad bar for dinner," Lex said.

I snorted. "If you want to see me again after today, you'll—"

"Good afternoon, ladies and gentlemen. If you'd like to come through for the stained glass demonstration."

"Saved by the bell," I whispered to Lex.

"Maybe I'll finish that thought for you," he said, keeping his arm around my back and his hand settled on my waist. It was warm and protective. I liked it. "If I want to see you again after today, I'll make sure to kiss you senseless when I return you to your car and find a way to clear your schedule for longer than a few hours so we can do all the things I've been dreaming about since the day we met."

My head was going to explode from the sudden rush of heat. Even my curls felt tightly coiled.

I barely paid attention as the man continued his introduction. "Creating pieces with stained glass is a process that can take weeks. Today, we'll demonstrate each step of that process, and you can try your hand at it too. This isn't a sales pitch, but we'll soon be running a few stained glass-decoration-making courses. If you're interested, there's information about them at the end."

We followed as he showed us a variety of colored glass and which one to use for the effects required. The person at the cutting table showed us how to trace the design onto the glass using the glass cutter and the special pliers.

"This is so interesting. If I had enough time on my hands, I'd totally be up for doing the course. Can you imagine the beautiful things that can be created?"

"I can, and I think you'd be great at it," Lex said.

I laughed. "You haven't seen my drawing skills."

He smiled and placed a kiss on my forehead. "You can do anything you set your mind to, Emery."

God, I wished that was true because if it was, I'd have already confronted my parents about what Mr. Kowalski had said.

Lex took my hand as we observed the demonstration. Some of the other people in the group were quite excited about trying the tools out themselves, but I was happy to watch, so we moved along with everybody until the end of the demonstration.

As everyone spilled out of the museum, Lex and I held back until a tall guy in a suit came into the reception area.

"Lior, the demonstration was amazing. I already have some ideas I want to run past my brothers. This is Emery, by the way. Thank you for letting him take part too. We'll get in touch with you next week," Lex said to the guy.

"Thank you, Lex. I look forward to it. And nice to meet you, Emery. Feel free to come back to the museum any time."

Lior shook hands with Lex and then me before he showed us to the door.

"*That* was the guy you had your meeting with?" I asked.

"Yes, why?"

"Nothing, he's just very..."

Lex laughed. "Not stuffy?"

"Yeah...but also..."

"Stunning?"

I raised a brow. "Should I be concerned you're into older men?"

Lex walked me to my side of the car. "It seems each time we see each other, we end up in some kind of group activity."

"You didn't answer my question."

"About Lior? He's not my type."

"Good to know."

I leaned against the car door and hooked my fingers through Lex's belt loops, pulling him until he pressed me against the car.

He ran his nose up and down my neck, inhaling deeply and moaning my name.

"I have an idea of something we can do that requires no one else."

"I'm all ears," he said, pulling my earlobe with his teeth.

"Um...how about..." *What was I going to suggest?* I couldn't think with him pressing against me like this, especially when I could feel the outline of his cock against mine. My ass clenched, letting me know he would very much like to be up close with Emery's cock.

"How about...?"

"Oh right. Fuck, you're driving me insane. I can't think," I said.

"Good."

I took a long and deep breath. "How about we go camping next weekend? I know a spot I used to go to every year during the summer. I think I stopped going after I went to college, but I used to love it."

"You mean me, you, a tent, and no one else around?"

I bit my lip and nodded.

Our eyes met, and there was no way we weren't on the same page about what would happen.

"Pick me up Saturday morning?" he asked.

"Yeah."

"Okay," he said, kissing my lips for a too-short length of time. I'd have to place a formal complaint about that. "There's a diner on the way back to the city. How about some greasy and totally unhealthy food?"

Lex

"Okay, you have definitely overpacked," Adam said, pointing at my suitcase, the three different sleeping mats, the two sleeping bags—because it could get cold at night—the food and drink supplies, and my brand-new camping stove.

"How have I overpacked? Aren't these all essential things?"

He raised his eyebrows. "Yes, if you're going on a month-long trip to the Patagonia jungle."

"I don't know where I'm going. That's why it's better to be prepared." Why he wasn't getting this, I didn't know.

"You need all those lights?"

"They're safety lights. What if I go take a leak at night and step in bear poop or on a snake?"

He shook with laughter. "I'd say that if you're close enough to bear poop, the light won't help you. And the fairy lights?"

I touched my eyebrow. "Um...I guess those are extra."

"Extra? For what? Getting cozy with the bear under the twinkling lights?"

I shoved him, and he stepped back, laughing even harder. "How are you even at the stage of your life where you're getting married if you can't tell why I've packed the fairy lights?"

"Oh, I know. I just want to hear you say it out loud."

"Dickhead."

"Make sure you pack some condoms and lube."

I raised a brow. Adam never talked about his sex life but was always happy to impart his knowledge of ours to us, considering River and I were gay and Noah was...well, Noah.

"Have you told Emery to bring a truck? How big is his car?"

I grabbed him by the hand as he went toward my coffee pot.

"No can do. I need you gone before Emery comes."

He sulked like a kid whose toys were taken away. "Why? I could have brought River, but I didn't. Or Noah. But no, I did the responsible brotherly thing and came alone, and now you want me gone?"

"Yup." I crossed my arms over my chest. I wasn't going to budge on this. If he stayed, then he could say something...he shouldn't.

He sighed. "When are you going to tell him?"

"I don't know."

"Lex." He drummed his fingers on the kitchen table. "You can't keep this a secret. When he finds out, it's going to be worse."

"Don't you think I know that? Do you think I like deceiving him?" Frustration bubbled inside me. "I'm fucking in love with a man who thinks he just met me. What do you want me to say? Hi, Emery, wanna go out today? Oh, by the way, a year ago, before your accident, you said yes to marrying me. That was before you disappeared and broke my heart. I know it's not your fault, but I was angry and sad. Anyway, how about a quick fuck before we go down to the town hall, get married, and *then* we can go for ice cream." I was panting by the time I finished. Adam stared at me like he was looking at a wild animal.

We both jumped when the doorbell rang.

"Fuck." I gave my brother a pleading look.

"Fine," he relented. "But please be careful, Lex. It's not just his heart on the line. You spent so much time in the darkness. You deserve to have all the love in the world." He gave me one parting shot before he walked over to the back door. "And we're going to talk about the fact you never told anyone he said yes."

Fuck my big mouth.

The doorbell rang again, so I grabbed my earbuds from the counter and ran to the door.

"Hey, I hope you didn't ring a lot. I forgot I had these on." I raised my hand.

"Just twice. Are you ready?" He shifted on his heels from side to side.

"Almost." I pulled him by his T-shirt until he followed inside, where I closed the door behind him and claimed his mouth. He let out an adorable squeak, which only helped me because I took the chance his lips were parted to deepen it into a hot, tongue-thrusting kiss.

His arms went around my neck as his fingers threaded through my hair, something old Emery never did before, but I liked in new Emery. He matched the pass of my tongue with his until the only thing I could taste was him and maybe peanut butter and chocolate. Had he had ice cream already?

"Wow," he gasped. "Do we have to go anywhere? Can't we stay in all weekend?"

"You're saying I went and bought the contents of The Outdoor Outlet for nothing? Besides, why would I miss the opportunity to do the things I want to do to you outdoors?" I asked.

"You keep saying that, but I'm still here, untouched like a virginal offer, waiting for my knight to come to save me with his gentle but calloused hands, riding from the east with the sun."

I practically growled. "Oh, baby, my hands aren't calloused, and I'm no knight. All I can promise is a lot of debauchery."

He pretended to faint like a damsel in distress before he saw my pile of supplies.

"Are we emigrating? I didn't bring my passport."

"Very funny. I've never camped before. The guy at the store said I needed all these things." I pointed to the sleeping mats, bags, and stove.

Emery tried to hide his laugh behind his hand, but when I wrapped my arms around his waist and tickled him, he let it out.

"I'm sorry, I'm sorry. I should have told you I have all these things, although mine are all very old, so for the sake of your camping-virgin butt, we should probably take some of your stuff."

I wasn't going to lie and say my chest didn't puff up a little as Emery grabbed most of my stuff and took it out to his car.

"We'll leave the stove behind because there's a diner near the campsite."

"Okay." I guessed I would be eating all the food I bought for the trip during the week, but I still grabbed the bag with the camping snacks and the cooler full of drinks.

I'd locked up everything and was walking toward the door when I noticed Emery staring at the empty space on my wall where our photos used to hang.

"Maybe we can take some pictures this weekend and fill

these empty spaces," he said like it was the most natural thing in the world.

"Yeah, we can," was all I could say because my throat felt so tight. Adam's words came back to haunt me. Emery would hate me when he found out the truth, but I couldn't bear to give him up. So I pushed all those thoughts into the same drawer where I'd put the photos.

It took us an hour to arrive at our destination and another hour going back and forth from the parking lot to bring all the stuff to where we were setting up the tent.

"There's a river," I said. "A river."

Emery smiled. "Yeah, this is my favorite place. I used to camp here every summer with a childhood friend who went to the same school. He moved to Australia, so we lost touch."

"And now you're here with the ultimate city boy. I'll be lucky if I get out of here with only a few scratches," I said.

"Don't worry, my nails are blunt."

My jaw slacked. What had he just said? Suddenly jumping into the river felt like a good idea because my dick needed to cool down. We hadn't even set up camp and it was already getting ideas.

I got put to work helping Emery set up the tent. Although I'd argue I was more of a hindrance than a help, he was patient enough to earn himself a kiss at the end. However, in the process, I stepped on a small rock and nearly made us fall on top of the tent.

"I never knew you were a walking accident waiting to happen. My expensive first aid kit might not be enough for someone like you," he joked.

There was only one thing I needed from Emery, and it wasn't inside his first aid kit.

"What else can I do?" I asked.

"Can you make the tent cozy inside while I check the

perimeter to make sure we're not likely to get visitors during the night?"

"Yes, Mr. Liv—Teacher."

Shit.

He smiled, but I didn't take a proper breath until he was gone. That was a close call.

"Keep it cool, Alexis. Just this weekend, and then you can tell him," I muttered to myself. With that resolution made, I unrolled the sleeping mats and made the inside of the tent more comfortable than a four-star hotel.

Despite Adam's jokes about the lights, I was happy I'd brought them. I couldn't wait to see Emery's reaction later.

By the time he came back, our living area was all clear and we even had a couple of portable chairs in front of the fire pit. I'd packed marshmallows, chocolate, graham crackers, and roasting sticks because I wasn't going to roast marshmallows on twigs from the ground where animals may have done their business. Just the thought made me gag.

"Race you to the water," Emery said, removing all his clothes except his underwear.

My brain was slow to catch up because it was busy staring at Emery's almost naked body for the first time in so long.

"Come on, what are you waiting for?" he shouted before he dove under the water, coming up a few meters away, his curls all wet and bouncy.

I removed my clothes too and walked carefully to the water's edge. It wasn't as cold as I thought it would be, so I didn't hesitate as I walked all the way in, making my way toward Emery.

"Hey," I said, taking in his freckles that would no doubt be sun-kissed by tomorrow, the green eyes I would never get tired of looking into, and the curly hair he never managed to tame. Emery was a whole look, and my eyes were addicted.

Suddenly, something touched my leg. I jumped too

quickly and lost my footing, going underwater for a few seconds before Emery pulled me back up.

"What was that?" I asked, looking into the water. It was too dark to see.

"What was what?"

"Something touched my leg."

He laughed. "It was probably a fish."

"A fish? You never said there were fish." I started making my way out, but Emery pulled me back.

"It's only a small one. Did you seriously expect a river to not have life in it?"

"Stop laughing at me. I'm life. You're life. That's enough life for one river."

He came closer and held on to my shoulders. His legs went around my waist, helped by his natural buoyancy in the water.

"I disagree." He swooped in for a kiss. "I think we can liven it up a lot more."

The small pecks turned into heated, open-mouthed kisses. My cock hardened without the restraint of other clothing and pointed at Emery's perfect ass.

"Lex," he moaned, tightening his grip on my waist.

I looked down, and his cock was hard and barely contained by his underwear. Both my hands were busy holding him in place.

"Take yourself out, Emery. Let me see you." My voice was thick with need.

He nodded, trapping his lower lip between his teeth. I wasn't sure what I wanted to see more. His expression as he stroked himself, or the thick cock I'd been so familiar with a year ago.

Ultimately, the cock won. "That's it, baby. Show me how you like it."

"It wasn't supposed to be like this," he said, even as his voice faltered.

"Like what?"

"I wanted to wait until later. Didn't...fuck...didn't want you to think this is all we came here for."

I pressed my mouth against his, sucking that trapped lip into my mouth before letting go. "I know, baby. Do you know how much I've wanted to see you like this? How long I've waited?"

"Lex."

His name on my lips was almost enough to bring me over the edge, but I knew I needed more.

"Stand on your feet, Emery."

He did as I asked, so with my hands now free, I pushed our boxers down and took us in my hand.

I wanted to cry at how good it felt. Our throbbing cocks were hard and slippery in the water.

"Emery, god, you feel so good."

I was on the brink of my best orgasm in a long time. I tightened my grip and twisted my wrist in an up-and-down motion I knew was a surefire way to get Emery to come.

"Oh my god. Yes! Like that, Lex."

There was a huge chance campers up and down the river heard me shout, but I couldn't exactly be blamed for it. Lex was doing all the right things like he'd been given a play-book of my cock and studied it until he had it memorized for optimum performance.

My body was coiled and primed for release.

"You're so beautiful," he said. His magnetic eyes were pools of desire trained solely on me like he didn't want to miss a single beat.

I didn't think I looked that beautiful with my wet curls plastered to my skin and a very likely red face from what Lex was doing to me, but I took in the praise nonetheless.

The sounds of the sloshing water around us brought an added element of eroticism to what we were doing. We were on the river, exposed. Anyone walking past could see us, and there was no mistaking that Lex was giving me the best hand job of my life.

"Next time, I'm going to take my time with you, Emery. I'm going to taste you everywhere, and then I'm going to open you up nicely before I fill you up with my cock."

"Nghnnn."

"Do you like that, baby? Is that what you want?" he asked between broken kisses.

"Uh-huh." My orgasm was right there, on the verge. My breathing became more labored. I latched my mouth to Lex's neck and sucked his skin.

"Oh fuck, fuck, Emery. I'm so close."

I nodded against his skin because I was incapable of words.

One small stroke and twist and I came with a full-body shudder. Lex was right there with me, our mixed releases disappearing into the stream around us. I liked the idea that even when we couldn't see it, parts of us were all swirled and mixed together.

Lex released our cocks to wrap both his arms around me. It was the only move we made for the longest time, even after both our cocks were soft, and I felt the stretched elastic band of my boxers digging into my legs.

"That's one way to forget about the fish," Lex said, and I released a burst of laughter.

I'd messed around with a few guys at college, but nothing had ever gotten this serious, this intense, this quickly. It had also never been this much fun.

The dirty talk, the urgency, the warmth of his skin even in the cool river stream. Everything about being with Lex was perfect, and it scared the hell out of me.

"Shall we grab a drink while we dry out?" I asked.

He held my hand as we walked out of the water and shared a towel to wipe down our bodies before we changed our underwear and sat on the foldout chairs.

"Did you always want to be a teacher?" Lex asked, taking a beer from the cooler.

"Not until I went to a private school. It was one of those where you stay there all week and go home over the weekend."

"You went to boarding school?"

I chuckled at the way his eyebrows knitted together. "Yeah."

"I never knew that," he muttered, and I laughed.

"Of course you didn't. Anyway, I didn't mind school because it was easier being there than home, where I'd practically been raised by nannies until I was old enough to be shipped away during the week. The teachers were strict, but one particular teacher was different."

"Less strict?"

"Not really. He just knew how to talk to us like we mattered. You can imagine a bunch of rich kids who grew up under the shadow of their family's expectations for their futures. They rebelled because it was the only way to feel in control."

Lex stretched out his hand over the arm of the chair, and I did the same until our fingers touched.

"I can't imagine you being a rebel," he said.

"I wasn't. The kids listened to that teacher, so I decided I wanted to be like him. I wanted to teach and give kids a voice. I was very naive then. I thought I was different from the other kids because while my parents always talked about me taking over running the family estate, they didn't make me take extra summer placements or force me to attend boring events. At least most of the time."

He rubbed circles on the back of my hand, and with the sun warming my skin, I could've easily fallen asleep from the contentment.

"So you became a teacher."

"I became a teacher."

"My parents always thought my brothers and I would take over the restaurant, but the only person who ever showed an interest was our best friend, River. That made it easier for them to let go when we said we wanted to open the agency together. River now manages the restaurant, but his main job is keeping my dad away so he can do his job."

I turned my face to look at him. "Ellie said Lusitana is your parents' restaurant."

"Yeah, they opened a million years ago because my dad was obsessed with the food my mom and grandmother cooked, and he wanted everyone to experience it. Three kids, a vegetable patch, and a pet rabbit later, they're still going strong."

"Even the rabbit?"

He laughed. "No, he died years ago."

I turned my hand over so our palms touched. He hadn't been wrong. His hands were soft.

"My parents want me to quit teaching," I practically blurted out. "They said I have to do it at the end of the year and then go work with my dad."

Saying the words aloud made them so real that my stomach churned. Lex got up from the chair and kneeled in front of me. I opened my legs to accommodate him.

"Can you say no?" he asked.

I shrugged. "I owe them everything. From my education to the support they offered after the accident. My therapist alone is more than I can afford on my salary."

Lex ran his hands over the tops of my legs. Such a comforting touch. It made me want to jump onto his lap and stay there for a long time.

"Emery, it's not my place to say what you should do, but I strongly believe in chasing your dreams. What kind of person will you be in twenty years, doing something you don't want to as opposed to something you were born to do."

I gave a scoffing laugh. "You don't know that. Maybe I'm a horrible teacher and my students will be glad to see the back of me."

He tipped his head to one side. "Do you really believe that?"

"No. But maybe if I say it often enough…"

He let out a long breath and then reached over to touch my cheek. "How much more do you have to lose, baby?"

I opened my mouth and closed it again. "What do you mean?"

"You lost three years of your life. Do you have any idea what happened in that time that you may never find out? That might be lost forever? Don't lose yourself too."

I stood, shoving my chair back. Lex fell back on his butt, but I didn't care. How dare he say that? He didn't know what it was like to live every day with a piece of me missing. I picked up a rock and threw it in the water. It didn't skip. It just plopped, splashed, and sank straight to the bottom of the river.

"Emery…"

I didn't turn around, but I could tell he was right behind me.

"I…I don't want to talk out of turn, but…I know what it's like to lose a part of yourself overnight. To have to continue living like everything's okay, but it's not, and it never will be because you're missing the one thing that made you…you. When everyone around you moves on. They celebrate life milestones, as they should, but there's always that spare glance at poor Lex, who's not okay. Maybe he will one day. But I know I won't…"

I closed my eyes and forced the tears back inside.

His boyfriend. That's the person he lost.

When I turned around, Lex's face was pained, but there was a smile.

"I'm sorry," I said.

I wanted to kick myself for being so selfish and thinking

only about my own pain. We both carried something we didn't want.

"Can I hug you, please?"

He didn't need to plead. I walked into his embrace, feeling all the pain radiating from him slowly dissipate until we were just holding each other. I wanted to comfort him the same way he was comforting me because he was right.

If I didn't stand up to my parents' demands, I'd end up being just like them, with the exception that they actually enjoyed the life they had. The pretense. The money.

"Do you believe in second chances?" I asked. My heart pounded as his blue eyes scanned over me. His hand reached up to cup my face.

"I didn't, but...I do now."

"Do you think we could be each other's second chance?"

He nodded.

Our lips met in a slow and tender kiss.

"Hey," I said between kisses.

"Hmm..."

"Do you want to take a walk to the diner?"

He stopped kissing me to look into my eyes. "How far?"

"About a twenty-minute hike up the river or a thirty-minute drive around the park."

"Wait, why did we have to drive a hundred miles into the forest to get here?"

"Because I secretly wanted to torture you. It was a test of your bravery."

I squealed when he grabbed me in a fireman's lift and carried me into the water.

We both surfaced from the water at the same time, gasping for air and laughing. I took my revenge by dunking his head under the water again, to which he retaliated by tickling me until I cried uncle.

"We're both wet again," he said when we finally stopped

messing around. I loved how bright his eyes were in the sunshine, his lashes covered in water droplets.

"Whose fault is that?"

I came closer, wrapping my arms and legs around him like before.

"Don't you even think about it," he said, although he held me back and started kissing the skin on my shoulders, so I'm not sure how determined he was to not repeat what we'd done earlier.

"I'm not thinking about anything," I said innocently.

"You can't fool me. I knew you just wanted me for my hot body and astounding refractory period."

I laughed. "You caught me there." I kissed him on the lips again. They were just there, so close, I couldn't help it. "How do you feel about cheeseburgers and fries?"

"I'd be very impressed if you can make that happen from the contents of the cooler, but there are enough beers in there that I can just sit back and watch."

"I mean the diner. Let's get dry...again...and walk up there."

"Will our stuff be okay here?"

"Yes, city boy. People around here respect each other's stuff. If you take someone's supplies, you could put them in danger for the sake of a new sleeping bag, so people don't do it. It's like a camper's unwritten code."

A big smile spread across his face. "Really?"

I chuckled. "No. No one cares, but it's unlikely anyone will come this way. People tend to stay closer to the amenities, and not many people know you can get to the diner from here."

"You're just begging to get spanked, aren't you?"

I winked. "Maybe."

"Well, shit. Let me dive under the water to cool down before we get out because you're killing me here."

"Come on, let's get out of here. The sooner we go, the sooner we'll return, and then..." I pulled him by the hand back to where we'd left the towel.

"And then?"

I was teasing him in a way I didn't remember ever wanting to tease anyone. It was playful and fun.

He groaned when I pulled down my underwear first and went looking for a dry pair after.

"I'm so fucked," he muttered.

With any luck, we'd both be pretty fucked by the time the sun came down later.

The diner, Emery had assured me, wasn't that far from our camping site, but it did require hiking through some challenging trails.

Challenging for me. Emery made it look so easy to avoid loose rocks and moss-covered ground.

I'd started off focusing on his perfect ass in front of me as we hiked in a single line. But soon enough, my two left feet made it practically impossible to stay upright unless I paid attention to where I put my feet.

"Your ass is too distracting. If I fall and break my neck, it's all your fault," I complained even as I tripped over another small rock and almost fell again.

Like me, Emery wore a pair of jean shorts, but while mine were navy, his were light blue and matched perfectly with his white polo shirt. I'd gone for the easy all-navy combo, but my T-shirt had a splash of rainbow on the front.

"I don't see how that's my fault," he said innocently, bringing his hand behind his back to pretend to scratch an itch, lifting his shirt and showing me more of his delicious curves.

We were approaching a wider part of the path, and I didn't see any death traps ahead, so I grabbed Emery's hand and pulled him against me. His immediate reaction was to relax under my hold.

He dropped his head back onto my shoulder. I fingered a loose tendril of his curly hair behind his ear, giving me better access to his freckle-kissed neck.

I sucked hard, knowing it would leave a mark, but he didn't complain.

"Everything about you drives me insane, Emery. Your ass, your skin, your hair, your eyes, your dick, your personality." I turned him around to face me. "Everything."

The hunger in his eyes as he fixed onto my mouth was like he was craving me as much as he craved his next fix of ice cream. I was very much okay with that.

"Are you going to kiss me, or are you—" I started before his head crashed onto mine. "What the—" I rubbed my forehead. "That was really not where I thought we were going," I said.

"Something hit me in the back of my head." He turned around, and sure enough, there was a large orange on the ground.

Another orange flew in our direction, hitting me on my leg. The third one missed Emery by an inch.

"You didn't tell me there were killer orange trees in this forest," I said, pulling him away from the path of a fourth incoming orange.

"There aren't."

We rushed up the path until I could see the top of a building. The oranges kept coming.

"And this is for the time I missed watching Henry Cavill in the cinema because you had the flu"—an orange flew past— "and this one is for missing my little sister's birthday and then making me feel bad for not being a supportive boyfriend just because I picked my ten-year-old sister over the stupid ball game you had tickets for..." Another hit the tree we'd just passed with such force it smashed, leaving a trail of juice and bits.

As we neared the end of the trail, the thrower of the murderous oranges became clear.

The guy couldn't have been taller than five foot two, but he had a strong arm and a long reach. It was only when we left the trail that I realized how far down we'd been when we were first hit.

I'd take a guess that he was a baseball player, but he really didn't look like the type. In his pink jean shorts, light-blue T-shirt, and matching hair, he definitely didn't look like a ball player.

Despite his focus on the orange throwing, when I stepped on a small branch and it snapped, so did the guy. He turned to us with a murderous look, orange in hand, ready to throw.

We both raised our hands.

"Don't worry. They're not for you," he said, throwing the orange in the same direction we'd just come from.

"The back of my head begs to differ," Emery said.

The guy's head snapped back to us. He looked semi-apologetic. "You shouldn't have been on the path. No one ever uses it." And then he mumbled between his teeth, "Unless you're a fucking closet case and horny for a quick hand job." Two other oranges were lost to his rage.

"Why are you throwing oranges into the forest?" I asked.

"They're not oranges. They're grapefruit." He held another one in front of him, rolling it between his palms. "Look the same, but they're bitter, like me."

"Oookay...."

"Wait," Emery said. "I remember you."

The guy turned to face us fully. His T-shirt had a pineapple, and underneath it read: *Eat me now. Thank me later.*

His fists clenched around the grapefruit before he dropped them to the ground, looking defeated.

"Do you know each other?"

"Yes," the guy said at the same time Emery replied, "Kinda."

The guy's lower lip trembled like he was going to cry.

"I'm so sorry." He took a few steps to where a pink messenger bag was on the ground next to a bag half-full of grapefruit, took out a small bottle, and sprayed something onto his face. "A girl's gotta be prepared at all times, right?"

"What happened?" Emery asked the guy.

He took a long, deep breath and held out his hand in my direction.

"Hi, I'm Ren. I'm sorry you had to witness my emotional crisis. I promise I'm usually brighter than a ray of sunshine on a summer day, but..." The trembling lip came out again.

"I'm Lex. How do you know each other?" I asked.

"Ren works at the restaurant where I had my date with Frederick," Emery said.

Ren scoffed. "He's another one."

"Who?" I asked.

"The other guy. Frederick," Ren said. "He also said he was gay but then wasn't. It's all a game to guys like them. They know they can have anything, whether they really want it or not. And they'll take it all. Every single bit you give them." He looked toward the diner, letting out a long sigh.

Emery glanced at me, and I nodded my agreement. "Hey, Ren, we were going to the diner to grab some food. Do you want to join us?"

The smell of greasy food coming from the diner was making my belly rumble. It wasn't exactly the kind of dinner date I'd imagined, but I could tell Emery didn't want to leave Ren alone.

Ren shook his head but then held his shoulders back and

smiled the fakest smile I've ever seen. "Thank you. It would be a pleasure to join you."

The diner wasn't anything special at first glance. The usual formica tables and fake leather seats formed separate booths and a countertop ran the length of the diner with round benches.

What was unusual was that while the parking lot seemed fairly empty, the diner itself was filled with people.

Emery pointed to a table in the corner, so we took our seats.

Shortly after, a server approached us. "Hey there, welcome to Sustainable Saturdays at Poppy's din—oh, hi, Ren," she said.

"Hi, Poppy."

She turned to Lex and me. "Ren knows all about Sustainable Saturdays. It was his idea, after all. Can I get you a coffee while you pick what you're eating?"

"Sure, thank you," Emery said.

"So what's Sustainable Saturdays?" I asked.

Ren picked the corner of the old menu with his fingernail. "It's nothing special. Local farmers donate food to the diner during the week, so on Saturday, Poppy's dad, who owns this place, uses those ingredients in the food and only charges half price."

My brothers and I had come up with a similar campaign for a friend a couple years ago, and it had helped his business thrive.

"Poppy said it was your idea?"

"Yeah. I grew up near here. Everyone has their own veggie patch or buys their food from the farmers' market. The diner used to be really quiet unless there was a game on and everyone came over to watch it together. I figured that if people brought their own food, they could have dinner together and just pay the cost of having it made. It was a silly school project from years ago, but it stuck, and it's now a thing here."

"That's an amazing idea," Emery said.

"I agree. Do you work in marketing, by any chance?"

Ren laughed. "No, I'm a...was a florist, a server, a personal shopper, a dog walker, a cat sitter, and a secret boyfriend. Anyway, the burgers here are great, and they add paprika to the fries. They're delicious, especially when you dip them in mayo. God, I didn't realize I was so hungry."

Emery and I exchanged a look.

"What's really going on, Ren?" Emery asked.

"Nothing much, just the end of my life as I know it."

"We only met on the most fortunately disastrous date of my life," Emery said to Ren, giving me a wink. "But I could tell that night you're not this person in front of us. You were flirty and spunky, and you certainly rattled Frederick a little."

"That was old Ren. Old Ren had a job doing the thing he loves the most in his whole life. Old Ren was someone's secret boyfriend, but he didn't mind because he knew it was only temporary, and he spent so much time with his boyfriend that it rarely felt like it was a secret anyway."

Poppy interrupted him by bringing us coffee. We quickly looked over the menu and ordered burgers, fries, and milkshakes.

When Poppy left us, I gestured for Ren to continue.

"New Ren...no longer has the job he loves, only the five other side gigs he does to make extra money, which he'll need now more than ever. New Ren can't be the secret boyfriend of someone who is also dating a woman. The worst is the boyfriend doesn't know I know. As soon as I tell him, everything is going to crumble like a house of cards."

"What's the connection with your job? Do you work for him?" I asked.

"I work in his parents' flower shop. They've been talking

about selling so they can retire, and I'd hoped to buy it from them one day. Chad told me he'd come out and we'd be together properly. No hiding. I guess my first clue that nothing would ever come true was his name. Who names their children Chad and expects them to be good people?"

I snorted, and Emery kicked my leg under the table. "He's kinda right, baby."

While it wasn't the first time the term of endearment had escaped my lips, I was finding it harder and harder to stop it from happening. Emery's eyes softened, and a small smile graced his lips. He'd always liked it when I called him that. He'd said it made him feel like he truly belonged to me.

"Aww, you guys. Ugh, the way you look at each other is like you've been together for years. You're making my cold, bitter heart melt," Ren said, and we both smiled.

"Believe it or not, we met just before my date with Frederick," Emery said.

Ren's expression was comical. "What? You're telling me you already knew this hunky piece of human pecan pie and you went on a date with that...that...person?"

"It's a long story," Emery said, "but Frederick isn't a bad guy. He was just a little misguided."

Ren scoffed. "Yeah, like my soon-to-be ex."

"I, for one, am glad Frederick turned out not to be the perfect date," I said, holding Emery's hand over the table.

"I'm gonna need my burger now if I have to watch you two be all smooshy," Ren said.

Right on time, Poppy brought our food, and as Ren promised, both the burger and fries were delicious.

"So, how did you find out about the girlfriend?" I asked Ren.

"You learn a lot about everybody working in the flower shop. I overheard two women talk about it. They didn't know I could hear them, and since no one knows about us, there was no need for them to be particularly quiet. That was this morning."

"And the grapefruit throwing?"

He shrugged. "No one likes grapefruit, so I figured taking them from the tree in his backyard was as close as I could get to pretending it was his head smashing against the trees."

"Or the back of my head," Emery said.

"Sorry about that. What were you doing on the trail, anyway?"

"We're camping by the river."

"It's a good spot down there. Me and Chad used to go down there all the time. That was before he got too busy with 'work,'" Ren said with air quotes. "I guess now I know what he was working on. God, I feel so stupid. I hate lies."

I wanted to say something to make him feel better, but his last words cut through me. I hated lies, too, and here I was, living the biggest lie of my life alongside the biggest truth.

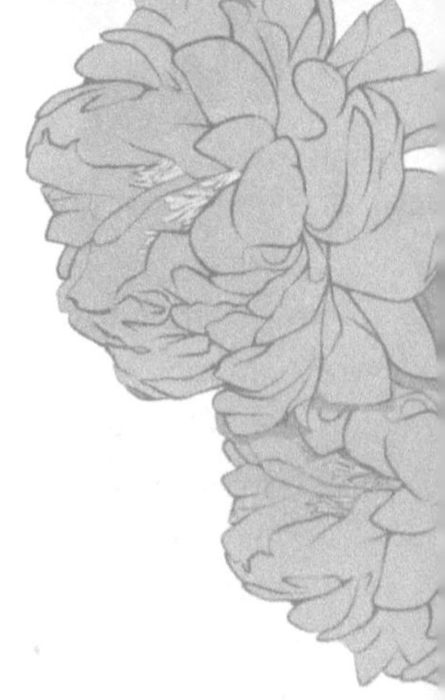

Emery

Ren let out the longest sigh. "If I'm honest, all the signs were there. Every time we talked about the future, he never got into the specifics. He complained that I worked too much because I was saving to buy his parents' store, but he never offered to buy it with me, even though he works there too."

I put my hand on his. "I know you probably aren't ready to hear this, but maybe it's all for the best. If you've been doing all the work alone, you deserve to own your flower shop."

"Well, I can't be around him now and not want to strangle his neck, so I need to quit the job. I suppose I could pick up more shifts at the restaurant and more pet-sitting gigs to make up for the loss of income."

"There you go," Lex said. "You already have a plan."

"I think I need a drink. Do you want to come to Fizzy Pops with me?" Ren asked.

Lex and I shared a look. Our evening was so not going according to plan, but we couldn't leave Ren. I barely knew him, but he seemed like a good guy.

"We're not exactly dressed for a...what's Fizzy Pops?" I asked.

"It's a bar, but it's not fancy. Your clothes are fine. I'll call us a cab."

We paid the bill, and twenty minutes later, the cab dropped us off in front of Fizzy Pops. The roadside bar had so much LED lighting on the facade of the building that I was pretty sure it could be seen from outer space.

"I'm not sure if I'm going to get a headache from the lights or diabetes from the illuminated food," Lex said as we walked to the line to get in.

"This place is fantastic," Ren said. "They have amazing cocktails but also desserts, hence all the illuminations. The wall is basically their menu. Anything you can see, they sell it inside."

"A bar that sells dessert. I could get on board with that, especially if they have ice cream," I said jokingly.

Ren turned around in the line. "Their milkshakes are made with ice cream, and they're delicious. The owner went to school with me. I suggested they add flower flavors like lavender and rose, and they did it. I can tell you which ones they are when we get in."

"Are you sure you don't want a job in marketing?" Lex asked, laughing. "I could get an opening for you in my PR company."

"That's very kind of you, but my brilliant ideas only strike during the waxing crescent moon when my neighbor's goat feels particularly thankful toward the cosmos and stops eating the hedge between the gardens."

"Um...huh?"

I snorted as Lex looked completely befuddled.

"I mean, they're unreliable at best and completely unlikely to happen when I need them," Ren clarifies.

"Right..." Lex said. "The offer is there if you need it."

"Thanks, hun," Ren said, and then he turned to me. "You picked a good one. Don't let him go."

I smiled and looked at Lex. He wrapped his arm around my shoulders and kissed my forehead. "Don't worry, Ren. I won't let him let me go...or something like that."

Heart sufficiently overflowing.

I didn't have much time to consider my feelings toward Lex's open display of his hopefully growing affection for me because our turn to get inside the bar came too soon.

After that, there was no space for introspective thoughts because even if they happened, there was no way I'd be able to hear them in my head over the noise in the bar.

Ren shouted that he wanted a Lemon and Lavender gin with extra ice, and then he disappeared onto the dance floor.

Lex shook his head and smiled at Ren's parting figure.

I nodded toward the bar. He took my hand, and together, we navigated through the crowd.

Somehow, the sound of the music and people talking didn't seem as loud around the bar area. We took two stools at the bar and waited for the waiter to make his way over.

Lex rested his elbow on the bar and swung in his seat to face me. A teasing smile graced his lips.

"You seem familiar. Have I seen you here before?"

I turned to face him. My hair, as usual, was all over the place, so I tucked the lock covering my eyes behind my ear. "You could have, but you see, I have this memory problem in which...I have none. Maybe we've met, maybe we haven't." I shrugged nonchalantly.

He tapped a finger over his chin. "Hmm, I wonder if there's anything I could do to make you remember."

I tilted my head. "Feel free to try, handsome."

He took my hand in his and flipped it palm side up. A shiver ran down my spine, spreading all over me as he ran a single digit from the inside of my wrist to the tip of my middle finger.

"The first time we met, you asked if you could read my palm," he said.

"I did?" Oh, he was pretending, of course. I smiled and went along with it.

He nodded. "You touched me like this." His finger followed the path back up my hand and over my arm. "I asked you what you saw." His voice was calm, and his gaze steady.

My whole being seemed locked in place by the magnetism in Lex's eyes. By his soft touch.

"What did I say?"

A tap on the bar made us both jump.

"What can I getcha, guys?" the bartender asked.

Lex turned to the bartender and placed an order. As far as I cared, he could have ordered a triple shot of vodka or something equally revolting. I didn't know because my hands were trembling from the power of Lex's touch.

"Hey, is my drink ready yet? I'm parched," Ren said, appearing out of nowhere, still dancing like he was surrounded by men who wanted to eat him alive.

"Coming right up," Lex said.

"Having fun?" I asked.

Ren nodded. "Uh-huh. Best idea ever. Now I just need to get drunk enough to find the courage to break up with Chad and rescue my succulents."

"Your what?"

"Succulents."

I laughed. Ren was definitely a character to be reckoned with. I had a feeling he was as much fun as he was hard work but loyal down to the bone.

The waiter brought our drinks, and Ren went for his straight away, drinking half of it in one go.

"Argh, brain freeze." He scrunched his eyes.

"You might want to take it easy. The night is still young," Lex said.

"And just like the night, I'm not getting any younger." He drank the rest and put the glass down, waving to the bartender to give him another one.

Two guys approached Ren, each placing a hand on either side of his hips and moving with the music.

Maybe it was the lingering effects of Lex's touch and needing more, but watching Ren dance with the two guys made me horny. My orgasm earlier, the first at someone else's hand in at least three years, had only made the fire inside me burn hotter.

To think I'd spent the last year avoiding contact with other men because I was so afraid. Lex made me feel so wanted, so desired, and I craved more of that feeling.

I sipped my beer, thankful Lex didn't pick something from the alcoholic shake menu. After dinner, I wasn't sure my stomach would handle that much dairy, and that was saying something, even for me.

I also needed to be careful with how much I drank, or I'd struggle while getting back to the campsite.

The campsite. Shit.

"We need to figure out what to do," I said to Lex, leaning forward so he could hear me.

"About what?"

"Ren. Going back to the campsite."

Lex kept his eyes on Ren, who turned around and started groping the two guys as if we weren't right there. "God, you're hot. Do you tag team? I'm in need of an above-standard dicking. My boyf–ex-boyfriend wasn't good at...being good. Who wants to relieve some stress with a guaranteed happy ending?"

"We can't leave him alone," Lex said. "God knows what trouble he'll get himself into." Then he moved forward until his breath brushed over my hair. "I'm not gonna lie, Emery. I want to get inside that tent and zip the rest of the world away. Just you, me, and the ridiculously expensive fairy lights I bought."

I moved my head to kiss him so he knew how much I was on board with that idea. Ren pushed us away from each other to grab the fresh drink the bartender had just left next to ours.

"What do we do?" I asked Lex. He shrugged.

"About what?" Ren asked. "Oh, I gotcha. The restrooms are very clean here, and if you're feeling a little adventurous, there's a passage through into town. It's usually quiet until people start going home, and as you can see, no one's going home anytime soon." He hiccuped, put the newly empty glass on the bar, and dragged the two guys onto the dance floor.

"Shit," Lex said. "I just remembered. River is working tonight, Noah is at a conference out of state, and I doubt Adam can come out tonight. I think he was having dinner with Victoria and her parents."

"There must be someone we can—wait." I grabbed my phone and sent a message.

"Who did you call?" Lex asked.

"The only other person I know who also knows Ren."

An hour and a bit later, I saw Frederick moving through the crowds, trying to find us.

"Here," I shouted as I waved at him.

"Your message was a little cryptic, but I was bored, and it's Saturday night, so what can I do for you?" he asked.

I laughed. "Let me introduce you to Lex," I said as they shook hands. I didn't bother introducing Frederick because Lex had seen us outside the restaurant on our failed date night.

"Nice to meet you, Lex."

I glanced at the dance floor where Ren had been for the last hour. His pineapple T-shirt was tucked into the waistband of his shorts and he was now dancing with someone else who was shirtless.

"We have a mutual acquaintance that requires some...assistance," I said.

"We've only just met. Who else do we...oh no, you mean the waiter from the restaurant? You have to be kidding me. I drove an hour out of town to do what, babysit a rude twink with an attitude?"

I cringed. The only person I could think to call for help was Frederick. If he didn't want to help, we'd have to stay with Ren all night and leave all our stuff unattended by the river. We'd never intended to be away from there this long as it was.

"Heeeeyyy, it's Mister I'm Not Gay, even though he has too many muscles to be straight, and this fitted shirt? Gay. Gay. Gay."

I groaned. Lex took my hand and squeezed it gently. He was fine with staying longer, but dammit, maybe I was being a brat, but I wanted to go back to the tent. I wanted to see the fairy lights.

"Believe in whatever makes you sleep at night, Tiny," Frederick said.

"Not thinking about you...you...Gigantor," Ren replied. "Whatever, I'm dancing. There's too much fake testosterone in here."

Frederick crossed his arms as he watched Ren disappear into the crowd and then turned to us.

"What's going on?"

I sighed. "We're camping nearby and need to get back to our stuff. Ren's going through some...stuff today, and he shouldn't be alone."

"Doesn't look like he has any problem with that. He's dancing with at least two guys who look more than happy to be his company and a third who looks like he'd love to watch."

I raised a brow. "Since when do you read gay?"

"Since a bunch of my friends in London are gay. I may not

pull off the accent or the gay thing, but it doesn't mean I can't read when two guys are willing."

Despite Frederick's words, I wondered if Ren was right in his assessment of Frederick. It wasn't for me to push or find out. Like he said, he had gay friends.

"We'll owe you forever. Pleeease." I did my best puppy-dog eyes.

He groaned. "Fine. But this is us getting even."

Lex looked confused, but I shook my head. I'd explain later.

When I stepped down from my stool, Lex pulled me between his legs and whispered in my ear, "How about a dance while we wait for the cab?"

We were settling the bill when Ren came running, practically crashing into Frederick, who only had time to hold him back by his shoulders.

"Ew, you're sweaty."

Ren shrugged. "Nothing wrong with a hot, sweaty, dirty romp in the sheets, but I guess you wouldn't be up for that, would you?"

"No," Frederick replied.

"Fine. But you're coming with me to help me break up with my boyfriend and take my succulents back," Ren said, taking a stand with his arms crossed over his chest. Well, as much of a stand as a five-foot-two man wearing pink shorts and nothing else could take.

"Are you drunk?"

"Yes, but we're still doing this because I need muscles and you need a workout."

"I'm not fighting someone for you."

"Who said anything about fighting? God, you straight boys only think with your fists."

"So you admit I'm straight."

Ren threw his hands out. "I'm standing here half-naked,

and you don't even have the tiniest stir in your pants. I guess I'll admit defeat."

That drew a smile out of Frederick. Maybe there was hope for both of them yet.

"Our cab is here," Lex said.

Frederick nodded toward the door. "Go. I'll look after mini-twink here."

I took Lex's hand, and we walked out of the club and into the cab.

It took us half an hour to get to the campsite parking.

It was practically pitch black after the cab drove away. I turned on the flashlight on my phone and guided us slowly to our camping site.

I didn't know if it was because of the dark or knowing what was about to happen, but a shiver went through me.

"You okay?" Lex asked, wrapping his arms around me.

"Yeah, just...nervous."

He ran his hands up and down my arms. "Nothing has to happen, Emery."

I nodded even though I wasn't sure he could see me. The moon didn't provide that much light where we were. "Maybe you can start by showing me your fairy lights."

"Is that a euphemism?"

And just like that, all my tension evaporated. I laughed and pulled Lex in for a dirty kiss. "Let's get there so you can take me inside the tent, Lex."

Lex

"*Take me inside the tent, Lex.*"

That was exactly what I intended to do. I hadn't lied. I'd be happy sleeping with Emery in my arms, like the old days. How I'd wake in the middle of the night and find that Emery had drifted into my space and wrapped his legs around mine, or how he'd turn over in bed and pull my arms around him like I was his own personal blanket.

Those nights were wonderful. Knowing that, at a subconscious level, Emery wanted me that much.

I never thought I'd have that again, so this moment right here was so much bigger than Emery could imagine. If he was nervous, I was scared shitless because I needed to make this good for him. For both of us.

"Are you sure no animals can creep inside?" I asked when we approached the tent.

He laughed. "We're outdoors, and bugs can get anywhere they set their mind to, but the tent is a single piece, so once the zipper is closed behind us, nothing else should come in."

The tent wasn't huge, but it was big enough for two

people to sleep comfortably, and because it was an igloo shape, we could also sit up without our heads touching the ceiling.

We both removed our shoes and put them inside bags since they would stay outside the tent for the night. We didn't want to give creepy crawlies a chance to snuggle up inside. Once in the tent, I searched for the button on the battery pack for the lights.

"I don't think I've ever seen these many blankets inside this tent," he said. "And I'm pretty sure I've never camped with actual proper pillows."

"Is it okay? I wasn't sure if we'd need more if it gets cold." I hadn't been sure of anything when packing and figured we could take blankets away but couldn't make them appear out of nowhere. This was as close to sleeping on a bed as we could get, and I liked that.

"The sleeping bags are enough to keep us warm, but this is a whole new level of comfort." Emery laid on his back. "I could get used to this."

As soon as I found the button on the battery pack, I lay next to him, my finger grazing the button.

"Ready?" I asked, turning my head to see his face.

He held my hand. "Ready."

I pressed the button, and we were surrounded by tiny lights. In the dark, we couldn't see the string holding them together, just the glow of the light bulbs.

Emery gasped. "It's like we're under the stars."

"But without bugs."

He shifted to his side, holding his head up with his elbows.

"You really don't like bugs, do you?"

"I've never paid them particular attention. I'm a city boy, remember?"

He smiled. "So what do you pay attention to, city boy?"

I cupped his chin, feeling the smoothness of his skin glowing under the lights.

The first time I saw Emery, I was stunned by how effortlessly beautiful and authentic he was.

He accepted his curly hair and freckles. He accepted that he was never as tall as most of the guys he'd been with, including me. And he was happy being who he was.

Even after having his memory taken away, he was still my Emery, whether he knew it or not.

I didn't want to bring my doubts and ugly thoughts into a moment like this, so I simply answered, "You, Emery. I pay attention to you. Every time you smile and your freckles smile with you, every time you lose yourself to a scoop of ice cream, every time you stare at something so hard like you're trying to figure out how it works so you can tell your students about it."

He parted his lips like he was about to say something. Had I revealed too much? Sometimes, it was hard to remember what I wasn't supposed to know about him. But I'd made up my mind that I'd tell him about us after the weekend, so those thoughts were sealed until it was time to face the music.

"Lex..." he whispered.

"Yeah?"

"You know when you said you wanted to do all the things to me?"

"Yeah."

"I need you to do them all." He moved forward, connecting our lips in a searing kiss that left my mouth burning with passion.

Emery's tongue sent shivers of desire racing through me. Every pass of his tongue over mine was a symphony of perfect sounds, a rainbow of bright colors.

I was hard enough to pound nails, and we were wearing far too many clothes.

"Off," I growled, peeling his shirt over his head and then practically ripping mine off too. I pushed him onto his back again and covered his body with mine.

"Lex," he said, his voice husky with desire.

"It's okay, baby. I'll make it good for you. I promise."

"Can you do it today?"

I chuckled and pecked him on the lips before I explored the skin on his neck. The spot I sucked earlier was raised, and I could feel his rapid pulse in the vein beneath.

"I'm going to worship every inch of you, Emery." It was a promise I intended to keep if I could fight the insane need to be inside him.

He moaned as I grazed my teeth over his left nipple and then sucked it into a hard peak before I did the same with the right one.

I kissed and licked my way down his chest. His shorts were a little loose. I undid the top button and peeled them off, along with his underwear and socks. "God, you're so hot. You make me want to draw you, just like this. Hard and wanting."

"Ugh. I love all the nice words, but I need you to touch me, suck me, or fuck me. Anything."

I chuckled. Emery had been the calmest person I'd ever met. Never demanding, unless it was for ice cream, of course. When it had come to sex, we'd always had fun together and it had been definitely the best sex of my life, but he'd always let me lead like it was something he craved. It seemed that had changed.

"I never knew you'd be so bossy." I went for his cock, but at the last minute, I kissed his hip instead.

"Lex!"

"What will you do if I don't give you what you want?"

"I'll sulk and call you a liar because you promised me things. Dirty things." His voice was defiant but desperate. I'd never deny him anything.

"You want dirty, huh?"

He nodded. I raised myself on my knees and shimmied out of my shorts, underwear, and socks. It was too dark to see, but

I felt the wet patch on my boxers. I wouldn't last long whatever we did.

I gave my cock a long stroke, but the relief was only temporary.

"Let me suck you," Emery said.

"If you do, it'll be game over, and I haven't even started on you yet."

I resumed my earlier position, but this time, I made good on my promise. I started by sucking his balls one at a time, rolling my tongue around them and licking a path up his cock, savoring the taste of his warm skin.

Emery hissed when I wrapped my lips around the head of his cock and sucked hard. A hand gripped my head, and I'm not ashamed to admit I wanted him to take everything. Fuck my mouth hard, hold my hair, and make me his until I could no longer breathe.

I held myself up on one elbow so I could work his cock with my other hand.

"Fuck, Lex. That feels so fucking good. Don't stop."

Like that would ever happen. If there wasn't a danger of us being found dead in this position and that news having to be broken to my parents and grandmother, I'd happily leave this world like this.

The sounds coming from him only spurred me on, but I could tell he was close, so I'd need to ease up. We had all night, but that didn't mean I wanted to rush that first orgasm.

I ran my thumb over his hole, applying a little pressure to test if he was ready for more.

When he shouted my name and practically tried to impale himself on my finger, I stopped sucking him and reached for the toiletry bag.

"Thank fuck," he sighed heavily.

I took out the small bottle of lube, but when I went for the condoms, I paused. Lex was the last man I'd been with, and we'd stopped using condoms after getting tested. Not that I minded using them, but I felt like it was adding a layer of distance between us. Which was ridiculous because he was here. I was already getting more than I ever thought I would. I was being given a second chance.

"What is it?" he asked, raising himself on his elbows. "Did you forget the condoms? I'm negative and on PrEP, so if you've tested negative recently, we don't need them."

"You're on PrEP?" I wanted to take the surprise out of my voice but was clearly unsuccessful because I could see Emery frowning in the soft hue of the lights.

"Yes. When I had the accident, I was tested because I couldn't remember if I'd been with anyone, and my doctor recommended going on PrEP. I haven't been with anyone, Lex." He sat up. New tension radiated from him.

"No. I know. I'm sorry. I'm doing this all wrong. It's been a while since I've been with someone too. My last test was almost a year ago. I was with someone before, but they were negative, and there hasn't been anyone since. But I'm not on PrEP. I didn't think I needed to be."

"Your boyfriend. He's the one you were with," Emery said.

I whipped my head around to face him. "What?"

Emery's hand came up to cradle my jaw. "Ellie mentioned your boyfriend left you. I'm...really sorry that happened to you."

"Are you?"

He looked around us, and then his eyes met mine again. "Well, no, because it means we can be here now."

The words were on the tip of my tongue, but no matter how much I knew I should utter them, they wouldn't come out.

Instead, I put the bag away and kissed Emery until he was

on his back again. He wrapped his legs around my waist. Our cocks were still hard and rubbing against each other.

"I wouldn't be anywhere else but here, Emery. I'm sor—"

He shut me up with a searing kiss before he pulled away again. "Stop apologizing and finish what you started. Everyone has baggage. We can deal with it later, but now? This tent is only big enough for two. You and me."

After that, things ratcheted up a few levels until we were both out of breath. The bottle of lube made its way into my palm, but I couldn't tell if I'd grabbed it from where it'd been laying on the blankets or if Emery had given it to me.

I sat on my knees, uncapped the bottle, and squeezed a little dab onto my fingers. Emery turned around and got on all fours, his ass practically in my face.

Even in the low light, I could see the puckered flesh eager and ready to receive me.

"Good lord, I'm not gonna survive this," I said, sweat beading on my forehead. If I'd been afraid we'd get cold tonight, I had nothing to worry about now.

"Come on, Lex."

"God, how I love hearing the need in your voice. Your desperation to take me inside you, Emery." I lathered my cock with the lube. "Next time, I'm going to eat you like you're the only meal I'll have all week, but I'm too far gone now. I need to be inside you."

"Do it."

I chuckled. "Just a moment longer, baby. I need to prep you first."

He groaned his frustration, but it turned into a moan when I ran my lubed finger over the rim of his hole. He opened eagerly, sucking my finger inside his tight heat.

I was going to lose my mind once I was inside him. I was almost too scared of doing it, something my dick had no issue with because it was throbbing with the need to get things moving.

"I'm good, Lex. I'm good," he said once I'd taken my time to ensure I wouldn't hurt him.

I aligned my cock with his hole and applied enough pressure to get through the first ring of muscles.

"Fuck," I shouted as he impaled himself until I was fully seated inside him. "You're fucking insane, Emery. Are you okay?" As much as I was eager to fuck him, I didn't want to hurt him.

"I am now. You were taking too long, so I took matters into my ass."

When I laughed, he moaned. "Can I move now, baby?"

He nodded.

I put a hand on his hip while the other ran gentle circles on his back as I pulled out a little and then thrust back in.

The tent was soon filled with the smell of man, arousal, and sex. There was probably steam coming through the fabric into the forest outside.

I kept a steady pace, following Emery's moans as a guide.

"Lie on your back. I want to see you," I said.

"Can I ride you?" he asked.

I rested my forehead on his back and took a deep breath.

Please don't come too early. Please don't come too early.

"You're going to be the death of me, Emery."

"Good." He pushed forward and moved from under me. I lay on the blankets, and in a swift move, Emery straddled me, reaching for my cock and guiding it back inside him. "You fill me up so fucking good, Lex."

My breath caught in my throat as I watched Emery lower himself on my cock. He was so tight, so hot, I felt like I was going to explode at any moment.

I took his cock in my hand and stroked it while he fucked himself on me. Emery raised his arms above his head in abandon. His hair was wild and his body undulated above me like it was in a dance.

Under the fairy lights, Emery was the most exquisite, sexual being I'd ever seen.

"Fuck, baby, you feel so tight. That's it, take everything you need. Let me watch you come like this," I said as I held on to the last tiny remnants of my sanity.

He leaned forward on my chest until we were face to face. "I want to come with your lips on mine. I'm so close, Lex."

I let go of his dick and drew my legs up to drill into him every time he came down.

"Fuck! Lex!"

With his cock trapped between us and mine thrusting in and out of him, all that was left was to slam my lips onto his. I silenced his moans with every single thrust of my tongue.

I knew he was about to come when his body locked up. He opened his mouth to take in a breath, but I just sucked his lips between mine.

As he wished, he came with our lips locked. Hands-free was a novelty to me. We'd never managed that before.

Emery became rubber in my arms. "You haven't come yet."

"Trust me, baby. I'm hanging by a thread."

I flipped us over again so Emery was on his back. I pulled one of his legs over my hip and fucked into him until my orgasm drew up from my balls.

"Emery..." It wasn't a cry or even a whisper. It was a prayer, a wish, that this was only the start of us.

In my post-orgasmic vulnerability, I felt tears stinging the backs of my eyes. I willed them to remain inside and focused on worshipping the man I was so in love with.

Eventually, sleepiness and the need to clean up won.

Emery reached over for the wipes I'd put in the toiletry bag and started cleaning us. I couldn't move and had no words. He was looking after me when it should be me looking after him.

"I can hear your thoughts, and if you're thinking what I think you're thinking, you can quit it," he said.

"I'm thinking, *how did I get here*?"

He laughed. "Your brother is marrying my meddling best friend's sister."

I smiled.

"And you're insanely hot."

"Of course."

Emery

Waking up wrapped around Lex was easily in my new top five favorite things. Sex with Lex was right up there, taking the prize.

Last night was extraordinary. I'd never felt so free, so myself, so in tune with someone else. I just hoped I didn't mess it up because I wanted more of this in my life.

Okay, so Lex ran hotter than the surface of the sun and the extra blankets we had under us didn't make it any better. Add to that the morning sun shining on the tent, and I wondered how long it would be until this lazy morning cuddle would become too unbearable.

"You're so hot," Lex mumbled against my neck, placing a soft kiss there that perked up my already interested dick.

I chuckled. "Says the oven to the stove."

My mouth searched his, reclaiming his lips. I opened my eyes to find Lex's blues staring at me, half-lidded but intense, like he wanted to visually memorize the kiss.

I pressed my cock harder against his thigh in a way of suggesting another round of sex, but my stupid belly rumbled. I ignored it, choosing instead to kiss Lex more and rub against him. A few minutes of this, and I could come without even touching my dick.

"Stop laughing," I said. "I could be so close. Help me out here. I'll take you back to the diner, and I'll even pay for breakfast."

"You promise?" His hands gripped my ass, keeping me in place, molded against his body. I opened my legs, which allowed our dicks to line up.

"Is this what you want?" he asked, his voice deep and husky.

"Yes," I breathed back.

I sought the crook of his neck to burrow my face in. His hair smelled so good, like expensive shampoo and sweat. I was aware that I sounded like a desperate, incoherent mess, but the only thing I could focus on was the feel of our dicks rubbing together.

"I'm going to finger you until you come in my hand," he said.

I nodded fiercely because I was already incapable of words, and we were only frotting. When I felt the pads of his fingers caress my hole, I relaxed to let him in.

"I love how much you need this, Emery. Come on, baby. Rub up against me. Make me come by watching you come undone."

"Ngh..."

Thank god I was still lubed from last night. The first finger was easy to take. The second was a little harder because of the position we were in, which meant he also couldn't go as deep.

My whole body trembled with the need to orgasm. The friction of our dicks and the sensations caused by his fingers in my ass were too much to take in.

When Lex hit my prostate, I came hard, spilling all over his stomach.

"Oh god...oh fuck," I cried.

"Emery," he shouted, coming soon after.

Aftershocks ran through my body from my core as I devoured Lex's mouth. He wrapped both arms around me, and even with the discomfort of the cooling cum, I didn't want to go anywhere.

Until my belly rumbled again, of course.

"Okay, time to get out of this smelly tent. We should wash up and go to the diner," he said.

"I'll race you to the river," I said, standing on my knees and turning over to open the zipper of the tent.

"That water is going to be freezing."

"Then you'll know you're properly awake."

He slapped my ass. "I *am* properly awake." And then he grabbed me by my waist, causing me to fall against him. "Even though sometimes it feels like I'm dreaming."

I was blissfully happy, fully alive and ready to take any challenge the world threw at me. Positivity coursed through my veins. It was a heady feeling, like I was so powerful that nothing could bring me down.

"I know what you mean, more than you can imagine."

That was as much as I could admit about my feelings aloud. I left the tent and ran to the river, diving into the icy cold water.

Lex joined me a second later.

"That was a bad idea," he said when he surfaced.

"It's the only way in when the water is this cold."

"I'm concerned for the health of my favorite body parts."

I ran a finger across his lips. "I think you'll be fine."

Despite being fairly hungry by the time we were drying, we decided to break up the tent and pack the car since we weren't staying another night.

We were on our way back to get the rest of the stuff from the campsite when my phone dinged twice, almost simultaneously. I pulled it out and saw two incoming messages. One from my mom and one from Frederick.

I opened Frederick's first. I still felt guilty about calling him to help out with Ren.

FREDERICK

> You have to come home. It looks like our moms have booked us all dinner.

Crap.

MOM

> Good morning, sweetheart. Jeanelle and I don't want to intrude on your and Frederick's time together, but we were hoping to all meet up for dinner tonight at Pierre's.

"What's wrong? Bad news?" Lex asked. I put my phone down with a sigh.

"My parents want to go out for dinner, and I need to stop at Frederick's place first to check in on last night. He lives in the city, so I'll still need to drive out of Cliffborough to get home. I'm so sorry, but can we head back earlier?"

Lex wrapped his arms around my waist, nuzzling my neck. "Of course we can."

"I wanted to take you on a hike and maybe mess around in the river some more." *And suck your dick until you come in my mouth so I can taste you. And I wanted to know if you like bottoming too because I think I'd like to top you.* But of course, I didn't say any of that. It was bad enough that I'd woken him up in the middle of the night for a hand job. He was going to think I was a sex addict or something.

"Answer the messages, and I'll carry the rest of the stuff to the car, okay?"

I nodded, and he gave me a soft kiss before we went back on the trail.

When I got my phone out to reply to the messages, there was a new one from Ellie.

ELLIE

What's up, lover boy? Did you get your itch scratched?

I snorted.

EMERY

There was no itch.

ELLIE

Yes, there was, and it was on the verge of turning into a medical condition.

EMERY

You'll be happy to know Dr. Spencer has a very good bedside manner.

ELLIE

Ooooh, tell me more…

EMERY

Maybe another time. Gotta deal with some
family stuff.

ELLIE

Talking about family, grab an extra-large,
extra-strong coffee tomorrow because I had
to sit through a family dinner yesterday, and
I need therapy.

EMERY

Coffee will be on me.

ELLIE

And ice cream after work…

EMERY

We'll see about that…

She replied with a sassy emoji that made me smile.
Okay, time to deal with real life.
I replied to Frederick's message first.

EMERY

Why does my mom think we were
together?

FREDERICK

Because my parents were at my place
when you messaged last night. I could tell
them the truth and explain exactly where
you are and with whom, if you want.

Emery

No! I'll drag you into every single gay nightclub in the state if you tell them. Trust me. You wouldn't have trouble scoring.

FREDERICK

No thanks. Come to my place, and we'll meet them together. Besides, we need to talk about last night.

EMERY

Okay. See you later.

I opened my mom's message and replied with a simple *looking forward to it* and *meet you there*.

"I'm free. How can I help?" I asked Lex, putting my phone in my pocket.

"We're all done," he said, closing the trunk of the car and looking at me intently.

I held out my hands, and he took them, raising them to his lips and kissing both knuckles.

"How about we take the long way back?"

He smiled. "And spend more time with you? Where do I sign up?"

I didn't want this weekend to end, so I took the long way back to the point we had to stop for gas and snacks. By mid-afternoon, we were pulling up at Lex's house.

"I have all this food in the fridge we didn't take with us. It can't go to waste," he said, pouting.

"I tell you what, I'll come back tomorrow and help you eat it all. We can even camp out in your backyard. You have one, right?"

"Yes, to the first, but the second..." he said, running his

hand down my back as I molded myself to his shape, "I'd rather take you to my bed."

"I'd like that very much."

We grabbed all of Lex's stuff and took it inside.

I hadn't really taken time to properly look around Lex's apartment when I'd picked him up yesterday, so it took me by surprise when I saw a tank with a goldfish.

"Oh hello, Goldie," I cooed. "You've been all on your own this weekend. Sorry for taking your roomie away from you."

I smiled as the fish did a few laps around the tank before coming back. When I turned around, Lex was standing still, his eyes wide.

"What?"

"How did you know his name?" he asked.

I shrugged. "Aren't all goldfish named Goldie? You named it, so you should know." I chuckled.

"I didn't name it."

"Well, whoever did clearly knew the rules. Anyway, I should probably get going."

He sighed. "Okay."

I took a step in his direction when I noticed. "Um, Lex? Why do you have a gecko on your shoulder?"

"I–what?" He snapped his head to each shoulder until he saw the gecko. What followed was a comedy of jerky moments, squirming, and Lex almost falling over his coffee table as he shrugged the gecko away. "Where is it? Is it still on me? Oh my god, take it off, take it off!"

"Calm down. He's not on you. You scared him under the couch."

Lex squeaked. "I scared *him*? What the fuck is a lizard doing in my apartment?"

I went over to the couch and crouched slowly. Maybe if he could see I wasn't a threat, he'd let himself be caught.

"It's a gecko, not a lizard. And he probably hitchhiked a ride with us from the forest."

Lex groaned. "What am I going to do now? How will I find someone to fumigate this place on a Sunday? I'm going to have to crash with Noah and his weekend hookup."

I laughed. "You don't need to call anyone. Geckos are harmless. They actually make great pets."

"Well, I'm not in the market for a pet." He paced back and forth. "Shit, I just remembered Noah isn't home."

"Do you have another tank like Goldie's?" I asked.

"Why?"

"Because if I manage to catch him, you can keep him there until we figure out what to do."

"Why do I have to keep it?"

"Because he came with you. If he wanted to be with me, he would have stayed in the car," I joked.

"This isn't funny, Emery. What the hell am I going to do with a gecko?"

"Shhh," I said when I saw the gecko by one of the couch legs. "Do you have one of those net things to cover up fruit?"

"Um, yeah, it's covering up fruit."

"Can you bring it to me and also cut a small piece of fruit?"

I kept my eye on the gecko while Lex went into the kitchen.

"Okay, where do I put them?" he asked.

"Put the fruit on the floor by the couch," I said, pointing to the precise location. "And give me the net."

It took a few minutes for the gecko to feel safe enough to test coming out from under the couch. As I'd hoped, he went straight for the fruit. When I placed the net on top of him, he tried to escape, so I had to hold it down.

"Now what?"

"Now you get your spare tank so we can move him."

A moment later, Lex was back with the tank. It took a few failed attempts in which the gecko almost escaped again, but we managed to secure him in the tank, which thankfully had a lid and an air vent.

"We'll put the rest of the fruit inside with him."

Lex kept away from the tank like it was poisonous. I wanted to joke, but he was clearly scared. There was a certain advantage to having grown up in a large countryside property instead of the city. I'd spent my childhood catching all kinds of bugs with Mr. Kowalski's son, who was just a little older than me.

"Okay, Gordon. You be good for Daddy Lex, and we'll see what we can do for you tomorrow," I said to the gecko before I turned to Lex.

"I am not that thing's daddy, and why are you naming him?"

I placed a soft kiss on his lips. "We'll see. Geckos are super adorable and friendly. You'll fall in love in no time. And everyone knows geckos have to be named Gordon. Like Gordon Gekko from the movie *Wall Street*."

He looked at me like I was certifiable. "But seriously, should we release him back to the forest?" He ran his fingers through my hair. I closed my eyes, enjoying the way his nails scraped against my scalp.

"Yeah, if you really want, we can take him back."

Between the long drive and the Gordon adventure, I was going to be late getting to Frederick's place, but I was also not leaving without a last thorough kiss from Lex.

My smile didn't leave my face the whole drive, but as soon as I pulled up in front of Frederick's apartment, it dropped. Being here was a reminder that my perfect weekend had ended and it was time to put on an act.

"You're late," he said, jumping into my car.

"Sorry, we had a gecko issue...and if I'm honest, I was prolonging having to do this as much as I could. I hate lying."

"Me too, but if it wasn't for that lie, you wouldn't have had this weekend. I take it things are serious with Lex?"

I pulled the car back out on the road. "I don't know. We had a great time...maybe things could be serious?"

"At least you're not stuck babysitting a hundred succulents," he groaned, crossing his arms over his chest.

"What do you mean?"

"That tiny terror of a person you asked me to look out for is completely insane. He made me break into his ex's apartment to steal not two or three but a fucking hundred tiny pots with succulents. Whatever succulents are. I guess some are pretty, but why the fuck are there so many?"

I tried to keep my laughter in, but it just burst out of me.

"What's funny? You owe me big time."

"Aww, boo, wouldn't you do anything for your new boyfriend?" I joked.

"If yesterday isn't enough proof of my love for you... boyfriend, I think we need to reassess."

I laughed. "Anyway, what's with the succulents?"

Lex

"Earth to Lex. Calling Earth to Lex."

I swiveled in my chair. "What?"

"We get that you probably got laid a lot this weekend, but we have work to do," Noah said.

"Yeah, I know," I replied defensively. "What's the issue?"

Noah raised a brow and sat back in his chair. "The issue, little brother, is that you can't repeat anything said in this meeting so far because you're too busy looking out of the window and spacing out."

"I don't have your twin telepathy, and even I feel slightly horny this morning," Noah said.

"When do you not feel horny?" I asked.

"Good point, but we need to wrap this up because I have places to be."

Adam and I looked at each other and then at him before Adam spoke. "You were out this weekend. Don't you have stuff to catch up with?"

"Yes, and that stuff requires me to visit a client." He grabbed his coffee cup and took a sip.

"Speaking of clients, how's the Van Stern account going?" I asked.

Noah coughed suddenly, almost spilling his coffee. "What?"

"How is it going with the stained glass museum? Lior seemed very interested in working with us."

"He is...very interested. We actually bumped into each other at the conference this weekend..."

Adam leaned forward on the conference table and groaned. "Please tell me you haven't slept with a client."

"I resent that you think I would."

Adam raised a brow. Those brows were working overtime this morning. I snorted.

"What are you laughing at?" Adam asked me.

"You, taking everything so seriously today."

"Someone has to. With you daydreaming and Noah potentially fucking a client, someone has to be the adult here."

He was right. I should have paid more attention, but I was struggling today. Apart from having seemingly gained a new pet that I was totally going to release into the wild if I couldn't convince Emery to take him back to the forest, all my brain wanted to do was replay every moment of the weekend.

Laughing with Emery, watching him, touching him. His face as he came. The desperate race to the finish. Him waking me up in the middle of the night for sex.

It had been the perfect weekend.

Even the distraction named Ren had brought a moment of lightness. I hadn't realized how much I'd missed just chilling. My brothers dragged me to our weekly after-work drinks, which River occasionally joined, but it hadn't been the same in a long time.

Adam was busy with Victoria. Sometimes, he had to go straight home because they had some kind of dinner to attend.

And Noah was living his best single life. If he didn't score at the bar, he'd go out to a club.

He'd always been the independent one. Never afraid to do stuff on his own and never phased by anything.

"And he's spaced out again," Adam said.

"I'm not spaced out. I'm just...it's hard coming back to work after the weekend, that's all."

Noah snorted. "It happens every week, and you don't usually have a problem with it. Emery must have learned some new stuff in the last year."

I threw my pen at him before he saw it coming and laughed when it hit him square on his forehead.

"I'm sorry, that was wrong," he said.

"Anyway," Adam said, bringing us back. "You're not sleeping with Lior Van Stern?"

Noah took a moment to answer but sounded convincing when he said there was nothing sexual going on between him and Lior. It wasn't Noah's usual MO to lie, so maybe he had some interest in Lior. But I knew he wouldn't jeopardize the account by sleeping with the client. At least not until the job was complete.

"Weren't you hooking up with Tanner?" Adam asked Noah.

"As the old adage says, you don't shit where you eat, so I don't fuck where I drink. Besides, we'd have to find a new bar when it ended, and I like that one. So, no, I'm not doing Tanner."

I looked at the paperwork in front of me with the mockups we needed to approve. "Okay, now that we've established who's sleeping with whom and who's *not* sleeping with anyone—"

"I didn't say that," Noah interrupted.

"God forbid we ever thought you spent quality time with your right hand," I continued, ignoring his stare. "Mom and

Dad have approved this design and River has approved this one." I pushed them to the middle of the table so they could both see.

"They couldn't make it easy on us and agree on something for once, could they?" Noah asked rhetorically.

"The day that happens will be filled with tragedy because the world will be too off balance." I chuckled. "I came up with an alternative design that combines the two. Adam, I need you to check the words for me. And, Noah, I need you to not tell them anything about this."

"Why?"

"Because if we keep running every detail through them, we'll never get this to the printers. There will be no menus and no advertising or social media campaign."

Adam scratched his head. "You know they're gonna kill us if we do this, right?"

"They keep telling us the business is ours too, that we need to be more involved. What design do you prefer?"

They both stared at it for a moment before pointing to the new, alternative design.

"Perfect. As soon as the wording is agreed on and proof-read, I'll get the ball rolling with the team."

Noah stood. "If this is all, I'll be out of here."

"Wait," Adam said. "Has everyone cleared their schedules for the party? Mom and Dad will kill us if we're not there."

We all nodded. "Time to dust off the old black slacks and white shirt," I said. "At least the new aprons we're getting made are much nicer."

"Who else already has nightmares about dropping plates with food or spilling wine all over customers' clothes?" Adam asked.

Noah and I both raised our hands.

"It'll be fun though. It's been a long time since we've all chipped in together," Noah said. "Família acima de tudo." We met our hands in the middle of the table for a collective fist bump.

"Família acima de tudo." Family above all.

As Noah left the room, I closed my folder and stood to leave too.

"Lex, do you have a minute?"

"Sure."

"I was thinking, how about we have a double date this week?" Adam asked.

"Double date?"

"Yes, you know, one of those things where me and my fiancée and you and your boyfriend hang out together?"

I raised a brow. "I've never seen Victoria hang out with anyone. Does she even know how to hang out?"

Shit. I regretted my words as soon as they came out of my mouth.

"I'm sorry, that was uncalled for."

Adam stood and moved to sit on the couch we had in the corner of the conference room. So many of our best ideas had come from that corner, sometimes late into the night over a bottle of scotch Noah would inevitably have stolen from Lusitana.

"She doesn't do it on purpose, you know? It's hard for Victoria to come into a family as close as we are, especially when she's not as close to her sister."

I sat next to him. "I know. I guess I never appreciated how hard it must have been for her to experience that, especially when River has been part of our family for years and Emery fitted in so easily."

"Did you know she's been practicing cooking Portuguese food so we can have the family over for dinner after the wedding?"

I turned to Adam in shock. "Really?"

"Yeah. She really wants to impress everyone. I want her to

feel like she's part of the family. Lately…I don't know. I feel like there's this distance between us. Like, all of us. Even River has been busier than usual. He's missed some of the Friday drinks, and whenever I ask if he wants to hang out, he says he's at the restaurant working."

I'd felt it too and had blamed myself for being in a different space from my brothers. I'd been sad and grieving Emery's loss. Since he'd come back into my life, I'd practically ignored everyone. My evenings were spent on the phone with Emery or messaging. Every time I could see him after work, I would.

But what I hadn't realized was that I wasn't just pulling away from my family. I was also pushing them away, and maybe unfairly, I wasn't giving Victoria a chance.

"I think it's a good idea. Let's do a double date," I said. "I'll check with Emery to see when he's free and will let you know."

Adam's instant smile was mirrored by mine.

"Do we go to Lusitana?" he asked.

I grinned. We couldn't risk being seen by my parents. "No, can we go somewhere else? That Italian restaurant by the river?"

"Lex…"

"I know. I was going to tell Emery the truth, but we got distracted by a gecko situation, and then he had to go. If I'd dumped all that on him, he would have left, and then I wouldn't know if he'd ever come back."

He laughed. "A gecko situation?"

"Don't ask." I sighed. "Look, I thought I'd lost him forever. Do you know what that feels like? I didn't go to a funeral. We didn't break up. He was there one day, going away just for a couple of days to sort out some family stuff, and then he was just gone."

Adam wrapped his arm around mine like we used to do

when we were little. "I know. I remember how hard it was for you. I felt it too. For weeks, I couldn't sleep well and was always on edge. I had to watch you grieve a relationship that ended but never ended. I get it, Lex. You're scared to lose him again."

I nodded, a lump forming in my throat. "He was in an accident. He *could* have died, and I would have never known. I think that's why I freeze up whenever I try to tell him. I don't think I could bear losing him again."

"Then make sure you know how to find him always. Make sure that if something were to happen to either of you, the other would know. What kind of family secrets was he hiding that you didn't even know if he had a family? How were you going to be engaged to a man you knew nothing about? How much do you know about him now?"

Adam was right, but once again, I was avoiding conflict and being ruled by all-consuming fear.

"He's mentioned his family and his upbringing. I don't know why he's sharing those things now and didn't before. I can't press him for more information because it's not something you'd tell someone you've been dating for five minutes."

"But you haven't, Lex."

"He doesn't know that."

He squeezed my hand. "Just make sure you don't end up hurting yourself in the process. Your heart also matters. I hope that one day, whether it's Emery or someone else, you'll get your white wedding, your partner for life, and we'll see our lookalike kids growing up together."

I smiled, and then laughter burst out of me. "This conversation would never happen with Noah here."

"Hell no. He's allergic to relationships, let alone marriage."

"Like you said, maybe one day he'll find someone who'll make him reassess."

Thanks to the meeting and my talk with Adam, I had to work through lunch to catch up. When Emery messaged me, reminding me we were going to eat the weekend's leftovers, it was the burst of energy I needed to get everything done.

With any luck, I'd have my favorite man as the main meal before we got to the leftovers.

Emery

I glanced at my watch again and sped up until I was practically jogging.

"Ugh," I muttered out loud. This was not a good day to get all hot, sweaty, and disheveled. I couldn't even bear to imagine what my hair looked like.

When Lex suggested a double date with his brother and future sister-in-law, I panicked. It was one thing meeting the family, but another altogether meeting the person who was a carbon copy of the guy you were dating.

What if Adam didn't like me? Would Lex reassess us?

"Stupid thoughts go away. I'm already flustered as it is."

I was almost there. Just another corner and I'd see the restaurant. Hopefully, Lex and his brother would be running a little late too. Just my luck that my car had broken down today of all days.

Getting an Uber to the city this morning was costly, but it had been fine. I'd been counting on getting another Uber from the school, so I'd declined a ride from Ellie. Then, I got distracted working on a project for the kids. By the time I realized how late I was, I took the earliest ride, but traffic was so heavy that I paid for the full trip and walked the rest of the way instead.

I stopped a hundred yards from the restaurant to take a breath. My reflection in a store window wasn't actually too bad. Maybe the gods were on my side today. I took a deep, calming breath and walked the rest of the way to the restaurant.

As I approached, I immediately saw Lex, and thankfully, he was on his own. From behind, in his gray slacks and shirt, he was my personal definition of sex on legs. I noticed straight away that his hair was different, so he must have had a haircut.

It made sense because we hadn't seen each other in a few days. Ever since I'd stayed over and we'd had the food he'd bought for the camping trip. I'd missed him.

Was that silly? We talked every day. How could I miss him? It was ridiculous at best. I was a grownup, for goodness' sake.

"So this is where all the hot men hang out," I said, walking up to him.

He turned around, but I didn't give him time to reply before I was on him.

God, I missed his mouth. I wrapped my arms around his neck and sucked his lips. It took me a few seconds to notice Lex hadn't reacted to my kiss at all.

I stepped back slowly, my brain already catching up to the mortifying truth that it wasn't Lex I'd just kissed.

Especially since Lex was a few feet away, accompanied by a tall woman.

I covered my mouth with my hand, but I doubted it hid my humiliation in any way.

"I'm...I'm so sorry," I said.

Adam was the first to react by bursting out laughing.

"Interesting first impression you're going for. I'm Victoria, and the man you just kissed is my fiancé, Adam." Even though her hand was stretched toward me, her voice was icy cold.

"Nice to meet you, Victoria. Please accept my apologies. I thought he was Lex." I turned to Lex. "Please believe me. I would never kiss someone else. His back was to me and he was on his own... I thought..."

"Hey," Lex said, coming over and placing his hands on my waist. "I know. It was an accident. You didn't mean it."

"You promise you're not mad?"

He laughed. "Why would I be mad at you for wanting to jump me anywhere, even in the middle of the street?"

"But it wasn't you."

"But you thought it was."

I nodded. I did think it was him, but now I also felt guilty for thinking his brother's ass was sexy.

"Let's go inside. Our table is ready," Lex said, holding my hand.

Adam gave me a pat on the back. "Nice to meet you, Emery. If you greet everyone like that, I'm going to start crashing all your dates."

My cheeks heated. Okay, so he wasn't mad that I'd kissed him, but Victoria didn't seem impressed with me.

The waiter took us to our table. I sat next to Lex, Adam took the seat in front of me, and Victoria took the spot next to Adam.

"I haven't been here in forever," Adam said, holding the menu. "What's good here?"

"The ziti," Lex and I said simultaneously. Our eyes met and we smiled at each other. Who'd have thought my failed date would eventually lead me to Lex?

"Wow, you're not even finishing each other's sentences. You're merging into the same person," Adam said.

"I think it's important to retain your individuality when you're with someone. If they fell in love with you, you don't want to change, or neither of you will recognize each other years down the line. Don't you agree, honey?" Victoria asked, holding Adam's arm.

"I agree," Lex said. "But having important things in common makes a relationship work. Speaking of which, Adam said you're learning to cook Portuguese food."

Victoria shrugged. "Yeah, I mean, it's not that hard, right? It's always the same ingredients."

"Right. Yeah, I guess you're not wrong there," Lex replied.

Under the table, I put my hand on his leg and squeezed it gently. He placed his hand on mine, so I smiled and turned it over so we could lace our fingers together.

The conversation stalled until a tiny squeak got our attention.

"Lex. Emery. How great to see you. I can't thank you enough for saving me that day. I would have done something stupid that I'd regret because that's the kind of stuff I do."

"Hi, Ren," I said. "I'm so happy it all worked out in the end. Frederick told me he's babysitting your succulents."

His face dropped into a scowl. "That caveman. I swear, if he wasn't so huge, I'd have clocked him already. Can you believe he threatened to overwater my babies?"

"He threatened?"

"Well, he said he would make sure he didn't forget to water them daily. I had to give him detailed instructions to ensure he didn't murder my succulents. They've come so far already from being stuck in Chad's apartment. Not that Freddy is less of an animal. He might actually be worse." I exchanged a look with Lex as Ren rambled on. "I mean, he's not cheated because, as he says, he's *straight*, and we're not together. Ew, that would be awful, right? Who needs that many muscles anyway? Did you know he has an actual six-pack? What normal human being has a six-pack?"

"Out of curiosity, how do you know he has a six-pack?" Lex asked.

Ren waved him off. "Oh, I was at his place, and he came out of the shower practically naked. You should have seen him jump. Even I don't pitch that high."

"He didn't know you were there?"

Ren shrugged. "He gave me a key so I could visit my babies. You really can't be surprised to find someone in your apartment after you gave them a key, amirite?"

A cough from Victoria got our attention.

"What are the specials today, please?" she asked.

"Oh, um, the ziti is always good. Today, we also have vegetarian lasagna and veal chops with thyme-roasted potatoes and arugula. If you ask me, I'd always pick the ziti. It's comfort food at its best and the chef's favorite dish, which is why it's so good."

Victoria moved her gaze back to the menu. "I'll have the mixed salad, please."

"Of course. And what will you have with it?" Ren asked.

"Water with a slice of lemon and a single ice cube." She closed the menu and handed it to Ren, who was staring at her like no one had ever asked him just for salad.

I could see the challenge in his eyes. He wanted to change her mind. But from what I'd heard from Ellie about her sister, that would end badly.

"Ren, could I have the ziti, please?" I asked.

"Same for me," Lex said, and Adam seconded.

He took our drinks order and left, sparing a last confused look toward Victoria.

"So what do you do, Emery?" she asked me.

"I'm an elementary school teacher. I actually work with Ellie."

"My sister?"

"Yeah. We're good friends."

"Huh."

I didn't know what the *huh* meant. The conversation

moved to the topic of their wedding, which meant a lot of the talking came from Victoria while the three of us simply nodded along.

I was starting to see what Ellie meant about her sister. She was just borderline rude, which could be excused with nerves for meeting someone new or the stress of her impending nuptials. In reality, I found Victoria a little aloof and disinterested in anything that wasn't about her.

The best part of the dinner was being able to eat the ziti with one hand because it meant I didn't have to let go of Lex. Every time I glanced at him, he smiled. Not his usual smile, but a version of a smile that you reserve for people you're trying to make an effort with.

About halfway through, Victoria said they'd need to cut the dinner short because she had a call with her wedding planner. She apologized and seemed sincere, but I didn't like how Lex seemed to deflate.

I waited until we were outside the restaurant to ask him the question I'd wanted to ask all day.

"Um, my car broke down yesterday. I took an Uber into the city this morning. I could crash at Ellie's tonight—"

"Stay with me," he said, pulling me close and tucking me under his arm.

"Are you sure? This isn't too soon? I mean, I already stayed over on Monday."

There was a tingling in the pit of my stomach as Lex's eyes shone bright in the pale light of the moon. "It's not soon enough, baby. Call me crazy, but if I could have you in my bed every night, I'd be the happiest man."

I bit my lip to stop from grinning. I could be cool about this.

"Fuck it. I'll never be cool." I slammed my lips onto his and gave him the kiss he'd missed out on earlier.

"Christ, Emery," he said, panting. We were still outside the restaurant. "No wonder Adam was stunned."

"You mean traumatized."

He laughed. "You're not the first guy he's kissed."

I raised my brows. "Isn't he straight?"

Lex shrugged. "I guess he is, but we all experiment at some point when we're young, and he's always been super close to his best friend, River. I don't think anything big ever happened, but I caught them kissing when we were fourteen. I waited for him to come out to me, but he never did. And he's only ever dated girls."

"When did you come out?"

"When I was thirteen."

"I was thirteen too," I said. "My parents weren't exactly happy when it happened. They said it would ruin my chances to get good jobs and no one would ever take me seriously."

Lex cradled my cheek, rubbing his thumb over my chin.

"I'm so sorry that happened to you. Did they accept it eventually?"

I shrugged. "Yeah, they're okay with it. I guess it's cool these days to have a gay son when you're in high society. I just wish my mom wouldn't try setting me up with all of her friends' gay sons."

"She really does that?"

"Uh-huh. Well, not anymore. I'm dealing with it," I said. "How was it for you?"

"It was super easy. Noah had already come out. He's pansexual. Once my parents understood more about being LGBTQ+, there was never any fear or reticence about coming out."

I ran my hand up his shirt, feeling the warmth of his skin beneath the fabric. "Your family is really close."

"Yeah, we are. It's the most important thing to us. Family

always comes first. Did you know that in Portugal, you often see multiple generations living in the same household?"

"Really?"

He nodded. "Yeah. There's respect for the older generations, and even though everyone is always up in everyone else's business, it's because they care."

"Is that why you looked so sad earlier?"

He let out a long sigh. "I'm trying to get closer to Victoria. I don't want to feel this distance with Adam, but it's there. I thought it was my fault, but... Maybe I need to try harder."

"Lex, you're trying hard enough. I've heard all about Victoria from Ellie, and yeah, I guess it's only one side, but from what I saw tonight, I think Victoria could do with maybe being a little kinder and more observant of those around her."

"Adam loves her."

I smiled. "He does, and he also loves you. I'm sure you two will find a way to nurture both relationships."

"I'm really glad you came tonight."

"Me too. But guess what." I wiggled my brows.

He chuckled. "What?"

"I know this little place on the other side of the bridge with the best ice cream in the world. I've been assured."

"I see where this is going..."

"Oh, do you? Pray tell."

He placed a kiss on my lips. "I think you want to get me high on ice cream so you can take advantage of me later."

I chuckled. "Dammit. My secret is out."

He took my hand and dragged me across the road to the bridge.

Ziti, ice cream, and spending the night with Lex? Best date ever.

"Promise me that when you get married, you won't make me go through all this again," Noah said, dropping onto the chair next to mine.

I bumped his shoulder with mine. "I've never thought about my wedding in that much detail, but I guess some events are part of the process. Besides, it's free food."

He looked at his watch. "I'd rather spend the morning in bed."

"I bet you would."

A week after our dinner together, Victoria had sent us all an email invite for a Saturday brunch. She wanted both families to get to know each other better and try the catering service for a company she was using for the wedding.

I thought it was a great idea, and it showed that Victoria was making an effort to include the family in the planning stages.

"This is important to Adam," I said.

"Then why does he look like he's bored to death?"

I chuckled. "He's not. He's hungover and trying to stay

alive. Have you considered why River is wearing sunglasses indoors?"

"Shit, dude. In that case, color me shocked because Victoria is handling this very well."

"Yeah, maybe it's time for us to start giving her some credit."

"No way. She's stealing Adam from us, and Friday after-work drinks will never be the same again."

I shook my head. "Big brother, I'll be here for the day you get that rug pulled out from under your feet by someone who will turn your life upside down."

"Will never happen."

The clink of a glass put a stop to the conversations around the room. Our parents and grandmother took their seats at our table.

Victoria stood with a beaming smile.

"Good morning, family and close friends. Adam and I"—she touched Adam's shoulder, and he stood, placing an arm around her waist—"are delighted to have you all here today. As you know, we both place a huge importance on the role of family in our lives, which is why we wanted you to be part of this process. We want to thank Luxury Catering for hosting us today." She gestured to the team on the outskirts of the room. "The man behind Luxury Catering shares the same values we do. Luxury, for him, is about the good things in life: good food and good company. They also regularly donate to LGBTQ+ charities as part of their mission to support the community, which is something else we value. This is why they were at the top of our list to cater the wedding."

A man walked up to Victoria, placed a kiss on her cheek, and shook Adam's hand.

"Fuck, he's hot," Noah whispered.

I rolled my eyes but couldn't disagree. He looked to be in

his early forties but already had a head full of silver hair that brought out his blue eyes.

"Good morning everyone. I'm Liam Harper, the co-founder of Luxury Catering. I grew up with weekly family Sunday lunches. My mother loved nothing more than to feed the people around her, and often, we had to borrow tables from the neighbors to fit everyone she welcomed into our house. Sadly, she was taken from us too young, but in her honor, my brother and I founded Luxury Catering. Please don't be fazed by the term. For us, luxury is the precious time we have with those we love. Which, of course, doesn't mean it can't be locally sourced, good-quality food. We're honored that Victoria has chosen us. I won't bore you anymore, as I'm sure you're eager to dig in."

He raised a hand to the back of the room and servers holding trays came in.

"Damn, my gaydar isn't pinging? Why are the good ones straight? It's so unfortunate," Noah said, his eyes tracking Liam as he left the room.

"You mean, how dare anyone not be into Noah Spencer? Shocker."

He looked at me, genuinely agreeing. God, I loved my crazy brother.

"We haven't seen each other much lately. What's going on with you?" I asked.

A server placed plates in front of us with pancakes, bacon, and eggs. Credit to Victoria and Liam. It looked delicious.

"I should be the one asking that, little bro. How's things with"—he glanced toward our parents—"that side project you were working on?"

I ran my hand through my hair, trying to disguise my smile and failing miserably. From the corner of my eye, I saw Avó pretending not to listen, but I knew her better than that.

"It's nice working on a project that is both familiar and presents new challenges," I said.

"You think this could be a long-term collaboration?"

"I hope so."

Thoughts of Emery flooded my mind. Waking up to him in my bed days ago. How he was so comfortable in my house, like he knew he belonged there. He'd even surprised me by bringing a framed photo of us at the lake and hanging it on my wall.

I'd wanted to cry at that moment, but Gordon, as it was becoming a habit, had provided us with a distraction.

He kept escaping the tank, even though he now had what had to be the most luxurious home any gecko could ever want or need, thanks to Emery sending me endless links for things Gordon couldn't be without.

And just like with Goldie, I was powerless to resist Emery's smile every time he came over and saw a new addition to Gordon's living space.

We hadn't talked again about taking Gordon back to the forest, and if I was honest, I think I'd miss the little terror. What I wouldn't miss would be waking up to find him on the wall right above my bed in the morning.

Somehow, when it was time for food, he always found his way back into the tank. So much so that I'd started leaving the lid off unless I was feeding him live crickets. Or, more accurately, if Emery was feeding him live crickets. Thank goodness Emery came over often enough, even just for a few hours after work, because I drew the line at handling more bugs.

"You two think I was born yesterday," Avó said, her left eyebrow rising to her forehead.

Noah hit my knee with his.

"Shut up, she can't see us if we don't move," I whispered, and he snorted.

"Don't know what you're talking about, Avó," I said.

"We don't keep secrets in this family, Alexis Spencer. We stick together and work it out."

"What secrets?" Mom asked.

"Who's keeping a secret?" Dad asked.

I felt like a spotlight was on me, making me hot to the point of burning. What could I say? I didn't want to lie to my family, but I also wasn't ready to tell them the truth. Not until I figured out what I was going to do.

"You're right," Noah said. "Someone's been keeping a secret."

I looked at him.

"I have a friend that works at the stadium, and he's really close with some of the soccer players. They've all bought tickets for the Lusitana anniversary dinner, and they're donating to our charity."

Immediately, my dad's ears perked up and he sat up straight. "You're telling me The Eagles are coming to our restaurant?"

"They are indeed. Lusitana has a great reputation, Dad. And you know a couple of the players are regulars," Noah said.

"Yes, but the whole team? This is huge. We're going to need to order flags." He turned to my mom. "How about we change the tablecloths to the team colors? Maybe have little soccer balls to give away."

Both Noah and I raised our hands. "Whoa, Dad, rein it in," Noah said. "This dinner is about Lusitana and our family. We have a brand to protect. You want every single customer to feel like they're at home, not catering to soccer stars."

I shot my mom a smile. She looked relieved at Noah's words.

"I guess you're right. But we'll need to take a bunch of pictures. This is going to be a historic moment."

I noticed Adam stepping outside the room into the

garden. I took the opportunity to follow him while our family was distracted with talk about the dinner.

"Hey. How rough do you feel?" I asked, approaching him.

"Dude, kill me now. I don't know how Victoria hasn't murdered me yet. Although considering the daggers she's sending River, it's surprising he's still standing."

"What happened?"

He shrugged. "I waited for him after the restaurant closed yesterday and forced him to come out for a few drinks. You know how it is. One drink turned into ten, and about three hours ago, I stumbled into the apartment.

"Victoria made me have a cold shower to sober up, but I'm dying here. She's going to stay behind after the brunch to discuss the menu for the wedding because Liam is leaving for Europe tomorrow and she has a business trip this week. I'm going home to crash so I can make it up to her tonight."

"Make sure you do. She's being great with everyone. By the way, where's Ellie?"

"Victoria said she has the flu, so she couldn't come."

"The food was great. You and Victoria picked well."

He laughed and then groaned, massaging his temples. "Fuck this headache. I'm never drinking again."

"Yeah, right."

"Seriously. But yeah, this was all Victoria. She's been working so hard on the wedding stuff. We'd like to get everyone together for a rehearsal weekend at Mabel's Vineyard on Peet Island. Maybe Emery can come too?"

I hesitated. "I'm not sure."

Adam put his hand on my shoulder, his expression shifting from a painful hangover to sudden seriousness.

"You know he's in love with you, right?"

"What?"

"Lex, I saw the way he looked at you the other night. I could tell you were trying hard with Victoria, and he was there for you. I noticed his hand on your leg, the way he leaned into you to make sure you were okay." He ran a hand through his hair. "God, you guys didn't even let go of your hold while you ate dinner."

I stepped back, my palms damp and mouth suddenly dry. "I'm scared to let go."

"You can't live in this limbo forever, Lex. You're going to break down. Besides, a guy who kisses like that? You wanna keep hold of him."

I grabbed his head in a chokehold and mussed his hair. "What would River have to say about you going around kissing other men, huh?"

"What do you mean?"

I released Adam, and we both turned around.

It was hard to read River's expression because he was still wearing the sunglasses, but his lips were in a straight line.

"Your boyfriend here"—I pointed to Adam, who rolled his eyes—"kissed *my* boyfriend."

"Ah, so he's your boyfriend now," Adam said, punching my gut lightly.

"You kissed Emery?"

Adam laughed. "He kissed me. He thought I was Lex."

"And you didn't correct him?"

Adam's eyes narrowed. "I didn't have a chance."

"Right. Um, I just came to say I'm off."

"Already?" Adam seemed surprised.

"Yeah, I have a bunch of laundry to do, and I want to stop by the restaurant later. We're two weeks away from the party, and there's a lot to do."

He walked away, leaving us behind to stare at his back.

"What's wrong with him?" I asked, and Adam shrugged.

"Don't know. I think the party stuff is stressing him out. Is there anything we can do to help him? It's not healthy for him to be at the restaurant every single hour of every day. Even Dad never spent that much time there when he was running the place full-time."

"Talk to him and let me know, okay?"

He nodded.

"I'm off too. Believe it or not, I also have laundry to do, and Emery is coming over later."

"Bow-chicka-wow-wow."

I winked and walked away, giving him the finger behind my back.

Emery

"Hi, honey. Are you going to see Frederick again?" Mom asked as I was coming down the stairs with my overnight bag.

"Um...yeah."

I was so going to hell for lying to my parents.

She patted my arm. "I'm glad things are going well for you two. Just remember, life isn't all about the fun stuff. I know it's nice having someone to spend time with, and god knows you deserve it after that terrible accident. We're all still recovering from it in some ways."

"I know, Mom."

I kissed her on the cheek, hoping she'd let me go. I wanted to stop by the pet store to get a gift for Gordon, and they were closing soon.

"Have you handed in your notice to the school yet?"

"Um, not yet."

Her smile turned into a scowl. "Why not? Emery, we agreed. Your father has been getting things ready for you."

"I know, Mom. It's... I'll do it, okay?"

She smiled. "Okay. Now go have a good time with your

241

Frederick. Make sure he treats you well and takes you to nice places."

I nodded my agreement to appease her. We'd never be into the same things. I didn't want to be taken to nice places. I'd rather spend the evening cuddling on the couch with a bowl of ice cream. I didn't need to be seen by anyone to prove I was having fun.

The door closed with a click behind me. I paused momentarily and looked at the view in front of me. A round driveway leading down a private road. Manicured gardens and perfectly cut lawns.

Sometimes I wondered if this was what my mom really wanted for herself or if it was her way of making everything around her perfect so she wouldn't have to deal with the fact my dad was a distant husband and father.

Could I blame her for wanting me closer? Maybe not, but I wasn't a socialite, and even though I would be forever thankful to my parents for everything they'd done for me after the accident, I still couldn't shake off the feeling they weren't being completely truthful.

Pushing those thoughts aside, I got in my newly fixed car and called Frederick as I pulled away.

"Hey, Loverrrr."

I laughed. "You almost sound convincing."

"Told you, I'm a great actor. What's up?"

"I need you to cover for me tonight."

"Another date with your lover boy? Things are getting serious."

I sighed. "I don't know. Sometimes I think he's holding back something, but other times, I feel like I can see all the way to his soul. You know what I mean?"

"Um...no, but it sounds like big L kind of stuff."

"Yeah, it's getting there. For me, at least. Anyway, did you have any plans tonight? Am I messing them up?"

"Nah, I was staying home anyway. Ren is coming over to visit the kids and we're watching a movie."

"You two would be the perfect picture of co-parenting if we weren't talking about plants."

He groaned. "He's a pain in my ass, that's what he is. But he's somewhat entertaining. And since I can't exactly go out on the dating scene, it's better than being home alone."

"How long are we going to do this for, Frederick?"

There was a long-held breath on the other side of the line. When he released it, I knew exactly what he would say.

"When something changes."

"Okay. Thank you for tonight."

"You're welcome. Say hi to Lex for me, and enjoy your time together."

I ended the call and spent the rest of my drive into the city thinking about Frederick. He really wasn't the person I'd thought he was, even after we'd decided to keep up the pretense that we were dating.

When something changes.

What would that be? And if nothing ever changed, did that mean we'd forever live a double life? I had Emery for now, but Frederick also deserved to find a woman who made him happy.

The fact he was pretending to be something he wasn't, in addition to the lie that we were together, sat heavily on my chest.

I knew that one day, everything would crumble like a house of cards. I just hoped we were prepared for the day it happened.

Once I picked up Gordon's gift and an additional gift for Lex, I headed over to his place. As I got closer to Lex's place, a thrill of anticipation touched my spine.

Would he like my gift? Ultimately, it didn't matter, but part of me wanted him to like it.

I parked in my usual spot on the road and climbed the stairs to his door. I was about to knock when I heard a shout.

"For heavens' sake, Gordon. Just go inside the tank. Yes, I know you miss him too, but I swear to god, if I don't get laid tonight because of your shenanigans, I'm withdrawing your fruit privileges."

I covered my mouth with my hand to stifle my laugh. I'd seen a change in Lex's approach to Gordon recently. He was almost protective of the little gecko. I didn't want to take him back to the forest, and if he was happy and healthy, we could keep him.

Lex had sent me countless photos of where he'd found Gordon around his place. It wasn't surprising that an animal that came from the wild wouldn't be afraid to break out of his shelter to explore his surroundings.

I was starting to think Gordon had also befriended Goldie because he was often found near the fish tank.

"That's it. Good boy," Lex said.

I rang the doorbell. Lex must have been near the door because he opened it almost immediately.

"Hey."

His smile didn't fail to make my belly tighten.

"Hey, I come bearing gifts." I raised my hand carrying the bags.

He rolled his eyes. "Gordon is too spoiled."

I followed him inside and closed the door behind me.

"It's not just for Gordon."

"Goldie?"

I shook my head. "For you. I mean...us, um...if you want."

He gave me a heated look, and immediately, I felt warmth pool in the pit of my stomach.

I found myself pressed against the wall, my knees shaking and my hands struggling to hold my duffel and the bag with the gifts.

Lex ran his nose up my neck, causing me to shiver. "A gift for us, huh?"

I bit my lip to keep from moaning when his fingers circled my nipples over my shirt.

"Lex..." I begged, not that I knew what I was begging for.

"You want to take a shower with me?" His lips pressed gently against mine and then covered my mouth. Lex tasted like coffee and he smelled like his aftershave. Woodsy, citrus, and man. It drove me crazy and got me hard every time.

"Can we...um, can we open the gifts first?" I asked, reluctantly pulling away.

He took us to the living room, where Gordon was again outside his tank.

"Not again, G," Lex said. "Come on, give me a break." Then he turned to me. "This is all your fault. If you get blue balls, don't blame me."

I snorted, but he was right. Gordon had taken to breaking into Lex's room when I was over, and he'd just watch us. There's nothing creepier than being on the brink of an orgasm and suddenly finding yourself staring at a small lizard.

"I'll give him his gift first. It's guaranteed to make him go back into the tank. He'll be busy there for a little while." I opened the bag containing the feeding rock, the crickets, and the powder supplement to coat them with. In the kitchen, I opened the rock and put the crickets and powder inside before closing it and shaking it a little.

"This is really good for him," I said. "The powder will give him the supplements he needs, and he'll be busy hunting crickets for the next couple of hours, at least."

"I've gotta say, this sounds a lot like parents who try to find time for sex around the kids' nap time."

I placed the rock inside the tank and stepped back, letting curious Gordon come take a look.

"Do you want kids?" I asked.

"Yeah. I'd like a few, and you?"

"Same. It sucks being an only child. I'd like at least three."

Lex came over and wrapped his arms around me from behind, resting his chin on my shoulder. "Three? That would require military-level organization for sexual activities."

"Lots of people have more than three kids. I'm sure sex is possible." I pushed my ass back, molding myself to his body.

"Hurry up, Emery, I'm dying to get you naked."

"Tell that to your kid."

After much encouragement, Gordon was curious enough to get inside the tank and stay. I took the cap off the rock to let the crickets out and put the top of the tank back on. I also used a paperweight Lex had on his coffee table to make sure Gordon would stay inside.

"Oh my god, why did I not think of that?" he asked, groaning.

"Because you secretly love Gordon and want him to be free to explore the house."

He smiled. "Lies, all lies."

"Uh-huh."

He waited until I washed my hands before he pulled me toward his bedroom. I hooked the gift bag through my finger as we ran past it.

This was happening. I was going to be brave.

In the bedroom, Lex practically threw me on the bed, sweeping me effortlessly into his arms. His demanding lips caressed mine with an intensity I'd only ever experienced with Lex.

When I was boneless to the point he could have done anything he wanted with me, he pulled away. "Can I see the gift?"

"Okay."

He reached for the bag.

"Before you open it," I started. "I was wondering...do you like to switch?"

Lex stared at me for a moment before what I asked sank in. "Yes. God, yes. Wait, has this been bothering you?"

My face became too warm, but I couldn't back out now. "No, it hasn't bothered me. In case you haven't noticed, I've thoroughly enjoyed everything we do."

He turned his smile up a notch. "I noticed."

"But I've wondered what it would feel like to top you. I think. I'd really, *really* like to know."

"Wish granted," he said, stealing a kiss. "Now, what's in the bag?"

He opened it and took the box out. "A plug and a Fleshlight?"

"I thought maybe I could wear the plug, and you could use the Fleshlight while we're...you know."

This is it. DEFCON 1 level of embarrassment achieved.

I closed my eyes, waiting for Lex to laugh at my stupid idea, but instead, I was dragged out of the bed and into the bathroom.

"Clothes. Off," he commanded. I did as he asked. My dick was so hard I thought I would come if anything more than a breath of air touched it.

Lex took the toys out of the boxes and gave them a good cleaning with soap and water. Then he grabbed the water-based lube from his drawer.

He paused for a moment, placing his hands on the sink.

"Is everything okay?"

"Christ, Emery. You've just turned my world upside down, and I don't know if I want to rush to the end goal or take my time. I just want everything with you, and I want it now."

I wrapped my arms around him and placed a kiss on the bare skin of his back. His nipples hardened when I grazed my blunt nails over them. He hissed and opened his legs to steady himself, creating the perfect cocoon for me to snuggle my erection in.

"I want everything too, Lex. We can have it all now, and we can have it later. I'm not going anywhere."

"Promise?"

"Promise."

He turned around and reached for the shower to get the water running, and then he maneuvered me so I was facing the sink.

"Keep your eyes on the mirror and watch what I'm doing to you." He knelt behind me and ran his hands up my legs, encouraging me to widen my stance. "Look at you, Emery, all exposed to me. You want me to put the plug in you?"

"Yes, please." I almost didn't recognize my gravelly voice.

He encouraged me to bend forward with a gentle hand on the low of my back. His hands massaged the globes of my ass before he spread them apart, leaving me wide open and vulnerable.

"Nhghhh," I cried when the warmth of his tongue caressed my hole. I'd expected a finger, or maybe for him to tease me with the plug, but not his tongue. He'd made many promises, but every time we were together, we could barely get our clothes off before chasing our pleasure.

Tonight was the night of slow and steady teasing. I loved it, and I was going to die because of it.

My legs struggled to keep me upright. I remembered attempts at rimming from previous partners when I was in college, but nothing came close to the sensation of being penetrated by Lex's exploratory tongue. He sucked and licked like we could do this all night. When a hand crept up my thigh, I had to stop him before I came too early.

"The plug. Please."

I uncapped the lube, drizzled a small amount on the plug,

and passed it to him. He didn't try to open me with a finger first. I suspected he knew I could come any moment now.

The slight pain from the intrusion helped stave off my impending orgasm.

"That's it, baby. Nice and slow."

With the plug fully inside me, Lex stood and dragged us into the shower.

While everything up till now had been slow, the shower was so quick that I was glad I hadn't been dirty to begin with.

Moving to the bedroom, however, was an exercise in self-control. Every time I took a step, the plug rubbed up against my prostate. My dick throbbed with the need for any kind of friction.

Lex lay on the bed, both legs wide open, showing me his hole.

"Touch yourself," I commanded.

He stroked his dick slowly, paying attention to the head. With the other hand, he reached down to his hole, massaging it with his fingers.

"Lube," I said. "Get yourself ready for me."

I got on my knees on the bed and watched him intently.

He drizzled some lube on his cock and his fingers. I was mesmerized watching him pleasure himself, hearing the slick sound of skin on skin and his moans as he fucked himself with his fingers.

"You're too hot for words, Lex. I can't wait to be inside you."

"Then come here because I'm ready."

"I feel so full from the plug, and now I'm going to fill you up too."

He dragged in a breath and closed his eyes. "Emery, don't tease, baby. I need you now," he said between gritted teeth.

I coated my cock with lube and placed myself between his legs with one hand keeping his knee against his chest. I pointed my dick at his hole and pushed through slowly. The thought that I would leave part of me behind inside him when I came made my already hard dick throb.

"Faster," he begged.

"I'm trying to keep you safe and stop from coming too early."

"If you need to work on your stamina, I can be your subject. Just fucking do it."

He swallowed his words when I did exactly as he'd asked, but I paid dearly for it because, in this position, the plug felt like it went deeper inside me.

I groaned in pleasure, pulling out of Lex and pushing back in. I kept a steady pace at first, but the sensations were too good.

Lex must have felt my struggle because he drizzled some lube over his cock, grabbed the Fleshlight, and started fucking it.

"Oh Jesus Christ, this is too much," he gasped.

"You have no idea how perfect you feel, Lex."

With the speeding up of my pace, we soared higher toward the peak of ecstasy.

"Fuck, you're filling me so good, and this fucking toy. I'm getting close, baby."

So was I. This wasn't just dirty, erotic sex. My feelings for Lex flowed through me like warm honey. Did he know how important, how unforgettable this moment was?

I hoped he did. He had to be feeling the same as me. No one can fake sex and a connection this good.

I pushed his hand aside and grabbed the Fleshlight.

"I'm gonna take us to the edge of ecstasy and then let us jump together. You with me?" I asked.

"I'm with you."

Everything was pure and explosive. My ass was on fire and

my dick was surrounded by fire. But I didn't let up. The involuntary tremors of arousal began deep in my spine.

As it built, I increased my pace. The bed was ramming against the wall, adding to the sounds of our skin slapping.

I kept going until Lex started coming in a full-body shake. I pulled the Fleshlight off just in time to watch him spurt jets of cum onto his belly.

"Oh fuck...oh fuck...yes. Yes!"

My orgasm picked up where Lex's left off, and I put everything I had into him.

Each of his aftershocks caused a new aftershock for me. With the plug still in my ass, my cock was rock hard. I was sure I could go another round right now.

Lex pulled me down and joined our lips. Each pass of his tongue over mine made me soar higher and higher to the point I didn't feel like I was coming down from my orgasm. I stayed up there, in the clouds, floating above my own body.

"I'm glad you're staying the night," Lex said.

"Oh really?"

"Yeah. This was fucking incredible, and we're not done with these toys."

I let out a contented sigh. "You say all the right things."

"How about dinner?"

"See? I was right."

I hissed when he raised his hips because I still had the plug inside me. As much as I would be happy to cuddle, we both desperately needed to get clean.

"Shower first?" I asked.

"Yes, please. You wrecked me."

I winked. "Not sorry."

My ass was sore. That was the first thing I noticed as soon as I woke up in the morning. My dick was hard. That was the second thing. The only difference between them was that the first was new to me, at least with Emery.

The whole year we'd been together, Emery had always bottomed. It hadn't been something we discussed. He'd assumed the role, and I'd figured he was happy with it.

How had we gone a whole year without talking about this? Would he have ever told me that he liked to switch? And equally, why hadn't I told him I enjoyed bottoming sometimes?

The birds outside chirped happily, mirroring my own disposition.

Yes, there were a lot of questions unanswered. We'd get to them one day. But for now, I was going to experience one of my favorite moments: opening my eyes and seeing Emery for the first time. Every time we woke up together was like a dream. I preferred waking up before him because I liked to watch his expression as he woke up and saw me.

Each time we did this, I savored it and locked the memory

away, just in case the moment would never repeat. I wanted to be able to close my eyes and feel Emery's presence even without him here with me.

I quietly inhaled, smelling my shampoo on his hair. As usual, his legs were wrapped around mine. It was the only way he'd settle in his sleep. I always wondered how he managed without me. Did he cuddle a blanket? Did he have trouble sleeping?

His eyelashes fluttered, but his eyes remained closed. I admired the smattering of freckles over his nose and cheeks. He also had some on his neck and shoulders. They brought out his bright emerald eyes.

I resisted the urge to push a curly lock of his copper hair from his eyes. He'd wake up in his own time, which was right about...now.

He stretched his arms out and pushed his hair away from his face. When he opened his eyes, I had the same revelation I'd had every time since the first night we slept together in that tent in the forest.

I was more in love with his man now than I'd ever been, and it was the scariest feeling in the world.

"It's a little creepy, don't you think?" he asked.

"What is?"

"You. Staring at me while I sleep."

I smiled. "Creepy or adorable? I think it's adorable."

His hands came up to cradle my cheek. "I mean, it's not as creepy as Gordon, that's for sure, but I'm not sold on adorable."

"Okay, what if I told you that when I watch you sleep, it's the most at peace I feel in my whole life? What if I told you that counting your freckles is my favorite pastime? What if I—"

His mouth crashed into mine in a searing kiss that took

my breath away. I kissed him back with all the love I felt but couldn't declare.

Our bodies collided in a sensual tango. Legs intertwined, erections pressing together, hands hastily groping all the skin they could hold on to.

A crescendo of energy built inside me. My balls drew up, and with each pass of Emery's cock over mine, I got closer and closer until I cried my orgasm into his mouth. A hand came between us, and I gasped as Emery took the remnants of my release to coat his cock. Then, in a slow and steady motion, he brought himself to orgasm.

"That," he said, trying to regain his breath, "has to be the quickest we've ever gone from zero to a hundred."

"Agree."

"Me too. I agree that you're an adorable voyeur."

I laughed. "How about a shower and then breakfast at the farmers' market?"

"I'd like that."

Lazy Sunday mornings at the market with your boyfriend. There wasn't a more perfect way to spend the day if you had to be out of your bed.

"I love farmers' markets," Emery said as we weaved through people. "You can try so many different foods you can't get anywhere else. There's a baker at the farmers' market by the school that makes the most amazing bread. Sometimes, I bring my own filling to make a sandwich for my lunch and sometimes I buy theirs. I swear it's like being in a Mediterranean country, soaking up the sun and watching people from a balcony."

"Have you ever been to Europe?"

"A few times with my parents when I was younger, but it'd be a different experience as an adult, you know?"

I nodded.

"When you're following someone else's schedule, you can't appreciate the things you want. Besides, the country I'd really love to visit is Portugal, and I've never been."

"Why Portugal?"

He shrugged. "I don't know. I think I saw a show about the food in Lisbon once, and I guess I've wanted to go there ever since. Wait, you're Portuguese. Have you ever been there?"

My heart tightened. We'd had a single conversation about our wedding after I proposed and before I last saw Emery. He'd told me we should go to Portugal for our honeymoon.

The thought that he wanted to see where I came from, part of my heritage, had made me incredibly happy. And now, despite his amnesia, there was still something of us left behind.

"No, I've never been."

He gasped. "That's a sin. I say we go there one day. We can eat all the food and go to the beach."

I circled my arms around him and pressed him against me, nuzzling the space between his neck and shoulder. His hair tickled my face, but I didn't care.

"You're really amazing. Did you know that?"

He turned his head to give me a chaste kiss. "Maybe you should keep me around then."

"I think I will."

"You might also want to feed me."

And right on cue, his belly rumbled.

We picked up a coffee and a couple of pastries from the coffee stand and sat at a table nearby, tucking into our late breakfast.

His phone dinged with a message. He laughed, replying to

whatever the message was. His fingers moved quickly on the screen.

Those fingers had caressed and teased me to no end last night. My cock swelled at the memory.

"Look," he said, passing me the phone. It was a photo of a distressed-looking Frederick with a bunch of succulent plants in the background.

"Wow. Are those Ren's succulents?"

Emery nodded. "Frederick is looking after them until Ren has a permanent living situation. At the moment, he's still commuting into the city for work, but I think he eventually wants to find a place."

"Maybe he should move in with Frederick. Then he'd be close to his plants."

Emery laughed. "They do seem to be getting along fine, despite Frederick complaining constantly about his space being taken up by the plants."

"Do you talk to him much?" I wasn't jealous of Frederick. After all, he was straight and didn't seem to have anything in common with Emery.

Emery stared at his coffee cup, expression changing all of a sudden.

"I have something to confess about Frederick," he said.

"Okay."

"We...me and him, we're kind of...in a fake relationship."

I stilled. "Say again?"

"We're fake dating." His fingers tapped the table like a little drum. I placed my hand on top of his and his eyes met mine.

"You told me he was straight. And you're with me." I ran my fingers through my hair. "We're exclusive, right?"

"Yes. Yes! It's not real. Between me and Frederick." He let out a frustrated sigh. "After our failed date, we didn't think we'd see each other again, but our moms are friends. Frederick wants his mom off his back so he can settle back here. He was in Europe for a long time and has just returned."

"And you?"

"And I...I met this really sweet, sexy guy I can't get enough of. In order to spend time with him, I agreed to fake date someone else to get my mom to stop wanting to set me up with other guys. I guess we're both helping each other."

"And this guy you met...the sweet and sexy one...how sexy is he really?" I asked.

The tension rolling off Emery dissipated in a heartbeat.

"Oh, he's easily the sexiest man I've ever met." He leaned forward on the table and half-covered his mouth with his hand like he was going to tell me a secret. "He also has a really big dick."

I laughed. "He does, does he?"

Emery winked.

"So how does it work?" I asked.

"It's not something we planned in detail. We mainly just agreed to put on an act in front of our parents, but since I've been spending so much time with you, my mom thinks I'm with him."

The fear that ruled me since I'd found Emery again stopped me many times, but I needed to know exactly where we stood with each other.

"I have to ask, Emery. Why can't your mom know you're dating me?"

He let out a breath. "My parents have expectations about who I should date."

"Ouch."

He took my hand. "It's not like that. They'd expect you to be of a certain social standing. It's not what I'm like. I don't give a shit about that, but they do, and I don't want them to get between us until...until I'm ready to tell them the truth."

I rubbed circles over the back of his hand with my thumb.

He'd built a house of cards right next to mine. Everything seemed so precarious that the tiniest breeze would cause it all to crumble.

This was it. I couldn't push it back anymore. I needed to tell him.

"Let's walk back to my place," I said.

"Okay."

My hands trembled with nervous energy. I couldn't go any longer without telling Emery about us. I owed it to him to tell the truth. What happened last night, and every single date we'd had before that, showed we were in the same place but were coming to it from vastly different baselines.

It was a risk, and I wasn't sure I'd survive if he didn't understand why I'd lied or omitted the nature of our relationship after we met the first time.

My brother was right.

"You're a little quiet. Is everything okay?" he asked. We were a few minutes from my place.

"Yes, of course. I just—" My phone rang. I pulled it out and saw Adam's name flashing. "Sorry, it's Adam."

He nodded.

"Adam."

"Bro. Code Red. Code Red. Come to Mom and Dad's."

"What happened? Is everyone okay?" My pulse shot up. "Avó?"

He laughed. "Dude. If it was something like that, I wouldn't be calling out a stupid code we made up when we were kids. Everyone's okay, but you should come here. There's a little non-medical situation."

I breathed a sigh of relief. "Shit, Adam, you just took years off my life."

"Sorry, Lex. I didn't mean to. See you soon then."

"Okay."

I stared at the phone after he ended the call.

"What's up? You look worried," Emery said.

"There's some drama at my parents' house. I'm really sorry to cut our day short, but I have to go."

He stepped into my arms and gave me a kiss. "It's okay. I have a bunch of work to do, so it won't do me any harm to get home earlier."

"Thank you." I held on to him tight. He would never know how close he'd been to having something so big thrown at him.

Maybe it was better to go our separate ways today. It would give me time to think about how to break the news to him.

On my way to my parents' house, I should've been relieved that I hadn't needed to do it today, but I wasn't. Maybe that was the sign I needed. Neither of us deserved to live a lie, especially when Emery didn't even know it.

Noah opened the door. He was rubbing tears from his eyes, but he was laughing.

"What the hell is going on?"

"Do you remember when Mom decided to throw a party when you and Adam finished high school?"

I groaned. "Yeah, the *my boys are all grown up* cringe-fest. I remember."

"This is that on steroids."

"Oh god."

Emery

I couldn't wipe out the smile from my face. It was permanently etched onto my face. All photographs taken of me from here on would record this all-consuming energy that rushed through my veins.

Happiness didn't begin to describe it.

I answered the incoming call from my phone by pressing the button on my steering wheel.

"Hello?"

"Wow. I can smell your love pheromones from here," Ellie said.

I laughed. "Jealous?"

"Only that this stupid flu put a temporary stop to my own sexual activities while you're clearly getting some...and then some."

"I won't confirm or deny."

"Oh, honey, you don't need to. I heard it at hello."

"Okay, Renée Zellweger."

Ellie laughed. "Anyway, what are you doing out of bed?"

"If you thought I was in bed, why did you call?"

"To cockblock you, of course. Also to remind you that we

263

have that meeting tomorrow after work about the last day of school activities. If you're thinking of getting laid, think again. We're having a girls' night afterward."

"How many times do I have to tell you I'm not a girl?"

She gave me a dismissive *meh* and said she had to go get dosed up on flu meds and nap so she was in top shape for tomorrow.

My smile was still very much on my face when I walked through the door to my parents' place.

My parents' place.

Why didn't I ever feel like I was coming home, but instead, I was just visiting?

Maybe this was the sign I needed to find a place to live. It was time to make my own decisions about even simple things like what brand of coffee to have in the pantry.

I went to my room to drop off my stuff and then searched for my mom. I'd tell her today. Not that I was rushing to move out, but I could make my intentions clear. And if she argued about affordability, I'd point out that I was about to start working with Dad and expected my earnings to increase from my teacher salary.

Besides, we had money. I never touched what wasn't mine, but it wasn't like we were poor. She spent all her free time in member's clubs and shopped in designer stores.

I couldn't pinpoint the time when I'd made the decision to not use the account my parents had opened for me when I was younger. Maybe it was one of the things I'd done during the period now lost to me. I trusted that if I'd made that decision, even if I didn't remember, it was for a reason.

At the end of the day, it wasn't my money, but I hoped that if I needed to use it to secure a place to live, my parents would be supportive.

With the decision made, I went searching for my mom.

I found her in the garden, reading a book.

"Hey, Mom."

"Emery. Sit down. I'm glad you're back."

The tone of her voice put me on edge.

"Is everything okay?"

"How was your weekend with Frederick?"

I kept my palms face down on my legs so as to not give myself away. "Um, it was fine. Why?"

"So you didn't have an argument or fight?"

"No..."

She closed her book and put it on the table, peering at me over the rim of her reading glasses. "So how do you explain Jeanelle seeing you this morning at the farmers' market in Cliffborough getting all cozy with a man that wasn't Frederick? She was simply livid when she told me."

I opened my mouth and shut it again. Since when did Frederick's mom go to farmers' markets in the city? Why had I not thought about being careful with PDAs?

"I...err..."

"Have you two broken up?"

"No, Mom."

She gasped. "Oh my god. It's even worse. You're cheating on the poor guy." She stood and paced in front of me. "This isn't how I raised you, Emery Livingston. I'm not a dinosaur. I know all about gay culture and your ideas on 'hookups,'" she said with air quotes. "I get it, but we respect family values here. We don't jump around from flower to flower like some butterfly drunk on hedonism. We have class and self-respect."

I wanted to shout back that she was wrong. Everyone had the right to love how they wished, and that didn't make them any worse than anyone else. Our so-called "family values" translated into a business- and money-obsessed father who hadn't spoken a word to me in at least a week. I had two parents who put on an act in public when in private, they spent very little time together.

But I didn't say any of that because I knew it would make things worse.

My head started throbbing. I rubbed my temples as she continued.

"This is an embarrassment to our family name. How will I ever face Jeanelle after what you've done?"

I flinched at her words. Okay, the picture didn't look good for me, I'd admit.

"Mom, I'm not cheating on anyone. I was with a friend this morning because Frederick had to help another friend." Well, technically, it was true. "I will arrange to take Frederick and Jeanelle out for a meal this week. We can clarify the misunderstanding."

She sat back on her chair and crossed her legs. Her dress fanned over her knees. "Do you promise this was just a misunderstanding?"

"Yes."

"Well...okay then. I think it's a good idea to take Jeanelle out to clear the air. It might be a good opportunity for you and Frederick to announce your engagement."

"What?"

"Let's make it a family meal."

"Mom, we're not engaged."

She stared at me with the coldest eyes I'd ever seen from her. "Then make sure there is one. And make it short. We'll start planning for a late summer wedding, so by the time you take over running the company for your dad, you'll be a married man."

I clenched and unclenched my fists and tried to keep my breathing steady. She couldn't make me do this. I was an adult, for goodness' sake.

Steady. Breathe in. Breathe out.

"Mom, I have only just met Frederick. Even if I was ready

to take that step in my life. And even if it was with Frederick, it certainly wouldn't be right now."

There. I'd said it.

She stood up and stared at me. "Remember who saved your life, Emery. Who nursed you back to health, paid the therapist bill, and kept a roof over your head."

"Is it true I had moved out and wasn't living here when I had the accident?" I asked.

She stepped back. "It doesn't matter. I did what any mother would have done. I got you the best doctors. I paid for the most qualified nurses to visit you daily to aid your recovery. I didn't raise you to be ungrateful."

You didn't raise me at all. I wanted to say.

"It matters to me. Because if you lied about that, what else have you lied about?"

She tucked a stray lock of hair behind her ear. "What do you want me to say, Emery? That you'd moved out? Fine. You had. And yes, I lied because I thought it was best for you if you felt like you were at home. I didn't know how to look after you if you weren't with me, so I brought you here."

"It's been a year, Mom. Why haven't you said anything?"

"I don't have to justify my actions when I had the best intentions."

She turned and left, disappearing through the double doors into the house.

The car keys were still in my pocket, so I avoided the house and went straight to where I'd parked my car.

My head was pounding from the argument, and I needed to be away from this place to think. I'd stood up to my mom. The adrenaline from that alone kept me moving.

I was grateful for what my parents had done, but my mom seemed to think I was indebted to them because of it.

How had I never noticed how unhealthy my relationship with my parents was?

Had I known before? Was this why I'd moved out? Where had I lived?

I turned onto the main road into the city, the tires screeching in protest.

My jaw hurt from clenching my teeth. I tried to relax, but every word my mother had spoken was playing on repeat in my head.

I thought back to when I first came home from the hospital. My room had felt foreign to me. I'd put it down to the brain injury and the stuff my mom fed me about growing up and getting rid of stuff, but now I could see it clearly.

My personal belongings were there. A few photos of me camping, on school trips, or on vacations, a stack of books. But there was nothing from me as an adult.

Now, the desk in my room was filled with paperwork and my bedroom mirror had drawings from my students stuck to it. I knew it was my room and not the room I'd walked into when I first got out of the hospital.

A flash of light went through my eyes. The car swerved a little, but I managed to control it. I'd have to stop somewhere to buy something for the headache, or it would get worse.

I pulled the window down, feeling the wind on my face. It didn't help calm me. Sweat ran down my face, making my hair stick. Suddenly, a sharp pain came from the back of my head.

There was only time to pull onto the side of the road before everything went dark, apart from the flashes of light behind my eyes.

A familiar image appeared inside my head. This time, it was much clearer.

The group of people standing in front of me had clear faces. I recognized Adam. My gaze went to the person on the other side of the group.

He stood by the peony trees. *Lex.*

"Uhghhhh," I cried with my hands gripping my head. The image faded and another replaced it.

"You weren't the first boy I kissed, but I knew even before I kissed you for the first time that you would be the last one. So what do you say? Want to spend the rest of your life kissing just one boy?" Lex was in front of me, holding tight like he was afraid I'd run, but his caress was gentle. His blue eyes were full of love but so afraid.

I searched my brain for the rest. What had I said? When had this happened? *Had* it happened, or was my brain making it all up?

The more I searched, the stronger my headache became until there was nothing.

"Emery...please wake up. Shit, what do I do now?"

The voice was familiar, but I couldn't place it.

I was still in my car. My hands gripped the steering wheel, but I wasn't moving. I opened my eyes slowly, ready for the impending pain, but it wasn't too bad.

"Thank fuck."

I turned to the voice and recognized him immediately. "Lior. I mean, Mr. Van Stern."

He chuckled. "Lior is fine. How are you feeling?"

"Like a steamroller crushed my head. I think I blacked out. Did I have an accident?" I tried to sit up. "Oh my god, is someone hurt because of me?"

"No, you didn't cause an accident. My guess is that you felt what was coming and pulled over. You're not exactly *parked,* so I stopped when I saw a car half on the grass, inches from the ditch."

I took a deep breath. Apart from a still-throbbing but milder headache, I felt okay.

"You were very lucky, Emery."

"Yeah, I think I was."

"Can I help you get somewhere? Do you need to go to the hospital?"

"No. I just should go home."

"Do you live nearby?" he asked.

"Yeah, a few miles that way." I pointed to the road behind us.

"Okay, give me your address. I'll get someone to come pick up your car, and I'll give you a lift home."

I didn't want to inconvenience him. He was probably on his way to somewhere important, but I also didn't want to drive.

"Thank you. I really appreciate the lift."

Lior dropped me off halfway down the driveway at my request. The last thing I wanted was for my parents to catch wind of what happened. Lior said the car would be dropped off in thirty minutes and not to worry about it.

There was no reason to not believe him.

I didn't want to go inside the house straight away in case I bumped into either of my parents, so once again, I went around the main house and followed the paved path to the pool house.

It was a part of the house I never used, and I didn't understand the need for it. Not when we never had guests that could benefit from it.

The pool house was bigger than Lex's place, and I found it utterly ridiculous. It had two guest rooms and a huge walk-in closet.

I was desperate to shower and lie down, so that's where I went to get a towel and a robe. The shower helped me feel a little better. I went into one of the rooms to lie down. As I put the towel I'd dried my hair with on a chair, I noticed the closet door was slightly open.

I was about to close it when something inside caught my eye, so I opened the door all the way.

The closet was mostly filled with bedding, but there was a box on the top shelf. The thing that had caught my eye because it had a metal label holder on the front.

I pulled the box out and took it to the bed.

The main house looked as quiet as always. Being a Sunday, my parents were likely getting ready to attend some function later. Since my car wasn't back yet, I doubted they'd come in here for anything.

I opened the box and my breath caught when I saw my passport on top. The passport that my mom had said was lost in the accident. It had never made sense to me why I'd been carrying my passport, but I couldn't remember, so I hadn't questioned. It was still in date.

Underneath it, there were other documents, mostly college stuff. I took those out and gasped at what had been hidden beneath.

A stack of photos and an engagement ring.

I had so many questions, but the first thing that came to mind was, *Did my mom know about this?*

Lex

"She's been at this since yesterday," Dad said.

"Has anyone tried to approach?" I asked.

Adam gasped. "You know the rules."

I rolled my eyes.

"Where's Avó?"

"She's in her room, too upset to come out," Noah said.

"What happened?"

Three shrugs followed my question.

"How does no one know why Mom is covered in flour, baking a fifth loaf of bread—"

"Sixth. There's one in the oven," Noah said.

"Regardless. There are four cakes on the table. One of them looks like it's trying to escape—"

"Too much yeast," Dad said.

I closed my eyes and took a deep breath. My family was deranged.

The four of us stood outside the arch leading into the kitchen from the hallway. Under normal circumstances, Mom would hear us from the kitchen, but when she was in one of her moods, she closed everything and everyone off.

We could have a full-blown argument out here, and she wouldn't hear it above the animated conversation in her head.

"Okay, let's look for some clues. What kind of bread is that? Sourdough?"

"Yeah," Dad said.

"And the cake?"

"Based on the shape, I'd say marble cake," Noah said.

"What else?" I asked.

Dad pointed at the kitchen table. "Look, there's condensed milk. Maybe she's going to make brigadeiros next."

"Wait," Noah said. "I think I got it."

We all turned to him. "Who loves all those things?"

"We all do," Adam said.

"Wrong. Almost. Yes, we all love those things, but if you were to ask Mom to make three things, what would you ask for?"

Adam scratched his head. "Marble cake, for sure. Brigadeiros and...oh minhocas. You know those cookies that look like caterpillars? I love those."

"Precisely," Noah said. "And I'd have gone for the cake, sourdough, and chocolate mousse. Who would have asked for those three specific things?"

I looked at Dad, whose expression was blank like there was no way there was anything Mom made that would take priority over the rest.

He'd never pick a thing, and Mom loved him for it. He was an easy man to please.

"Me," I said. "I'd have picked those three."

I turned back to Mom. "There's only one way to find out."

Adam put his hand on my shoulder. "We're right here for you."

Noah raised his hand. He was holding a box of tissues.

I shook my head. What could be so bad? And why was I involved?

Taking a determined step forward, I forced my lips to part in a curved smile and approached my mom.

"Hey, Mom, what have we got here?"

She raised her gaze to me and gasped. "Lex, baby. How lovely to see you."

Her arms went around my waist, covering me in flour. "Oops, I got you all dirty. Don't worry. You can grab one of your old shirts from your bedroom while I wash this one. Here, have a slice of cake."

She pulled a knife from the drawer, and I heard a collective gasp from the audience. Christ, they needed to chill.

I took a bite from the cake and almost spat it out. "Mom, um...have you tried the cake?"

"No, what's wrong?" She broke off a piece from mine and tried it. "Oh no, I'm so sorry, honey. I must have mistaken the salt for sugar. Hold on, have this one."

She cut a piece of another one. I was too scared to try but too scared *not* to try in case it upset her.

"Not as bad as the other one, but I think you forgot the sugar."

"Darnit. Let's try the other one. Third time's a charm, right?"

"Wait." I grabbed her arm to stop her. "Let's go sit on the couch, okay?"

"Yeah, sure. Ah, hold on. I need to get the bread out. Can I make you a sandwich? I have four fresh loaves. Now, one of them may have the sugar that's missing in the cake, but—"

"Mom. Leave it. I'm not hungry."

Her bottom lip wobbled. "But I need to have something for when you're upset."

"Why would I be upset?"

She relented and sat next to me.

"Emery is back."

I coughed. "What?"

"I knew you'd be upset." She hid her face in her trembling hands.

"I'm not upset, Mom. Tell me what this is about. How do you know Emery is back?"

She placed her hands on her knees like she was preparing to tell a long story.

"Tiana's son, you know, the one who had the funny eye but then got it fixed, so he went into the military? It looks really good now, and he has twenty-twenty vision. He even got married to this sweet young lady who works at the hairdresser downtown—"

"Mom. Focus."

"Sorry, honey. Anyway, the whole family has been coming to the restaurant for decades. You remember them. Right?"

"Yes?"

"They have a newborn baby girl too. So yesterday, I was doing the shopping when I bumped into Tiana at the grocery store. She showed me photos of her new granddaughter. She's adorable."

I kept gesturing for Mom to hurry up with her story and get to what I wanted to know, but a lifetime of Mom being Mom had taught me to just wait and she'd get there via five other people's stories.

"Then she said her son's wife already had a sweet little boy, who's six. She showed me his class photo, and there he was."

"Who?" I'd lost track by now of how many children and grandchildren Tiana, also known as Mrs. Kimble, had.

"Emery. He's Tiana's grandson's teacher." She stared at me. "Aren't you surprised? Oh my god, you're in shock. Let me make you a sandwich."

"Wait, Mom." I turned back to the audience in the hallway. "Can you get Avó and all come here?"

Five minutes later, my whole family was reunited in the kitchen. Everything my mom had baked was in the center of the table, but everyone was afraid to touch it.

When Mom cooked under stress, she always switched ingredients or missed them altogether. It was clear she was upset that Emery was back and how that would impact me.

"Mãe, Pai, e Avó, I know Emery is back. I've known for a few weeks, actually."

My grandmother, who never missed a beat, stared at Adam and Noah.

"Yes, Avó, they knew. I asked them to keep it from you until I could figure out what to do."

"But you're not upset." Mom said.

"No, Mom," I smiled. "I'm really not upset. I'm afraid, but I'm not upset."

"Afraid of what?"

"I bumped into Emery at the farmers' market. He was with Ellie, Victoria's sister. She introduced us. He had no idea who I was. He was in a car accident a year ago and lost his memory, which is why he disappeared from our lives, but it wasn't intentional."

My dad pursed his lips. "How can you trust him? Let's say he's telling the truth. How did he not check his phone for contacts, messages, and photos? Or in his apartment. Wouldn't he see spare toothbrushes, things you bought together? I watch True Crime. I know to look out for these things."

I chuckled. "I don't know, Dad. He lives with his parents now." I raised a hand when Mom tried to speak.

"I know you'll have a lot of questions. The reason I didn't want to tell you was because I don't have those answers. Emery and I have been seeing each other for a while. He's the same Emery I fell for, but he's also a new person. I'm enjoying getting to know this new person."

"You haven't told him about you, have you?" Avó asked.

I shook my head.

"Alexis. How is that boy going to feel when he finds out you lied to him?"

"I know, Avó. I know I haven't been myself over the last year. Emery appearing back in my life was like someone literally pulling the rug out from under my feet. I had no warning, so I reacted by pretending we'd never met. Everything else tumbled from there. I was going to tell him this morning, actually, but then I got a call from Adam about..." I pointed at the baked goods on the table.

"When are you going to tell him?" Dad asked.

"Next weekend, I want to take him out to the coast. I'll tell him then. If I'm lucky, we'll still be together for the party at the restaurant."

It seemed like there was a collective sigh. I felt it too. I'd been carrying this weight on my shoulders for weeks, and I knew I should have told my family before, but I'd been too scared.

"Thank you, everyone, for looking out for me. I couldn't ask for a better family. Yes, you're all a little insane, but I love how we all have each other's backs. I know you all loved Emery as much as I did. Still do. I can't guarantee he'll forgive me, but I will try."

Mom and Avó gave me a hug and Dad patted me on the back. I went in for a hug because he was a big old marshmallow, and I knew he really wanted a hug too, especially after seeing Mom so distressed.

"I'm going home, and I'm taking one of these loaves with me." I picked a random one, took a bag from the drawer, and said my goodbyes.

I felt lighter than I had in weeks. I hated lying to my family or omitting things. The fact they hadn't raged over Emery disappearing or the missing parts of his story meant a lot to me.

Now, I just needed to gain enough courage to tell Emery this weekend.

I pulled into my usual parking space and went up the stairs, nearly jumping when I saw Emery by my front door.

"Hey, what are you doing here?" I went straight to him and kissed him. He didn't respond how I'd expected. "Is everything okay? I didn't see your car. Has it broken down? How did you get here?"

"Can we talk inside?"

"Sure." I opened the door, and we went straight to the living room. I dropped the bread on the counter and checked that Gordon was still in the tank.

It seemed Emery's treat had worked because he was still there, bathing under the light. I'd removed the paperweight from the top of the tank in case he wanted to explore while I was out, but I was happy to find he was finally learning some boundaries.

"Okay. I'm here," I said, sitting next to Emery.

He was holding a box and passed it to me.

"What's this?"

"I hope you know because I don't."

That was weird. I removed the cover, and my heart sank immediately.

"Emery..."

"Why do I have pictures of us together, Lex?" His voice wobbled. "Why is there an engagement ring inside the box?"

I drew in a long breath. "I guess it's time to talk about us."

Emery looked like he was on the brink of tears and trying his absolute best to hold himself together. There was no time to practice. It was time to rip off the Band-Aid.

"We met two years ago in the Botanical Gardens. I want to

say I don't believe in love at first sight, but I'd be lying because as soon as I laid my eyes on you and you smiled, that was it. I was taken. We dated and fell in love. A year ago, I proposed to you." The memory of that day came flooding back. I wanted to smile and cry at the same time. "You said yes. It was bumpy because my whole family was watching and you seemed, I don't know, panicked, but you said yes. You said you had to deal with some family business, so we decided to keep the engagement to ourselves. A few days later, you left and never came back. I didn't see you again until we met at the farmers' market."

"Why didn't you say something then?"

Emery

I'd debated whether I should come to see Lex, but he was the only person who could give me the answers I needed. At least, I hoped he was.

My heart thumped against my ribcage so hard I thought I would be sick.

Lex shifted in his seat as if that would help shift his thoughts into the right gear.

"I was so madly in love with you, Emery. We'd had our life planned out. You said you were moving in with me. The last day I saw you, I gave you the ring. And then you were gone. You didn't answer your calls, you weren't at your apartment, and then your phone stopped working."

"I lost my phone in the accident. My parents bought me a new one."

"I went to your place, and your landlady said you'd moved. That destroyed me, Emery, so when I saw you again, I was floored. I didn't believe you were real." He let out a nervous laugh. "You probably thought I was so weird when we met."

I thought you were stunning. That's what I wanted to say, but the words never went past my lips.

283

"You lied to me, Lex."

He nodded. "I know. At the time, it seemed easier to go with it. I was trying to hold on to any bits of information to figure out how you came back into my life like nothing had happened."

"Nothing had. Not for me. You were a perfect stranger. I trusted you. I told you things…"

"Things you never told me before," he said. "You never mentioned your family until you said you had to visit them before you disappeared. You never talked about your upbringing or your childhood. We never camped. Although I do have Goldie because of you. You named him."

I looked at the tank.

"I don't know anything anymore, Lex. I don't remember us from before. I had a couple of flashbacks, but they're sketchy at best. I think…I think today's flashback was when you proposed." Tears ran down my face. "I blacked out afterward, and when I came to, I was confused. I'm not sure I remember every detail from the flashbacks."

He ran his finger over the lid of the box. "Where did you find the box?"

"In my parents' house. It was hidden, likely by my mother."

"This is the proof that there was an us, Emery. This photo was taken on my birthday. The first we spent together. You wanted to go into the photo machine and do stupid faces, but we ended up making out. This one"—he lifted another photo —"was taken by Noah when I bought this couch, and we couldn't get it inside because it wouldn't fit through the door. We ended up with it stuck, so we spent the night on the couch, one of us indoors and the other outdoors."

The more he talked, the more my tears fell. I wanted to remember those things. My brain had failed me, and I'd lost so much more than I'd imagined.

And the thing that scared me the most was that I was afraid I was no longer the same person.

Lex stood and went to a set of drawers in the hallway. He came back holding three frames.

"The first time you came here, you mentioned the gaps on the wall. This is what was on there before."

Photos of us. I ran my finger over the faces in the pictures. We looked the same but also not.

"I took the photos down a week before we met at the farmers' market. I'd finally made myself move on from your loss, but even then, I couldn't throw them out. Do you know how much you have to love a person that when they leave, you grieve for their absence instead of being angry?"

I took a tissue from the box on the coffee table and cleaned my face from the tears. "I...I always had this void in my chest. I talked to my therapist about it, and she said it was normal, that I was probably grieving the loss of something I didn't remember. Not knowing is the worst. You feel empty, like you don't exist."

Lex opened a small drawer in the coffee table. Inside, there was only one thing. A ring. He took it out and stared at it like it was painful to do just that.

"I wore this ring for six months, hoping you'd return. I took the ring off, but I never stopped hoping. I wanted to, but I don't think I ever let you go."

Lex stood and then knelt in front of me. He placed the ring on my palm and closed my hand, holding it. "This is the proof that we existed. We still do. I'm so sorry I lied. If I could do it all over again, I would tell you the truth as soon as I knew what happened. All it took was one look into your eyes, and I knew, Emery. I knew you were telling the truth about the accident. That it wasn't your fault that you disappeared from my life. But I can't go back in time and undo the things I did. I can only promise you a future."

He dropped his head on our joined hands. "Please tell me there's a future. I love you so fucking much, Emery." When he raised his head again, his eyes were pained and wet. "If you can't trust the past, then trust the present. Trust the time we've spent together. Don't you see that our story didn't stop and restart? It repeated, but it also got better. We would have met again at the Botanical Gardens if you hadn't had your flashback the day of the engagement party. You convinced me to adopt Gordon, just like you did Goldie. You've always loved ice cream, but your favorite flavor is different. You're different, and somehow, I still fell for you all over again."

I shook my head. "I don't know what to do. I'm so scared, Lex."

His hand cradled my cheek, and I couldn't help leaning into it.

"It's a lot to take in. I know. Not just me hiding the truth from you but also you finding out this whole part of your life that was missing. I can fill the gaps. My family can fill the gaps, but only you can decide how you feel about me. About us."

I nodded. "I should go."

He didn't stop me when I stood and walked to the door.

"Emery."

I turned around.

"Take these." He took my hand and placed the two rings on my palm. "I hope they help you find your way. I just ask you one thing."

"What is it?"

"If you decide..." His voice broke. "If you decide you don't want to come back, please tell me. Send me a message. Send a message through Ellie. Drop a card in the mail. Anything. It doesn't need to be more than goodbye, but please don't disappear again. I won't survive it."

I broke down and wrapped my arms around him. "I can't

remember how I felt, but I know, and hope you do too, that my disappearing wasn't a choice."

He held me tight. "I know, baby. I know." He kissed the top of my head and let me go.

I didn't know what I'd wanted out of seeing Lex. I'd gotten my answers. Some of them. But now, I had a lot more questions. Questions Lex couldn't answer.

No one disappears without a trace.

I walked to the nearest bus stop and sent Ellie a message.

EMERY

Hey, can I crash at your place tonight? I could use a friend.

My phone rang straight away.

"Where are you?"

"A block from Lex's place."

"I'm coming to get you."

I sat on a bench nearby and broke down again.

Ellie pulled up ten minutes later. I dragged myself into her car and slumped on the seat.

"I have ice cream. Whatever it is, we can work through it."

I nodded, but I wasn't sure I could talk any more today.

Ellie, my best friend and the most amazing person in the world, sent me to make myself comfortable while she scooped ice cream into two bowls. I had a few spare clothes at her place from when I stayed over, so I changed into a clean pair of sweatpants and a shirt.

"I don't want to talk about it," I said.

"That's okay. Let the peanut butter help you, and I'll be here when you're ready."

The next morning, I had to put on a brave face to go to work. I wanted to hide under Ellie's covers and not come out for a week.

"You should probably call your therapist, hun," Ellie said during our lunch break. "And you have to eat something. If nothing else, you need the energy to keep up with the kids."

"I don't want to go home today."

"You can stay at my place as long as you want. You know that. But, sweetie, you're worrying me."

I sighed and accepted the bowl of ramen she'd made for me.

"I want to talk, but I don't even know where to start."

"Shhh. Eat the ramen, teach something important to the kids, and then we can see about the rest."

"I love you so much, Ellie."

"I love you too, Em."

Surprisingly, I managed to eat the ramen and keep it inside my stomach. The kids served as a good distraction, but as soon as the bell rang for the end of the day, dread settled in the pit of my stomach.

I wondered how long I could avoid more confrontations or making decisions.

One more night wouldn't hurt, would it?

Lex

I ran to the door when the bell rang. I threw it open, but there was nothing but disappointment on the other side.

"Don't look so happy to see us. I gave up perfectly good company to hang out with your bright mood."

I flipped Noah the bird and turned back to the living room.

"Rude, little bro."

"You don't have to be here. You know where the door is."

"Lex."

I raised my hand. "Look, all week, I've acted like my life isn't falling apart. I've smiled, I've worked hard, and I've even networked, when all I wanted was to spend every second behind that door waiting for the man I'm in love with to knock. Give me a break and leave me alone."

I knew I was snapping at my brothers unfairly, but I was on the brink of a meltdown and holding on to my sanity by a thread.

Adam sat on the chair perpendicular to the couch and leaned forward, resting his elbows on his knees. "Last week, you said all that stuff about family. Was it bullshit?"

"What? No."

"Then why are you back in that place where you're dealing with your feelings all on your own?"

"Because I *am* on my own," I shouted.

Noah went over to Gordon's tank. "Go ahead, shout all you need. Get it out of your system so we can get in the car and go get Emery."

Just the sound of his name coming from someone else's lips was like a dagger to my heart. I fucking missed him so much. Had it been this painful the first time around? Or was this worse because it felt like I was losing him all over again?

This time, there was no hope that he'd suddenly appear out of the blue. I used to imagine stories where he'd knock on the door and just say, *"Sorry I was away. I got a promotion at work and had to travel for training"* or *"I'm back, and guess what, I'm a secret prince and I just renounced my throne to be with you."* They'd become wilder and wilder the longer he was gone.

"No one's gonna get Emery."

"Oh yes, we are."

"I said I'd give him space. Do you know what he's been through? He needs time to wrap his head around it."

Adam let out an audible sigh. "What if he's waiting for you to go get him?"

"He's not."

"How do you know?"

"I told him I love him more than anything. He already knows where I stand. And guess what, he didn't say it back, so I guess I know where I stand."

Noah laughed. "You're a jackass."

"Don't, Noah. I'll punch you."

He laughed harder. "You've never had a physical fight with anyone in your life."

"There's always a first, and sadly for you, I might get beginner's luck."

He came over and sat next to me. "Look, I know you didn't call it, but this is a Code Red situation. River is on his way. We'll figure it out together."

"Please," I begged, "just leave me alone."

"We can't, Lex. You want to know why?" Adam asked. "Because we love you, and we know Emery loves you. Yes, life has thrown some shit in your way, but if there's a love that can make it through, that's yours."

The doorbell rang again.

"That'll be River and our ally." Noah went to the door, and a moment later, River walked in with Ellie.

I was stunned. "Ellie."

She gestured for Noah to move and then took his place next to me.

"He's been at my place since last Sunday. He's sad, depressed, despondent, mopey, all the adjectives you want to come up with. It's Saturday, and I don't do teacher stuff during the weekend. My point is that Emery is not himself. Yesterday, I managed to get it all out of him. This morning, he went back home. It's like he had a purpose, a goal to meet, and nothing would stop him."

"What purpose?" I asked, willing the knot in my throat to come undone.

She shrugged. "I don't know. You're the only one who knew him before the accident and after."

"I lied to him."

She scoffed. "So would I. How many people do you know that have a car accident, lose their memory, and then are unfortunate enough to have parents who'll make their whole life disappear and reappear with a new look. Without them even knowing." The last few words were a staccato.

"You think Emery needs saving?"

She threw her arms up in the air. "Now you're getting there. To think you're the creative brains behind your company."

"Hey!" Noah and Adam complained in unison.

"Calm your testosterone, boys. He's the one who needs his feathers fluffed up today. Your turn will come."

A minute later, I found myself sandwiched between River and Adam in Noah's car as Ellie gave him directions.

"Just so you know, the cooler is stocked," Noah said.

"One of these days, you're going to get in trouble when you get stopped by the police," I said.

"For what? Taking my sick great-uncle his last beer on his deathbed and wishing for nothing but a cold brewski for old times' sake? Besides, carrying alcohol in the car isn't illegal, and so far, none of our Code Reds have required drinking on the move."

I shook my head. I couldn't even blame him. He'd probably gotten the idea from our grandmother.

"Does anyone have a plan? Because I'm shitting my pants here and have no idea what to do," I said.

"Nope," Noah said. "All my ideas are NSFHC. Not suitable for human consumption."

Over the next thirty minutes, as we left the city, I heard every idea under the sun and was still lost. Although, present company probably wasn't full of the best save-the-day idea givers.

We turned onto a long driveway.

"Fuck me sideways and hang me to dry. He lives *here*?" Noah asked.

While he was impressed with the grandeur of the place, I was starting to understand Emery. Truly understand him for the first time.

"I know what to do," I said, leaning forward. "Hurry up."

Emery's car was parked in front of the house. Although

calling it a house was an understatement. It was more of a palace than a house. To me, it looked like a prison.

We all got out of the car and looked at each other.

Now what?

The front door opened, and Emery came out dragging a suitcase.

"Lex." He stopped in shock. "What are you doing here?"

God, he looked good. Really good.

"I came here to get you. I wouldn't be here if it wasn't for them." I pointed to my brothers and Ellie behind me. "The truth is I was scared to push you in case you never came back, so I was giving you all the space you needed. But I've just realized something really important. You don't need space, you need love, and you need to be understood."

Emery walked down the stairs, stopping in front of me.

"And you understand me?"

"I do now. The first day we met, I was so fascinated by you. Your whole presence was calming, and I just wanted to be near you. On our second date, which you argued wasn't a date because there was no ice cream, your eyes were like two green beacons, captivated by everything you saw. The simple things. You noticed the sugar packets in the coffee shop and asked why they were the same color as the salt and what would happen if you got them mixed. Would they make you another coffee, or would it be your fault?"

I walked to him and held his hands. "On our third date, you said something to me that I'll never forget."

"What did I say?"

"Everybody deserves the chance to be free. If everyone went around killing the larvae because they're gross, we'd never see how beautiful butterflies are. That was the most beautiful observation I'd ever heard, but I thought you were talking literally. After all, we were at the zoo in the butterfly house. But now I know you were talking about you."

His Adam's apple bobbed as he swallowed.

"When you moved to the city, you had a purpose. So you kept something of you hidden from me. Even after we shared all our dreams, wishes, and vulnerabilities, after you showed me the real you, it wasn't complete. I think the reason was that you wanted a new start away from your past." I gestured to the grand house behind us. "I know this isn't you. You're not grand or stuffy, but this is where you come from. When I met you the second time, your guard was down. You opened up and told me things you never had before."

I pressed my lips over his knuckles and kissed them.

"The stuff you described when you were at boarding school. I think what your teacher passed on to you was a passion for life. For being yourself away from the expectations of all this."

"What's going on here, Emery? You've been gone all week, and now you're throwing a party? I thought your rebellious stage had passed."

The woman seemed familiar. It took me a minute to place her, but her dismissive look as she stared at everyone brought it all back.

"What is your old landlady doing here? Are you renting a new place?"

"What do you mean? She's my mom," Emery said, looking at the woman.

What?

I stared at her, unable to take the bite out of my words. "You told me you were his landlady and that he'd moved out."

She turned her nose at me. "No. You *assumed* I was his landlady, and I didn't lie. Emery had moved out. Home, where he belongs."

"Wait. You've met before?" Emery asked.

"Once. When you didn't answer my calls, I went to your apartment. I figured if I kept coming at different times, I'd catch you eventually. One day, she was there and told me you'd moved out."

Emery turned to his mom. "You told me I'd never lived away from home. That was a lie. You told me I'd said I wanted to quit teaching because it didn't pay and that I'd specifically asked to work with Dad. Was that a lie? What else did you lie about? Was my cell phone destroyed in the accident, or did you dispose of it so I'd lose all contact with the life I'd built for myself? I've already found my passport, photos, and engagement ring, which you knew about but failed to tell me."

"I did what was best for you. One day, you'll agree with me. A mother will do anything to keep their children safe and give them all the opportunities they deserve." She stood her ground with her chin up, looking defiant and almighty.

Emery went to her and placed a kiss on her cheek.

"If you want me in your life, you'll respect my wishes. I'm not quitting my teaching job, and I'm moving out. I can recommend someone to take over the family business. Frederick has the right qualifications, and I think not only would he be great at it, but he'd also enjoy it. We're friends, and I trust him to do what's best for our family."

"Friends? You're engaged!" his mom said.

"Only in your head, Mom. Granted, we made you believe we were dating, but I was clear when I said I wasn't ready to get married."

"To anyone?" I asked.

He walked over and put his hand in his pocket, retrieving something.

When he opened his hand, I saw the two rings. "I'll make an exception for someone really special."

A loud cheer erupted behind us.

My pulse raced. This wasn't happening. Fate better not be messing with me because I wouldn't survive this cruel joke. "Do you mean it?"

He nodded. "It seems I loved you enough once to say yes. And without knowing anything about our past, I still fell in love with you again. I'm sure that if we keep meeting life after life, I'll always be yours. Maybe we should make it official."

I released a laugh of relief that felt like it had been stuck in my throat forever.

Emery jumped into my arms, giving me a slow, drugging kiss.

"Okay, boys, that's our cue," Ellie said. "Emery, you can use your car to get you both back to Lex's place. Don't know where you were going with that suitcase, but now you have a destination." Then she turned around. "Who wants to go celebrate this elsewhere? I hear there's some beer in the trunk."

They all piled back into Noah's car and left.

Emery locked his gaze with mine. "I love you so much, Lex. Let's go do some celebrating of our own back at your house."

I smiled, pulling him toward his car. "I believe you're driving."

"Oh," he said, stopping me. "Maybe we should start wearing these, just so no one out there gets the wrong idea."

He slid one of the rings on my finger and the other on his.

This was everything right with the world.

I grabbed the handle of his suitcase. "Let's go. Gordon and Goldie have been moody all week because they've missed you."

"Of course they did. I'm their favorite daddy."

Emery

My eyes were on the road, but I kept glancing at Lex as I drove us away from my parents' place and into the city.

"Are you okay?" he asked.

I smiled and reached out my hand. Lex took it in both of his, resting them on his lap. "Yeah."

"It's a huge thing, what you did back there with your mom."

My smile dropped a little. "I've been avoiding conflict for a long time. I should have asked all these questions as soon as I came back from the hospital, but I guess I was dealing with the memory loss, and it was easy having someone make all the decisions. I should have known that if my inconsequential questions were avoided, they were hiding something bigger."

"Do you really think she kept your phone after the accident?"

I shrugged. "I don't know. I want to move forward, so I don't want to think about it. If she did it, it's done. I'm sure it's truly gone now if she ever had it."

"Where were you going with your suitcase when we arrived?"

"Don't know. My plan was a by-the-seat-of-your-pants plan. I wanted to grab as many of my things as possible before confronting my parents about what happened. Then I was hoping you'd take me back. If you didn't take me back, I guess I would have crashed at Ellie's."

I'd left Ellie's apartment without a plan. It was more of a concept, but with no idea how to execute it. I'd just known that I missed Lex at such a visceral level that I needed to be with him, or I'd make myself sick.

I'd spent the whole week thinking. Ellie had tried to pull me out of it, but I'd needed time to put all my thoughts together. In the end, I'd realized that the only thing that mattered was how I felt about Lex.

He'd loved me. He'd proposed to me. And after I disappeared from his life, even if unintentionally, he still took me back and got to know me as I am now. He still fell for me all over again.

If that wasn't worth fighting for, then what was? The void I'd felt for a year had started closing after I met Lex until I'd felt whole and strong.

Finding out about what happened a year ago had shaken my foundation, but I was here now because Lex had spent weeks putting me back together without even realizing.

I pulled up at Lex's place. He helped me take the suitcase out of the car, and we went up the steps to the front door.

"You'll find this is a really friendly neighborhood. The tenant occasionally has visitors, but they tend to leave when the alcohol and food reserves are low." He put the key in the door and turned it to open. "This is your typical single-story duplex. The apartment next door is a mirror of this one. The tenant has assured me they're nice people and very considerate."

I bit my lip to stop myself from laughing.

"The unit is ready for immediate move-in if you don't mind sharing your space with a gecko that has no respect for personal privacy and a goldfish that doesn't know any tricks."

I snorted. "And how about this tenant?"

He snaked his arms around my waist and pulled me closer. "That might be the only downside to this rental. You see, he also has no respect for personal space. He might insist you sleep with him in his bed."

"How many bedrooms are there in this luxurious duplex?"

"One."

"And he won't move out?"

He shook his head.

I pursed my lips. "Hmm, I don't know. I'm tempted. The place looks clean, and pets do bring a lot of joy. Maybe I'll get a dog—"

"No way."

I laughed. "And this tenant...how big is he on the whole taking-up-your-personal-space thing?"

"Huge. You might find yourself in compromising situations under him, on top of him, inside him..."

I wrapped my legs around his waist as he nuzzled his face into my neck and held me. "That sounds like a terrible arrangement. Where do I sign up?"

He took me to his bedroom and dropped me on the bed, covering my body with his. "In front of the justice of the peace as soon as humanly possible."

"This future roommate of mine seems quite possessive."

He growled. "You have no idea."

Our clothes ended up on the floor in three seconds flat as Lex showed me exactly how much of his own personal space he intended to share.

The air around us became electrified as Lex kissed every inch of my body like he was staking a claim.

"I love you so much, Emery, and I'm going to show you."

Every touch closer to my dick lit a fire inside me. My hips bucked from the bed when he finally wrapped his lips over the head of my cock. His hand gently stroked my length, teasing and drawing out my pleasure so slowly that I thought I would die.

"Lex, I need more."

"More what, baby?"

"Just...more." My dick was so hard it was borderline painful and my ass was begging to be filled. To have Lex's cock stretching it and stroking it.

He released my cock and moved up my body like we had all the time in the world. I'd take this into my own hands if I needed to.

"Three-second warning," I said.

He chuckled. "For what?"

"To be inside me, or I'm not responsible for my actions."

"Now that's a tempting offer. Both options sound equally appealing. Get inside you or see what happens when you lose your mind."

I groaned. "Don't tempt me, Alexis Spencer."

"Oh fuck, my name out of your mouth is the sexiest sound in the world."

He reached for the side table and got out the bottle of lube. I offered him my palm, and he dropped a dab of lube on it.

I eased my hand between us and gripped our dicks together.

"Yes," Lex hissed as he fucked my hand with abandon.

His tongue traced my lips before he covered my mouth with his in a hungry kiss. It was hard keeping up with all the sensations.

Kissing Lex affected me on an emotional level, but the sex? Oh god, the sex was indescribable. It was as if we'd been made for each other. No other dick could cause the electric current pulsing through my veins like Lex's.

I had a decision to make, and right now, there was something I needed more than an orgasm.

"Lex, I need you to fill me with your cock. I want to feel nothing but the pain and the pleasure of you inside me."

"You asked for it, baby. Remember that."

I trembled when the cold lube hit my hole, but after a minute of Lex working me open, I was ready to boil over.

He pressed his head against my hole, and as soon as I accepted him inside, he pushed through all the way.

My toes curled, and I screamed in pleasure. He stopped to give me a moment to adjust. His hand reached down to my ass, massaging it and helping me relax.

"Now, Lex. Now."

He pulled out and then pushed back in. The staccato of his thrusts made me reach new heights every time.

"Yes...fuck, yes." The aching need to come was overwhelming, but I didn't want this to stop.

Lex's breaths came in short bursts between his gritted teeth. "You feel so good, Emery. So fucking good."

Our bodies were in exquisite harmony, performing a dance they both knew by heart. My head would soon catch up as I made new memories and learned all the things that made Lex tick.

In a way, I was privileged with my memory loss. I'd get to experience all of Lex again for the first time. No one got that opportunity. If there was ever a silver lining for my memory loss, this was it.

"Alexis," I whispered.

He'd closed his eyes while ramming into me, so when he opened them, I saw fire and ice swirling in a steamy pool of desire.

"Emery."

He increased the pace of his thrusts. My ass burned and my cock, trapped between us, was a steel rod.

As he whispered my name over and over again, hips lips ghosting over mine, I felt the tell-tale signs of my orgasm. "I'm close."

His breath mixed with mine. Hot and sweet.

The ball of energy unfurled from the center of my body. I wrapped my legs around Lex's waist so tight there wasn't an atom of separation between us.

Lex shouted his orgasm, the vein on his neck pulsing as he thrust one, two, three times until he emptied himself inside me.

Without withdrawing from my body, Lex reached down to my dick and stroked it until I spilled my orgasm between us.

We didn't move while we caught our breaths.

"I love you, Alexis. In case I haven't said it enough."

"I love you too, baby."

He slid out of me slowly and sat on his knees. "I'll go grab a towel to—dammit, Gordon."

I followed his line of sight to the wall above the bed where Gordon was staring at us.

"Has he been there all along?" I asked.

"Probably. Pervert." He came back from the bathroom a moment later with a damp towel. My heart swelled as he made sure I was clean before he dropped the towel on the floor and joined me in bed.

Gordon moved to the foot of the bed where the early-afternoon sun warmed the frame.

"We need to set some rules," Lex said.

I placed my leg over his and my head on his chest.

"Shoot."

"Not for you. For him. During sex, the paperweight goes back on the tank. He can't be trusted."

I chuckled. "Somehow, I don't think he's going to tell anyone our sex secrets."

Lex drew slow circles on my back. Before I knew it, I'd fallen asleep.

I woke in the same position. I didn't know if I'd been out for a few minutes or hours, but the sun hadn't moved much, so it was probably a short nap.

Lex was flicking through something on his phone.

"Whatcha doing?" I asked.

"Looking at our photos. I wondered if you'd like to see them."

I raised my head to meet his eyes. "I'd love to."

Lex sat up and pushed me to snuggle between his legs. He handed me his phone and placed my thumb on the home button. The screen unlocked.

I gasped.

"We had no secrets then, and we have no secrets now, Emery."

I opened the photo app and went back two years from now.

Our first photo together was of me eating ice cream and Lex trying to lick my face. My eyes were shut, but I looked so happy.

Even though I didn't remember it, I felt the happiness seeping through the photo.

I scrolled to the next one and the one after. A hundred photos later, the lump in my throat was ready to come out in a sob.

We really had been happy and in love. I'd known it, but seeing it through the photos hit me differently.

"I probably need to call Frederick to tell him what happened. I hope he won't hate me," I said.

"I'm sure he won't. He seems like a good guy, and who

knows, if he still wants to sell the whole gay thing to his parents, he can always pretend to date Ren."

I laughed. "Good luck to Frederick proposing that to Ren and keeping his balls attached."

Lex ran his hands over my chest, settling one around my waist and the other over my heart. "I hate to ask this now, but do you have any idea what you're going to do about your parents?"

"I don't know. Right now, I just feel so much anger toward them for hiding everything from me. For manipulating me when I was so vulnerable. I don't know if I can forgive that."

"I understand. Just know you're not alone anymore. There are two older brothers, a mom, a dad, and a grandma who will love you no matter what."

I turned my head to kiss him. "Thank you. That means more than you can imagine."

"Hey, my parents are throwing a party for the restaurant's anniversary next weekend. I have to work because we're doing this whole throwback thing where we help like we used to, but I'd love it if you came."

I laughed because it had never occurred to me to tell him before. "I hope you're a better server than Ren because I'm already booked to attend the party with my lovely date."

His eyes couldn't have opened wider.

I straddled him and grabbed his hands, pinning them with mine over his head. "I'm taking Nadine, a teacher from my school. It's my first date with a woman, so you better make it special." I bit my lip, trying not to laugh.

"I'll make sure to brush up on my serving skills. Do you think she'll put out?"

A bubble of laughter escaped me.

"I don't know about her, but I can guarantee I will."

I feigned shock. "Mr. Spencer, is that an indecent proposal I'm hearing?"

"Uh-huh," he hummed as his lips brushed against my neck.

Lex

Emery's moans as I sucked his cock to the back of my throat were downright dirty but also doing everything for me. My own relief was coming from rubbing against the bed sheets because I didn't have a spare hand to use on me.

Not when I was teasing Emery with the butt plug, caressing his balls, and sucking him at the same time.

There was a lot to be said for spending the weekend in bed.

"Good almost afternoon, boys. Cover up your unmentionables if you don't want them to get seen."

"Shit." I scrambled up the bed and pulled the covers up just in time for the bedroom door to open.

River, Adam, and Noah spilled inside the room.

"Oof, it stinks in here. You do know where the shower is, right?" Noah asked, going to my window and opening it. "I can get some signs printed if you've fucked each other's brains out so much that you don't know what's left or right."

Emery tried to push me in front of him, but I knew that would only encourage them.

"Can someone explain what kind of emergency has been

called that you've entered my place using the key I gave you for *emergencies only?*"

Noah looked at Adam and Adam looked at River.

"It's Sunday," they all said like it meant something.

"Look," Noah added, pointing to his watch. "We gave you almost twenty-four hours, and you still have the rest of your lives. Get dressed. We have to be at Mom and Dad's in half an hour."

"Shit. It's Sunday." With all the time I'd spent with Emery recently, I'd missed a few lunches. It wasn't exactly a rule that we all had to attend every lunch.

"What does that mean?" Emery whispered in my ear.

I turned my head to face him. His face was flushed, which brought out his beautiful freckles. He was breathing in short bursts, as if barely holding it together.

He was still wearing the plug. Correction, he was sitting on it, so it was probably pressed against his prostate. My erection had taken a nosedive when my brothers arrived, but it was ready to play again.

"It means, baby, that you're about to meet the parents...again."

His eyes bulged.

I turned back to my brothers and River.

"Okay, message received. You can go now. We'll meet you there."

Adam shook his head. "No can do. We've been ordered to make sure you follow us all the way there. No delays or detours."

I sighed. "Fine. Can you at least wait in the living room? And close the door on your way out."

Emery let out a heavy sigh of relief when the door closed behind them.

"That was the worst. Do they do this often?"

I chuckled. "Not at all. They're just messing with us."

He looked down at his erection that was pointing up to his stomach. "I can't meet your parents like this."

I wanted to lighten the moment with a joke, but I knew this was a real worry for him. The first time he'd met my family, he'd panicked so much that I'd had to take him to get ice cream before to calm down.

For Emery, this would feel much like the first time, but with the added element that while he didn't remember them, they very much remembered him.

"Come with me." I stepped out of the bed and held my hand out.

I turned the water on in the shower and got the spray to face away from us.

"Hands on the wall, open your legs," I commanded.

A small puff of air escaped his parted lips. While he did as I asked, I grabbed the lube and coated my cock with a good amount.

I aligned my body with his. I was just tall enough that we fit perfectly together, like two matching pieces.

"This is going to be quick, baby. We don't have much time, or they might actually barge in again."

He nodded.

I pulled his plug out and replaced it with my cock. Emery shouted.

A second later, the stereo in my living room started playing loud music.

"Oh god," Emery groaned. "They know what we're doing."

"That's a given, baby. If they don't want to listen, they shouldn't have come."

I reached for Emery's cock and stroked it in sync with my thrusts. When he couldn't keep quiet enough, I put a hand over his mouth.

I thrust in and out of him, holding on to nothing but his

dick and his mouth. As my balls drew up, I whispered sweet nothings in his ear.

Emery came a second before me. His whole body went limp and was flushed from the freckles on his nose to his toes.

"You are so beautiful when you come."

We had to be super quick with the shower and getting dressed, but we still managed to get to my parents' in time.

My mom came running out of the house as we parked.

I gave Emery's hand an encouraging squeeze before we stepped out of the car.

"Ah, meu querido. Emery, it's so nice to see you again. Welcome."

She wrapped her arms around a very wide-eyed Emery.

"Mom, right now, you're just a strange woman with no boundaries." I laughed.

"Oh, right. I'm sorry, dear. I forgot about the...oh damn, that was probably insensitive, wasn't it?"

I burst out laughing.

"Welcome to my deranged family, Emery...again. This is Carla, my mom."

"Hi," he said shyly.

We went inside, where my dad, who had only a sliver more restraint than my mom, was waiting in the living room.

"Hi, Dad," I said. "Emery, this is Jack, my dad."

They shook hands, and then a gasp came from the door.

"Ai meu deus. I couldn't believe it was true." My grandmother's eyes shone bright as she approached Emery.

"And this is Jacinta Santos, the leader of the gang."

Emery smiled and hugged her. "It's really nice to meet you all again."

"Where are the rest of my boys?" Mom asked.

"They were right behind us but took a different turn a while ago," I said.

"Oh right, they're picking up Victoria. She's made Pão de Ló for dessert."

As if on cue, Noah's car parked, followed by Adam's.

We all gathered at the table. Mom had a smile the size of Texas. This was what she had always dreamed of: a big family to feed and everyone around the table together.

I reached out for the bread and cut a piece for me and one for Emery.

My eyes met my grandmother's, and she pointed at my hand.

I looked at Emery. My wallflower man, who was funny, loving, and also a little shy sometimes, smiled.

"Um...we have a small announcement to make," I said.

"Emery is pregnant already?" Noah asked.

I rolled my eyes.

"Well, it sounded like you were giving it the good old try earlier."

I picked up my bread and threw it, hitting him in the head.

"Boys," Mom said. "What was your announcement, honey?"

"Well, first, I have a confession to make."

They all stared at me expectantly.

"You may remember my failed proposal to Emery last year. At the time, we decided to keep it between us until Emery came back from a trip. Now we know why he never came back from that trip." I held his hand. "The proposal didn't fail. Emery said yes then...and he said yes again."

I raised our hands to show us wearing the rings the eagle-eyed Avó had noticed.

"There are a lot of things that are new to us as a couple, but one thing we do know. The way we feel about each other hasn't changed."

Dad opened a bottle of champagne, and we all toasted to our engagement.

The time would come when questions would arise. My parents were curious but polite enough not to ask Emery much about his past or what he'd been doing this last year. I loved them for that.

Now that I had Emery back in my life, I wanted us to find our way together. The movie nights, the farmers' markets, the restaurants, and spending time with my family.

Victoria cleared her throat.

"Um, thank you for inviting me today. I'm really happy, and I hope I was able to do justice to the real Portuguese Pão de Ló. Is that how you say it?" She looked at my mom for reassurance.

"Well done, dear, and you don't need an invite to come over. You're going to be part of the family, so you're always welcome."

"Thank you." Victoria smiled shyly and leaned against Adam, who put an arm around her.

I didn't know what had caused her behavior to take a turn, but it was nice to see a less confrontational, warmer person with my brother.

"Adam and I would like to host a prerehearsal weekend at Mabel's Vineyard on Peet Island. It's three weeks after the party at the restaurant. They had a sudden opening for a party our size, so we jumped in. We hope you can all make it."

I turned to Emery and wiggled my brows. "A romantic weekend at a vineyard, baby."

They all laughed.

Everyone was on board with the idea, so we toasted to that too.

"I'm not sure I can make it, actually," River said suddenly.

Adam's face fell. "But you're my best man."

"I know, and I'll be there for your bachelor party and

wedding. The restaurant is fully booked throughout the summer. I can't just take time off whenever I want to."

"Nonsense," Dad said. "This is family, River. When I managed the restaurant, I made sure to take time for the important things. This is important."

River smiled. "Thank you. That's very understanding of you, Jack. I'll see what I can do."

The food was amazing, as usual, and even Victoria's cake hit the right spot. It was nice seeing her smile and look proud of doing something with the family. I was even happier for my brother.

When we finished, Emery stood and grabbed our plates, saying, "I think we should do the dishes and let your mom and grandma take a backseat."

My mom rushed over to him, caressed his cheek, and gave him a kiss.

"The memories may not be here." She pointed to his head. "But they're here." She pointed to his heart. "That's what really matters."

Emery looked at everyone who was smiling at him. "What did I do?"

I stood, took the plates from his hands, and put them by the sink. Then I placed a soft kiss on his lips and said, "Mom raised three sons and a straggler," I looked at River, who smiled. "The only time anyone ever offered to do the dishes was when you came along. What you just said was word for word what you always said after a meal."

Emery's lower lip wobbled a little. "Do you think I'll ever get those memories back?"

"I don't know, baby, but we'll make many more memories to replace those you lost."

"Puke," Noah said. "I think you two should go take that smoochiness elsewhere. You're giving me hives. I'd rather do the dishes."

"Oh, Noah," Mom said like she wondered how on earth he could possibly be her son.

"I guess that's our cue," I said, pulling Emery toward the door.

"Wait. No. We can't just leave," he said. "How about all this?" He pointed to the table.

"And that's how you became Mom's favorite. Guys, we've all just downgraded one level again," Adam said.

"I don't know about that. My life has had a major upgrade recently," I said, wondering how I could be so lucky to have a second chance with Emery.

Emery

"Hey, what are you doing all the way out here?" Lex asked, snaking his arms around my waist and kissing the back of my neck.

"You mean all the way out six feet from the bed?"

"That's six feet too far. I can't cuddle if you're six feet away. I certainly can't do this from six feet away." He snaked his hand down my stomach, cupping my semi.

"You do present a very good point. However, we have a family breakfast to attend in approximately fifteen minutes, and you're not dressed."

"Hmm." He nuzzled my neck. "Clothes are overrated."

I chuckled. "Tell that to the servers and your family."

"Fine. I'll get dressed."

I shook my head as I watched him search for the jeans he had carelessly discarded on the floor last night because he'd jumped me as soon as we'd arrived at the hotel. Apparently, hotel sex was a hundred times better than regular sex. Or so Noah had told us when we went out for drinks last Friday.

Lex had wanted to test the theory, and I couldn't disagree. Hotel sex really was the best. Then again, all sex with Lex was the best, so maybe it wasn't so much about the location and more about the person you were doing it with.

"This place is stunning. Look at all the grapevines," I said, looking out onto the vast fields outside our window.

"That's how vineyards work."

I grabbed a decorative pillow from the chair and threw it at him.

"Don't start a war you can't win," he teased.

When he was fully dressed, he joined me by the window.

"This was a good choice from Victoria. It's been so busy at work lately that a weekend away is just what we needed," he said.

"I know. I've even brought the latest Aiden Lawton novel to read. It'll be nice to read for pleasure."

Busy was an understatement. I'd taken a placement at a summer school for neurodivergent children and was learning so much. It was hard work, but I loved it. I was also studying for the finals, which were during the summer because most of us already had teaching jobs, so this was the best time to catch up on our studying.

I didn't have to retake the final exams to gain my MA since I'd already passed, but it was something I wanted to do for myself.

"Do you think you'd want to get married here?" Lex asked.

I thought about it. From the little we'd seen since we arrived, the vineyard was the perfect wedding destination. But...

"I'm not sure. I don't think it's us," I said.

"What do you have in mind?"

"Honestly? I'd rather have a small, intimate wedding and then travel to Europe for our honeymoon. I'd like to visit Lisbon, maybe Florence and Paris. Or maybe just rent a car and tour around Portugal."

"I like that idea very much."

"Your mom has asked me a bunch of times when we are getting married."

I laughed. "That wouldn't be my mom if she hadn't. What did you say?"

"I'm becoming a master ninja at avoiding those questions. Your mom really likes hugs and help in the kitchen."

"Cunning. I like it. And what do you really think? When would you want to get married?"

I put my hand on top of his. The sound of our rings clinking against each other warmed my heart. I was engaged to Lex. If anyone had told me two months ago that I would not only be dating the most gorgeous man in the city but also engaged to be married, I'd have called them insane. But reality was a lot better than fantasy. At least when it came to us.

My parents had recently reached out and apologized for what they'd done. It had been a tense meeting, and I wasn't entirely sure it was their idea since they'd also announced at the same time that Frederick was going to work with my dad and would eventually take over the company as CEO.

Frederick had become one of my best friends. I wouldn't put it past him to refuse to take the job unless my parents did the right thing. Frederick was their absolute second-best choice to take over the company since I didn't want it, so I knew they'd do anything to get him.

Only the future would tell how much my parents would be in my and Lex's lives.

"I think we should wait until Adam and Victoria get married. They've been planning their wedding for a while, and I wouldn't want to take the spotlight away from them."

"That's an excellent idea. Besides, by then, I'm sure Mom will be delighted to not have a hundred wedding-related things to do and won't press us for a bigger party."

A sudden knock on the door made us jump.

"We're not late to breakfast, are we?" Lex asked.

"No."

He opened the door to a red-faced Adam.

"What happened?" Lex asked.

"Ugh, everything was going so well, why did he have to fuck things up? Victoria has been really great. She's making an effort. I know it's hard for her because she's not used to a super close family unit, but she's trying. Now he's thrown this shit up, and she's upset because this is all everyone's going to be talking about this weekend. And I'm not one to pander to tantrums, but I think she's right. She's worked so hard to bring our families together this weekend, and now it's all going to be about them."

He paced the room, his hands on his hair.

"What are you talking about? Who did what?" Lex asked.

"Noah. He's not here alone."

"That's not unexpected, is it? He could bring a date."

Adam stopped and faced us.

"He didn't bring a date. He brought his fucking husband."

Lex coughed. "I'm sorry, what?"

"What I said. Mom is crying in her room because she's hurt. Victoria is crying in our room because she's upset. Avó may or may not have gone down to the hotel kitchen to borrow a butcher's knife, and Dad...well, Dad is trying to keep everyone happy and failing miserably. It's not even nine o'clock in the morning. All because, apparently, our big brother went and got married."

Did you enjoy Lex and Emery's story?

Want to fast forward to their wedding day and find out how Gordon's little distraction almost makes Lex and Emery late for their special day?

Sign up to my newsletter (https://landing.mailerlite.-com/webforms/landing/t8o2l9) to read an exclusive bonus scene.

What's next for the Spencer brothers?

How much do you want to know what Noah got himself into?

Get The Fake Husband Deal (https://readerlinks.com/l/3610377)

In the meantime I have another happy ever after for you in this world. Find out in The Christmas Roommate exactly how Ren and Frederick's frenemyship developed into something a little deeper over the holiday season.

Get The Christmas Roommate (https://readerlinks.-com/l/3610533)

Acknowledgments

The Spencer brothers took a while to come to life from the plot bunny I had after my good friend Anka Papoog put a little seed in my head.

In fact, it's been over a year, but Lex, Noah, and Adam wouldn't leave me alone.

Since I've finished the first draft, four people have been my champions and superstar helpers.

Nora Phoenix and Saxon James have both listened to my rambles about the series and given me precious feedback when I was stuck and unsure.

Abbie Nicole always makes my books better. Without her, my books would be a mixed hot mess of Britishisms and weird Portuguese sayings.

Last, but not least, Alexander Cendese was the nicest person to work with while he brought my story to life perfectly.

Books by Ana Ashley

Single Dads of Stillwater

A spin off series from Chester Falls that can be read on its own. Each book features one or more single dads in this community of friends, family and found family. In this contemporary MM romance series you'll find heat, emotion and a guaranteed happy ever after.

Newcomer

Antagonist

Breakthrough

Heartstring

Datebook (Coming soon)

Finding You Series

A standalone series set across the Atlantic between New York and Portugal. Find your way home with this contemporary MM romance series with friends to lovers, star-crossed lovers and age gap with plenty of heat, feels and always a happy ever after.

Home Again

Together Again

Love Again

And for a special short story, Complete Again, plus bonus scenes, grab the Finding You boxset now.

Room for 3 series

This is a high heat MMM contemporary romance series set in an island resort.

The Resort

The Vacation (Free short story - dl.bookfunnel.com/dehgkmsb61)

Chester Falls Series

From a Prince to a Happy Ever After for all, enjoy this small town MM romance series that's as sweet as they come, with plenty of heat, humor and everything in between.

How to Catch a Bookworm (Prequel short)

How to Catch a Prince

How to Catch a Rival

How to Catch a Bodyguard

How to Catch a Bachelor

How to Catch the Boss (a Christmas novella)

How to Catch a Biker

How to Catch a Vet

How to Catch a Happy Ever After

Standalone books

Christmas Bubble: a low angst, standalone, Christmas novel featuring a petite but larger-than-life cheerleader, an older demisexual football coach and a winter cabin by the lake with only one bed. With cameos from Chester Falls and Stillwater.

Midnight Ash: a sweet Cinderella fairytale retelling with a sexy kinky twist on the side, and a cast who don't quite behave as you'd expect.

Stronghold: a sweet and sexy romance in Sarina Bowen's World of True North, Vino & Veritas series. This is a standalone story between two childhood friends who reunite after as decade apart, with some creative use of maple syrup.

Audiobooks by Ana Ashley

All of Ana's audiobooks are now available through her store.

Ana Ashley Shop (anaashleyshop.com/)

Dads of Stillwater narrated by John Solo

Newcomer

Antagonist

Breakthrough

Chester Falls narrated by Nick Hudson

How to Catch a Bookworm (a short prequel)

How to Catch a Prince

How to Catch a Rival

How to Catch a Bodyguard

How to Catch Bachelor

How to Catch the Boss (a Christmas novella)

How to Catch a Biker

How to Catch a Vet

How to Catch a Happy Ever After

Stronghold narrated by John Solo is available on Audible and wide stores as well as libraries.

About Ana

Ana Ashley was born in Portugal but has lived in the United Kingdom for so long, even her friends sometimes doubt if she really is Portuguese.

After getting hooked on reading gay romance, Ana decided to follow her lifelong dream of becoming an author.

These days you can find her in front of her laptop bringing her stories to life, or in the kitchen perfecting her recipe for the famous Portuguese custard tarts.

Ana Ashley writes sweet and steamy gay romance set in America, often in small towns where everyone knows everyone.

You can follow Ana on the usual social media hangouts.

For access to exclusive teasers, content, and general book and food related goodness you can now join Ana in her Facebook Group, Café RoMMance (facebook.com/groups/Cafe-RoMMance)

Ana's VIP Readers - bit.ly/AnaAshley

Facebook Page - @anawritesmm

Email - ana@anaashley.com

Instagram - @anawritesmm

Bookbub - https://www.bookbub.com/authors/ana-ashley

Goodreads - https://www.goodreads.com/ana-ashley